Dorian glared, but his hands remained at his sides.

As much as he wanted to punch Jules, it would probably find a way of coming back to him in a bad way. Things always did. When he didn't move, Jules laughed softly, biting his bottom lip and shaking his head.

"I knew it. You don't really want this. You just want to say you were here. You tried. And that's what matters."

It was the condescending tone that really snapped something inside Dorian and made him swing his fist around, inches from making contact with Jules' jaw, but Jules was quicker, and before Dorian knew it, the wind was knocked out of him and he was flat on his back against the mat. Struggling to breathe, he tried to fight against Jules on top of him, but Jules was bigger and stronger, and he pinned him down as easily as if he were a wrestler.

Dorian gasped for breath as it finally came back, pushing against Jules. "Get the fuck off me," he spat breathlessly, struggling under Jules' hands tight on his arms, his legs pinning him to the mat.

Also recommended...

You may also enjoy these other Forbidden Fiction works:

Checking Out by E.E. Grey

Dominic's dream is to run his own bed and breakfast, while Sean's is to be a celebrated chef. Dreams often require sacrifices and when Sean is offered a better job in the big city. Dominic is unable to give him a reason to stay at the Honey Creek Inn. With all the walls he's built up around himself, both real and emotionally, losing Sean threatens to have Dominic's entire world come tumbling down. In a place where people come and go, Dominic struggles to give Sean a permanent home in his heart. (M/M)

http://forbiddenfiction.com/library/story/EEG-1.000090

The Camillia Missions by Laylah Hunter

Jay is a young decommissioned solider who ventures into an online game with full sensations, Way of Illusion. Upgrades are too expensive for his veteran's pension until he discovers The Camellia, a house of ill repute and sensual software adaptions. Jay soldiers on into a world where gender changes instantaneously and blowjobs are digitally enhanced. Yet, Jay might find more of a connection to reality than he realized. (M/M)

http://forbiddenfiction.com/library/story/LH2-1.000159

Vaulted

E.E. Grey

ForbiddenFiction
www.forbiddenfiction.com

an imprint of

Fantastic Fiction Publishing
www.fantasticfictionpublishing.com

VAULTED
A Forbidden Fiction book

Fantastic Fiction Publishing
Hayward, California

© E.E. Grey, 2014

CREDITS
Editor: James L. Wolf
Cover Design: Siolnatine
Cover Art: Jeannie Bell
Production Editor: Erika L Firanc
Proofreading: Aislinn and Jae Knight

SKU: EEG-000138-01 FFP
ISBN: 978-1-62234-170-2

Published in the United States of America

DISCLAIMER

This book is a work of fiction which contains explicit erotic content; it is intended for mature readers. Do not read this if it's not legal for you.

All the characters, locations and events herein are fictional. While elements of existing locations or historical characters or events may be used fictitiously, any resemblance to actual people, places or events is coincidental.

This story is not intended to be used as an instruction manual. It may contain descriptions of erotic acts that are immoral, illegal, or unsafe. Do not take the events in this story as proof of the plausibility or safety of any particular practice.

To Zeus,
God of Thunder.
Creating the Olympics
For our general splendor
Since 776 BC.

Contents

Chapter 1

Don't Get Cocky

Dorian stared up at the domed ceiling towering over them, light reflecting off the silver panels and shining down on the stands that rose up on every side of the arena. At the moment, the floor before him stood empty, teams claiming spots alongside the arena and chatting amongst themselves. A huge banner with the China 2008 Olympics' logo stamped on it hung over his head as he stepped inside.

He stumbled forward as a shoulder knocked into him hard from behind. Looking over, he was met with Jules' cocky smirk as he stepped past.

Jules rubbed his hand over his head. He kept his head shaved and said it gave him better aerodynamics, but Dorian thought it was because he loved to let girls rub his head "for luck." His hair would have been dark had he let it grow in, the same color brown as his eyes. Instead, a dark shadow was all that remained on his head, darker than his tanned skin.

"How's the view from down there?" Jules asked, hooking his bag over his shoulder and glancing around.

The rest of the team filtered in behind them, all in their same USA logo jackets and pants. Dorian was easily the shortest on the team, barely reaching five-six, less muscular than the others, but that hadn't stopped him from making the US gymnastics team in time for the Olympics. No matter what Jules or anyone else said, he deserved to be there as much as they did.

"Fine," Dorian replied flatly, turning and following the coach down into the narrow pit that ran the length of the gym, below the performance area.

"Are you sure you're not Chinese?" Jules asked, following him down the steps. Beside him, one of the other guys, Carey, laughed. "Better be careful. You might blend in around here. Don't want you to get lost."

For the past month, Dorian had endured many similar jabs at his height and weight. He may not have been the tallest guy on the team, but he was a world champion on the vault and the rest of the team should have had reason to see him as serious competition for all-around champion this year. They didn't, though, probably because Jules made him the butt of every joke he could think of.

"Are you sure you're not a jackass?" Dorian shot back, dumping his bag on the bench and unzipping his jacket. How he could ever have idolized Jules, he couldn't remember anymore. He couldn't believe he'd ever had a crush on him, though they hadn't officially met until the Olympic trials a month ago. It seemed a lot had changed between now and then.

"Ooh." Jules grinned, unzipping his own jacket and flinging it on top of his bag. "Kitty's got claws. Thought you southern gentlemen were all about class."

Dorian jerked his shoulders. "Why should I bother when you don't have any?"

"That's enough." Brian stepped between them, a hand on each man's chest although Dorian had no intention of fighting with Jules. He couldn't afford an injury so close to the games, even a minor one at that. He needed to forget about how much Jules got under his skin and focus on training. He was here to win.

Even if he had wanted to hit Jules, he wouldn't have been able to get around Brian, their head coach, who was about a foot taller than he was and more muscular than both of them. Back in the day, Brian had won his own gold medal in the all-around. They were lucky to have him as a coach.

Brian shoved Jules back a step although Jules looked perfectly calm. Behind Brian, Georgia, the assistant coach, shook her head at Dorian, a silent warning. Georgia was the epitome of a gymnast—small, compact, muscular, and far too peppy in the mornings. She always wore her brown hair back in a bun or ponytail and didn't own any shoes that didn't come with arch support.

Brian dropped his hand from Jules' chest. "You're a team, remember? Now stop pissing around and get warmed up." He strode away, digging out the notebook he carried with him everywhere and shouting at Carey to get on the floor.

Jules grinned at Dorian, though Dorian merely crossed his arms instead.

"I'll try not to step on you out there," Jules tossed back to Dorian as he hauled himself up to the floor and stretched, muscles visibly straining under his shirt.

Rolling his eyes, Dorian turned away. He had bigger things to think about than Jules' ego, although he'd smash that too if he had the time.

Even for being a world champion, Dorian still felt amazed and so very small when he traveled to new countries. As a kid, growing up in tiny Cherry Grove, Mississippi, he'd never imagined that one day he'd be performing in front of crowds of thousands of people, in front of cameras broadcasting his wins, his falls, everything to the world. At the very least, he'd lost the southern drawl that had garnered plenty of teasing from his fellow gymnasts.

He had known about Jules before they'd both won spots on the Olympic team this year, but it was hard not to considering all gymnasts ran in the same circles whether or not they trained together. He had known who Jules was even before they'd started competing against each other. Four years ago, Dorian had watched him get a bronze in the all-around and thought it was a crime. Jules was better than a bronze.

To say he'd had something of a crush would have been a big understatement. He used to spend hours watching competitions on television, just for a glimpse of Jules. Dorian had spent far too much time in the past few years jerking off to the image of him in his head. Jules had been all that he'd aspired to, but since they'd been put on the same team, everything had changed. Dorian didn't know how he could have been so stupid as to look up to Jules, the guy who spent most of his time making fun of him. Now Jules just pissed him off. They were polite enough on the outside, though, only so no one would suspect anyone might pull a Tonya Harding at competition.

After all, they were a team.

The rest of the team, however, seemed to side with Jules against Dorian, laughing at his jokes whether or not they were funny. The only one who didn't was Mitya, the Russian guy who'd moved to the States at a young age with his parents. Mitya kept mostly to himself, which didn't help Dorian at all.

The team had been put up in the Olympic village hotel along with everyone else competing, but the rooms were small, a little cramped. It hardly mattered, though, since Dorian spent most of his time in the gym, working out and practicing his routine until he could do it in his sleep.

He wasn't going to leave anything to chance. This might be his only chance at an Olympic medal. He couldn't do what he'd done last year, trying to be normal and go to college while still training and doing all the international events. It was just too much stress and he knew his mother would rather he get a good education especially considering all the injuries he'd sustained over the years. If he had it his way, he would take a leave from university next year and go back when he had more time.

His ankle had healed completely from the last injury, and he wasn't worried about it interfering in the competition. The team doctor still checked him out daily on Brian's command. They couldn't risk anything. The most he was worried about were the reporters. He'd never been very good with reporters or with the public in general. Today, though, he didn't have to see the doctor. He didn't have to do anything but snuggle into his small bed and try to block out Mitya's snores in the bed next to him.

Georgia pounded on the door to the dorm room in the Olympic Village—really just a large cluster of dormitories, a cafeteria downstairs, and video cameras in every corridor. When no one answered, she used her key to open the door and step inside.

"Up and at 'em, lazy bones."

Of the two people on the beds squished in the small space, only one stirred at her voice. Dorian groaned, turning over into his pillow.

"Get up, Dorian," she commanded, and she yanked down his sheets to somewhere near his ankles.

Georgia smiled as Dorian grumbled. He wasn't really a morning person, but Georgia had been up for hours. She'd already taken her usual morning run around the compound which left her energized and ready to go. Dorian, on the other hand, was clearly not happy with this surprise if the way he groaned was any indication. Getting up early was a great way to start the day in her opinion, and Dorian should have been used to it by now considering the sheer amount of training they had daily.

Dorian peeked out of the pillow at Georgia's face planted right next to his. "I thought we had today off."

"We do," she agreed, stepping back and waiting for Dorian to drag himself upright.

In the next bed over, Mitya hadn't even stirred, but he could sleep through anything. Dorian rubbed at his eyes and pushed his hands through his short, blond hair, sighing. "Then why am I awake?"

"Because we are in China," she replied, grabbing his arm and hauling him up. There was no excuse for lying around all day. They'd long gotten over their jetlag. "And I want to see it. You know, a few years ago, coming to China wasn't as easy as it is now. You should feel lucky we're here."

Dorian was taller than her as he stood up, looking disgruntled with his hair mussed, pillow marks on his face, and yawning. Georgia had taken an immediate liking to Dorian despite his tendency to overreact at the slightest provocation. At his age, she'd already competed in an Olympics and officially retired from the sport.

"Can't you go with someone else?" Dorian asked as she gave him a shove towards his suitcase to get dressed. "Like Brian? Or Jules?"

"Shut up and get dressed," she replied instead. It was the perfect day to go exploring, and even if Dorian didn't want to, they were going to enjoy this.

She knew full well that all Dorian wanted to do was practice. He spent almost every spare minute at the gym, but that, in her opinion, was no way to enjoy the Olympics. Dorian was lucky. He was young. He was healthy. It was his first time at the Olympics and undoubtedly wouldn't be his last. Many male gymnasts went on to compete in multiple Olympics. It was Jules' second time, Carey's third, and she didn't doubt that they would all be competing for many years to come. Now was the time to enjoy it.

She wished sometimes that she hadn't been forced to retire, but taking care of her family had been much more important than some medal she could have won. Sometimes she wasn't sure that she had taken enough time to enjoy it before it was gone. This was her second chance, though, coming back as a coach. Sure, the accolades were fewer, but the experience was worth it. After all, she was there to see her team succeed.

Dorian glanced at her. "Can I at least have coffee?" he asked hopefully, and she laughed.

"Nice try, but you know coffee isn't part of the diet." Shaking her head, she smiled and turned around so he could get dressed.

"Where are we going?" Dorian asked resignedly once he was dressed. Georgia led the way out of the dorms and they crossed the large expanse of the grounds towards the exit.

"Everywhere," she replied. They passed the Bird's Nest, the national stadium supposed to look like a literal bird's nest, but Georgia thought it looked more like a thatched hat. On the other side of the path, the Water Cube glowed blue in the early morning sun. Even in the early hour, the air felt heavy with humidity, the sky overhead thick with smog. So far, China had been much of what she had expected, and at the same time not the same at all. The little food stands on the corner had to be unsafe, but she'd sampled from them anyway.

"Georgie," Dorian lamented as they kept walking—it was a long way to the metro stop across the six-lane road, traffic rushing past at full speed as they climbed the sky bridge to pass overhead.

She shot him a look. "What else were you going to do? Practice?" They'd been practicing every day for months straight, years in most cases, but there was no harm in taking a day off. In fact, that was what days off were for. She was a firm believer in preparing completely, then doing something completely unexpected.

Dorian frowned, kicking the ground and glancing over the bridge to the cars below.

"Part of being a world-class athlete is enjoying the places you travel to," she said, gesturing around them. There wasn't much to see except Olympic buildings out here, but the city of Beijing loomed up in the grey morning in the distance. In a few minutes, they would be inside the city. "Trust me, I know." Years ago at her own first World Championship, she had spent the whole time in the training gym, only seeing Prague through the van window on the way to and from the airport. Since then, she'd vowed to see as much of the world as she could, and given that gymnastics afforded her the chance to do it, she figured she had to take advantage.

They reached the other side of the road finally and headed for the metro station. It was clean and fairly empty given the hour and the fact that the Olympics didn't officially kick-off for a few more days.

There was only one way to go on the metro, but the rest of the subway map had so many lines it almost made her dizzy looking at it. As much as she'd traveled during her competition years, she still had never quite figured out the ins and outs of it. She sank into a free seat lining the outside walls of the train and Dorian slumped beside her, clearly not awake yet.

"Do you know how to get anywhere?" Dorian asked, and she frowned at him.

"That's part of the adventure. Will you stop being so grumpy and just enjoy it?" She intended on enjoying it, and she'd appreciate a travel buddy who would as well. She could have chosen Jules to come with her, but Jules would have been more interested in finding a way to break the diet with some strange Chinese food. She'd heard of food stalls selling scorpions on a stick and she wasn't sure she would have been able to stop him. Dorian, on the other hand, would have had no interest in eating scorpions or grasshoppers. Of all the gymnasts on the team, she knew no one else who followed all the rules better than Dorian.

In a way, she appreciated it. It was nice not having to constantly keep an eye on his eating habits, but it could also be incredibly frustrating when he refused to let loose at all.

"Sorry," Dorian muttered, and she sighed, slipping an arm around his shoulder.

"I don't want you to be sorry. I want you to realize that you are young and you are in the Olympics, and how could life get any better?" She gave him a look, waiting, and he sighed.

"I'm young, I'm in the Olympics," he said, and on her continued look, added, "and how could life get any better?"

"Exactly." She smiled. There had to be a way to loosen him up. If he didn't, there was every chance that he would freak himself out so much he would ruin his own chances at a medal. She knew the way his mind worked. She'd coached many more just like him, so incredibly focused on winning that they couldn't see anything else. It wasn't good to have a single focus. It was things like that that led to drinking at an older age and regret.

The next train they took was much more crowded than the other, a whole mass of Chinese people swarming together, pushing onto the subway car. Georgia wasn't sure they would all fit, but somehow, the doors closed behind them and the train took them onward.

She was glad to get off a few minutes later, pushed along in the wave of people exiting the train into the waiting station. It must have been morning rush hour.

"So how's it feel?" Georgia asked him as they climbed the stairs to the exit. They emerged at the corner of a busy road, yet another sky bridge stretching over the traffic. She had no idea where they were going, but she figured following the crowd of tourists was a good bet.

"What?"

"Being here." She gestured around. "In China, at the Olympics. It's your first time."

Dorian paused. "It's… unreal," he said finally. "I never thought it would actually happen, especially after the accident." He paused. "I was so afraid my career was over. I don't know what I would do if it was."

Georgia nodded. Dorian's ankle was certainly a sore spot, both literally and figuratively. "People have come back from worse," she assured him. "You made the team because you're the best."

Dorian smiled slightly. "And Jules made the team because he slept with the judge."

Georgia shot him a look. Jules wasn't the most hospitable teammate, but he was a teammate and Dorian had to remember that. At her look, Dorian looked away, a scowl wrinkling his brow as though he already knew what she was going to say. Considering either she or Brian said the same thing every other day, it wasn't surprising.

"You are both on the same team," she reminded him calmly. "If you want that medal, you're going to have to stop picking at each other."

Georgia really didn't know what their problem was. They were both under a huge amount of stress, and Jules' teasing didn't help anything. She only hoped that Dorian would be able to put it aside and focus on the task at hand. On the other hand, that might have been the problem considering how focused Dorian was already.

Of all the athletes she had coached over the years, none were quite like Dorian. Sure, most athletes were incredibly focused, but they usually knew when and where to loosen up. Dorian spent every spare moment training, and when he wasn't training, he was talking about it. If anyone had tunnel vision, it was him. Personally, it worried her. No one should be so focused on one thing. It closed them off to other opportunities. What might happen when he had to retire? She was sure he hadn't thought that far ahead. She hadn't at her first Olympics either, but circumstances could change in the blink of an eye.

"Tell him that," Dorian only replied, kicking a leaf off the ground in front of him.

"I'm not your mother," Georgia said as they came up on the Forbidden City, a tall, red wall running around the perimeter. At the front, large crowds milled, taking pictures of the painting of Chairman Mao on the outside. Security guards stood on each small bridge leading into the City. "I'm your coach. I'm just telling you what's best for the team. You both need to stop being immature."

What was best for the team was for everyone to get along. If Dorian couldn't handle it, she'd be forced to step in, though she was a firm believer in people sorting out their own problems. Unfortunately, that didn't always happen.

The sun had risen more fully now, the air heating up, almost suffocating and leaving her sweating even as she stood there. Her skin felt sticky and uncomfortable. She didn't understand how the locals handled it. She died in any temperature over seventy-five.

Dorian didn't reply, gazing up at the portrait of Mao. She hoped he would take her words to heart.

Crossing the little bridge to the entrance to the Forbidden City, she grabbed Dorian's arm and kept him close as they passed through the archway, brushing her fingers against the little golden balls attached to the door. Some had the gold rubbed clean off—for good luck, Brian had told her. Brian was big on cultures.

Georgia glanced over the large square bricks inlaid into the ground. There was another doorway in the distance, a long line weaving out as people waited to get in. They joined the line for tickets.

"Were you scared?" Dorian asked abruptly, and Georgia glanced at him curiously. "Your first time."

The line shuffled forward minutely. "Terrified. I was barely sixteen and all my hopes were hanging on a gold medal that I wouldn't ever get." Her first Olympics had been her last and mostly she remembered many sleepless nights, listening to her roommate's Cyndi Lauper tape. Cyndi had spoken to her soul for that brief year.

"But you got a silver."

She smiled, nodding. Her Olympics had really been a blur. "I did, but looking back, I really remember the time I spent with my team more than those few minutes I stood on the podium. And you will too."

"I just want a gold medal."

She shook her head, patting his arm. "There's more to life than medals."

"Not at the Olympics."

"Well, life isn't the Olympics," she told him. "And life isn't a competition. And someday you might regret it if your only memories are how much Jules annoyed you."

Dorian's eyebrow went up, but Georgia only laughed at him.

"Trust me. If you don't react, it'll stop. They have other things to worry about too. I need you to promise me that you'll try." She hoped Dorian could find something in him to let it go. There was no use rising to Jules' taunts except that Jules found it highly amusing.

At that, Dorian grimaced. "They don't try."

"You have to be the bigger person." She couldn't spend her time coddling Dorian. Just because she liked him didn't mean he could get away with murder.

"Can we work on my bars routine later?" he asked instead.

She smiled to herself. Dorian would never change. "Maybe after some much-needed sight-seeing," she replied, letting him get away with not answering this time. At least she'd said it. Maybe it would sink in later. "It's about time you had some fun." She smiled at his disgruntled expression. It was her job, after all, to keep them on track, and not just on track to win.

Chapter 2
Money Where Your Mouth Is

"Tuck your arms in tighter!" Brian shouted as Dorian hurtled over the vault and landed with a thud.

Reeling forward, Dorian felt himself tripping and barely caught himself from stumbling off the mat. That would have been bad. Rubbing his face, he stepped over to the edge where Georgia handed him a bottle of water. Brian didn't look too pleased.

"You're leaning too far into it before takeoff," he said. "Screwing up the angle when you land."

Dorian knew. He already knew what he was doing wrong. He could feel it when he was in the air, body twisting around in a move that was probably too difficult for him to attempt this late in the game, but if he wanted to win, he had to do everything in his power to up the difficulty level of his performances. The higher the difficulty, the higher the scores and the better chance of getting a spot in the all-around.

"He's so light, he's probably just floating up there," Jules commented from where he sat on the bench, waiting his turn.

Dorian shot him a glare over Brian's shoulder, but Brian ignored him.

"Just relax," he said instead. "I know you can do this."

Dorian pulled his eyes away from Jules' grin and took a swig of water. He tried to remember what Georgia had said. Ignore Jules. Ignore him and he would go away. Wiping the sweat off his forehead, he rose back up and rotated his shoulders once. He could do it. He'd done it before. He would wipe that smirk right off Jules' face.

"How's the ankle?" Georgia asked.

"Fine." Dorian set the water down and headed for the end of the runway again, pausing to gather himself. He could control his body, he told himself. He could control the angle and the landing. He could stick it.

He always hated the beginnings of routines. Even in practice, he felt nervous, as though anything could go wrong before he was up in the air and it was up to gravity to pull him through. He shook out the nerves in his fingers and drew up his energy as he started down the runway, gathering speed until the vault was just a blur as he launched forward and pushed off, twisting around three times and landing with a hard thud, but he kept his balance just barely, rising to his feet and letting out a breath.

"Much better," Brian said as Dorian trotted over and hopped down into the pit, grabbing the water again. Dorian smiled. That was much better.

"Yeah," Jules echoed, rising from the bench and passing by Dorian. "Just watch that ankle." He tapped Dorian's cheek as he went, and Dorian reeled back.

"Jerk," Dorian muttered under his breath, sinking onto the bench next to Mitya and taking the towel Georgia handed him. He looked away from Jules as he prepared to vault and watched Adrian on the rings instead.

"Good job, Jules," Brian said a minute later, and Dorian looked over to see Jules flash Brian a smile, charming as ever. "Watch the landing, though. A few more inches and you'd be out of bounds."

Dorian smiled this time to himself, shoving the towel in his bag and leaning back against the wall. Around the arena, other teams were practicing. He recognized a few competitors from other meets, but mostly everyone kept to their respective teams.

"You shouldn't look so cocky."

Surprised, Dorian turned to find Mitya watching him.

"I'm not cocky," he replied, and Mitya shrugged.

"You're world champion vault," he said, his faded Russian accent slipping in amongst his missing words. "You're cocky. So is Jules."

Dorian didn't know what to say, but Mitya seemed to be finished as he sat back and started wrapping his hands for the bars.

Slightly put-off, Dorian turned back to the floor, watching Jules do his second vault. He could tell just from watching that he'd angled too far forward, hadn't come out of the last twist soon enough, and watched Jules land on his hands and knees.

Maybe he was a little cocky, he thought as Jules pushed himself up and huffed at the mat. He allowed himself to feel vaguely satisfied, though. After all, Jules had one of the best, most competitive coaches in the country at home — Coach Harper, who came with a somewhat fearsome reputation — so Dorian expected him not to mess up.

"Walk it off," Brian told him as Jules returned to the pit, rubbing his head and looking annoyed. "There's plenty of time before it starts."

There were, in fact, only a couple days before the real competition started. The camera crews had already started coming around, filming promos and interviewing the coaches. Dorian had spotted Jules flirting shamelessly with the interview girl from NBC news. The sight made his stomach turn, but it wasn't his business if Jules wanted to whore himself out for a little media attention. When Dorian won all-around, he'd get plenty of attention.

"Nice vault," he said as Jules passed by him.

Jules paused a second, glancing back at him. He didn't get mad. Instead, he merely smiled, eyes burning into Dorian. "We'll see how you feel after the bars, tater tot."

He went on and Dorian sighed. So much for ignoring Jules.

"Cocky," Mitya said from beside him as he rose and headed for the bars.

Crossing his arms, Dorian sunk onto the bench. The parallel bars weren't exactly his best event, and everyone on the team knew it. No one's weakness was a secret.

"Drink your water," Brian said a moment later as he walked past. Dorian raised it to his lips but didn't drink.

Instead, he glanced over at Jules down the bench, laughing with Carey about something. Both their eyes flicked to Dorian a second later. Dorian had had plenty of experience with people talking behind his back. It came with the job, but it was usually competitors not teammates who did it. He wasn't really sure what to do, and

Mitya had a point. They were all cocky, but mostly, he just felt left out, especially when Carey sniggered into Jules' shoulder and Jules merely grinned and looked away.

Lowering his water, he slumped his shoulders and looked away from Carey and Jules. He didn't care what they said about him. He didn't, or at least that was what he told himself and ignored the sinking feeling in his stomach.

The next few days did not go well and Thursday found Dorian falling on his ass after a slip on the parallel bars.

"Fuck," he cursed to himself, not loud enough for the French guy waiting on the sidelines to hear.

"Come on, Dorian, get up," Brian called to him, and Dorian dragged himself up, rubbing his ass and glaring at the bars. He could do so much better than this. He had to do so much better than this if he had any chance of winning anything for the team or for himself.

In the pit, Jules said something to Carey, who merely smiled and nodded.

Shaking himself, Dorian forced himself back to the bars, hoisting himself up and restarting the routine. He couldn't be worrying about Jules now. The first half on the bars went fine, but it was always the double back release that caught him up, his hands just a centimeter off in one direction or another.

He slipped again but grabbed on tighter and managed to swing himself up. His dismount was shaky at best, but he was panting for breath, hating the parallel bars already. He knew he wouldn't be doing them for the team competition, but if he made it to all-around, he would have to.

"Better," Brian said as Dorian dropped into the pit, but Dorian knew he was just saying it. Bars were not his thing. "Jules, you're up."

Jules rose from his seat next to Carey, passing behind where Dorian stood, wiping the sweat off his face with a towel. He stepped in close behind him.

"That *was* better, Thumbelina," he muttered in his ear, and

Dorian jumped as Jules slapped his ass. Hard.

Staring after, mouth hanging open, anger bubbled up inside him, but Jules was already trotting up the stairs and stretching out his muscles.

Dorian caught sight of Georgia, though, who shook her head sternly at him. Frustrated, Dorian threw the towel onto his bag and strode off towards the bathroom. He knew Jules was only doing it to mess with him, but the fact that no one else seemed to find it distracting or necessary to correct really pissed him off.

In the bathroom, he stood at the sink, staring at his reflection in the tall mirror. His muscles stood out under his shirt, and he used the hem to wipe off the sweat on his brow, blue eyes staring back at him under his messy hair. The camera crews would be there full time starting tomorrow, and Dorian wasn't going to let Jules get away with that on live TV.

He splashed some water on his face, trying to calm himself down. He couldn't let this get to him. It was exactly what Jules wanted. He just needed to focus.

By the time he returned to the gym, Jules had finished and was back in his seat next to Carey. Dorian took the chair furthest from him and watched Mitya do his floor routine instead.

Dorian poked at his dinner, surrounded by the hundreds, if not thousands, of other athletes in the cafeteria. Across from him, Georgia cracked open a bottle of water and took a sip.

"Not hungry?" she asked. "You need to stay on the diet, especially now. Everything is going to start soon. Opening ceremony is tomorrow."

Dorian nodded. He knew. He knew that already. It was one of the many things he couldn't stop thinking about. The opening ceremony, the competition, his routines. They all took up valuable space in his mind. He paused instead of replying right away, glancing up at Georgia. She didn't look worried at all, but then, she wasn't competing. Her competing days were over.

"Is it always this stressful?" he asked, pushing a tomato around his plate. "Are your teammates always jerks?"

Georgia laughed, shaking her head. "Don't mind the guys. It's their way of testing you."

Dorian frowned at the idea. He'd made it to the Olympics already. That should have been his test. He didn't see why they had to pick on him all the time. It wasn't helping anything.

"Why do they have to test me?"

"Because you'll react," she said knowingly. "Dorian, it's no secret you're the least experienced here."

"So you think I don't deserve to be here?"

Georgia shook her head. "I think you're young, and the guys see that. Everyone here deserves to be. You've all worked as hard as anyone to get here, and the next few weeks are going to prove that."

Dorian was silent for a moment, reaching for his water.

Georgia leaned across the table. "Why do you want to be here?"

Dorian frowned then laughed slightly. "To win."

"Really," she said seriously. "Why do you want to be an Olympian?"

Dorian paused. "I've always wanted to be one, ever since I was six years old. My dad and I used to watch the Olympics every four years, and he always said that someday I'd be the one on that platform. I spent all my time practicing and he spent all his time working so that I could." He looked away from Georgia, away over the heads of the many other people in the cafeteria. "He died a couple years ago, and then I got injured, and I don't know. I just felt like I had to get here, like I have to win for him."

Georgia smiled, sitting back. "I'm sure he knows you're here."

Dorian smiled slightly at her, sighing. Sometimes it was all he could do to stop thinking about his dad. He felt like he never stopped. It was always there in the back of his mind, pushing him to go further, to do more, to never stop. Sometimes it could be overwhelming, but he forced himself to push through. This was no time to get emotional, not during the biggest competition of his life.

"Now if I can just win," he said simply.

Georgia reached across the table and patted his arm. "You'll do

the best you can."
    "Thanks, Georgie."

Chapter 3
Opening Ceremonies

Only a few lights remained on in the arena, casting a low glow over the equipment, and Dorian glanced around. The stands were empty, the pit cleared of people. It was just him and the bars. They looked so innocent in the dim light, and he ran a hand over one. The bars had always been his worst event, from the very first time when he'd fallen on his tailbone and limped around for a week to today when he felt like a complete failure, only barely able to hold on. He could do much better on the high bar.

He shook his head, sighing into the empty gym. He had to get this routine right.

Stepping in between the bars, he lifted himself up slowly, taking his time, arms straining against the flexible bars.

"You know you're not allowed to be in here."

A voice startled him, and Dorian dropped to the ground, turning to see Jules standing on the edge of the mat, an eyebrow arched.

"What are you doing here?" Dorian asked tiredly, ducking under the bar and crossing his arms. He really didn't want to see or talk to Jules right now.

"What are you doing here?" Jules asked instead of answering. "Trying to get kicked out? You can't be in here without a coach or a medical team. It's dangerous."

"Like you care if I injure myself," Dorian snorted. "You're probably hoping it will happen."

Jules shrugged. "Can't say I'm not." He smiled slightly. "But if you're kicked out, we have to use an alternate, and they're not nearly as fun to play with."

Dorian's eyes narrowed. He'd had just about enough of Jules' "playing."

"I'm not here for you to play with," he snarled, taking a step towards Jules. "And if you pull another stunt like you did today, I won't hesitate to punch you in the face."

Jules didn't laugh, but he looked like he wanted to, eyes shining, amused. "Really?" he asked. "Your southern code of ethics allows that? Go on. Do it."

Dorian glared, but his hands remained at his sides. As much as he wanted to punch Jules, it would probably find a way of coming back to him in a bad way. Things always did. When he didn't move, Jules laughed softly, biting his bottom lip and shaking his head.

"I knew it. You don't really want this. You just want to say you were here. You *tried*. And that's what matters."

It was the condescending tone that really snapped something inside Dorian and made him swing his fist around, inches from making contact with Jules' jaw, but Jules was quicker, and before Dorian knew it, the wind was knocked out of him and he was flat on his back against the mat. Struggling to breathe, he tried to fight against Jules on top of him, but Jules was bigger and stronger, and he pinned him down as easily as if he were a wrestler.

Dorian gasped for breath as it finally came back, pushing against Jules. "Get the fuck off me," he spat breathlessly, struggling under Jules' hands tight on his arms, his legs pinning him to the mat.

Jules hovered over him, eyes dark, keeping him stuck to the floor. "Do you really want this?" he whispered, close enough that Dorian could feel the warmth of his breath against his chin. He still struggled against his grip, but he could barely move an inch. Jules was too heavy, too strong above him.

Jules shifted, adjusting his legs to keep Dorian pressed in place. Dorian glared up at him, finally able to breathe normally again. He felt hot from Jules' body against his, and he cast around for any way to use Jules' weight to his advantage.

"Do you really want to be an Olympian?" Jules asked, and Dorian felt his thumb pressing against his pulse, the pulse that was already quickened from their precarious position on the mat, the anger coursing through him. "Or are you just a spoiled kid looking for the next thrill?"

Dorian's eyes flashed angrily up at Jules. If he could punch him, he would this time, no holding back. Jules didn't know anything about his past, how much work it had taken to get there, how much he'd had to sacrifice over the years. Jules didn't care.

He opened his mouth to spit back a response, but he sucked in a breath as Jules' thumb brushed up his throat, pressing down slightly, constricting his throat, though not enough to cut off his air. Staring up at Jules, he wasn't sure if he was scared or just angry, his heart pounding in his chest as he tried to swallow.

"J-Jules," he tried to warn him, squirming beneath him as Jules' thumb grazed over his Adam's apple, pressing in against his racing pulse. He could have moved, pushed Jules away, but he was stuck, brain ceasing to function as he tried to breathe normally, wondering what was going to happen. He wasn't afraid of Jules, but having him on top, bodies pressed together, was doing strange things to him.

For a moment, he couldn't force himself to move, unsure where this was going, if Jules was going to punch him or if he was going to do something else. But Jules' thumb slid away finally, back to his wrist, yanking it up above his head, and Dorian blinked quickly, breath coming quicker now.

Jules glanced down at him, impassive for a second, but then he shifted, and Dorian's mouth fell open at the flash of blinding friction against his hips. He was completely hard.

"You liked that?" Jules asked, rocking his hips down even as Dorian bit his lip against the heat rising on his skin, the tightness in his body. "Thought you might."

Dorian swallowed, exhaling a shaky breath. He stared up at Jules, unable to explain why he was hard, unable to explain the heat coursing through his body, the flush in his cheeks, the pounding of his heart in his chest. Even after all that, he wasn't prepared for Jules to smash their mouths together in a hard, unfinessed kiss that dazed him for a second, feeling Jules' tongue in his mouth, but he reacted a second later, using his shoulder to knock Jules back.

"What the fuck are you doing?" he demanded, hating the way his cheeks flushed pink and how his breath came in short pants now. His cock throbbed as Jules shifted on top of him again, pressing their hips together in a blinding flash of heat that almost had him moaning like a whore.

"Getting off," Jules replied, leaning in for another kiss, and even though Dorian knew it was coming this time, he didn't try to fight it.

He let Jules kiss him, bite at his mouth, push his tongue inside. He even kissed back, though not gently, the competitive urge rising in him, anger and lust surfacing as he responded to Jules' tongue in his mouth.

Dorian had done this before with other guys, guys he would never see again, guys who just wanted a quick fuck at a party and didn't care who he was. He'd never done it with someone who would remember his face the next day, but he couldn't stop now.

He wasn't going to let Jules have the last laugh.

Jules' body pressed in hard against him, hands loosening their grip, and when he had Jules licking into his mouth, teeth closed around his bottom lip, he moved, rolling them over with an agility that came from many years of training. He pulled out of the kiss, licking his swollen lip and taking the moment of control to lock eyes with Jules, who didn't look surprised or upset at all.

Jules only swallowed and quirked a brow. "What are you gonna do now, Dorian? Walk away? Pretend you don't want this?"

Dorian didn't want this, but his cock said otherwise, straining against the stretchy material of his pants. He wanted power over Jules and this might be the only way, except that Jules was watching him knowingly, knowing he wasn't going to walk away.

"Suck me off," Jules said a second later, leaning up into Dorian's mouth, whispering the words against his lips, tongue flicking out to taste him. "Come on, shortstack. Show me what you're made of."

It sounded so absolutely filthy when Jules said it, pushing his body up against Dorian's in a clear invitation, and Dorian felt his resolve slipping. It would be easy, so easy, just to get off right now, right on the mat where tomorrow they would have to compete. Though it seemed they were alone, he knew there had to be security all around. It wasn't safe at all, and it wasn't as though he wanted anyone to know about this.

He could feel Jules' hard prick pressing up against him, rubbing against his thigh, inviting him to make a move. He could see it in

Jules' eyes, the dark spark that danced there, daring him to do it.

"Suck me off," Jules repeated, licking up Dorian's neck, ignoring the way Dorian jerked back, but Dorian came back a second later, pressing their mouths together in a rough, greedy kiss that he felt all the way to his toes.

"Not here," Dorian hissed, though he was ready to rise to the challenge set to him. He would prove to Jules that he wasn't afraid of anything he could dish out.

"Locker room then," Jules replied just as quickly, struggling up and heading out of the gym.

Down the hall, Dorian's resolve didn't waver, though he could feel the blood rushing to his cock, something between excitement and anger at Jules. They made it to the locker room unseen, bursting through the doors. Dorian didn't waste time going slowly, shoving Jules roughly up against the lockers. He enjoyed the loud sound of his shoulders hitting the metal.

Reaching for Jules' jeans, Dorian yanked them open, tugging them down just enough to get his cock out. He slid to his knees, heart hammering in his chest as the realization hit him of what he was doing. This was Jules, the guy he'd had a crush on for way too long, up until he realized Jules was a complete douchebag. Still, that didn't change that Dorian had thought about this moment in the past, four years ago when he'd watched Jules on TV at the last Olympics.

Jules' hand slid into his hair as Dorian moved his mouth down, pulling Jules' prick out of his jeans, smoothing his hand over the hard, heavy length. He barely paused to swallow, moving in and running his tongue over the prick.

He sucked at the head, listening to Jules' agreeable hum of satisfaction, wincing when Jules' fingers tightened in his hair. He wasn't going to make this completely pleasurable for Jules, though, and let his teeth scrape against the sensitive skin.

"Shit," Jules cursed loudly, jerking Dorian back. "Play nice, kid."

Dorian didn't want to play nice, swallowing him further, sucking until Jules made soft noises, hips pushing up into his mouth. Dorian shoved them down sharply, taking complete control. He wanted Jules to come, to surrender to him, to admit that he was better at something, even if it was cock sucking.

"Looks like your mouth is good for something," Jules commented, quirking half a smile before he gasped and bit his lip.

Dorian didn't reply, reaching for the base of Jules' cock, hand wrapping around it and squeezing. He worked it hard and fast, licking over the ridges in his prick and sucking until he felt Jules' body tensing under his hands. He started to pull away, but Jules' hand tightened in his hair, pushing him back down.

"Fuck," Jules breathed as he came, holding Dorian in place though Dorian jerked back, wrenching out of his grip and wiping at his mouth, the come that hit his chin as he pulled away.

"Fuck you," he spat back, licking the taste of Jules off his lips. "Jackass." He looked away from Jules' cock finally, an overwhelming feeling of disgust and anger washing over him.

"A little come won't hurt you," Jules said lazily, rubbing his stomach and sighing.

Struggling up, Dorian adjusted his pants, glad they were roomy. How he could still be hard after that, he didn't know, but he wasn't going to give Jules the satisfaction of knowing that. He paused, wanting to say something, but he couldn't think what. Instead, he turned finally and strode away, back to the room to take a very long, cold shower and never think about this again.

Dorian was supposed to be focusing on the screaming crowds, on the people walking next to him, on this moment that he may never get to experience again, but instead, he could only think of Jules. He couldn't get the image of Jules from the night before out of his mind. It was ridiculous considering how much he disliked Jules and how much of last night was probably just a ploy to distract him.

It was the opening ceremony, and all Dorian could think about was Jules' infuriating smile, the way he'd practically ordered Dorian to get him off, and how Dorian hadn't bothered to fight him at all.

He should have said no and left. He should have reported Jules to Brian or Georgia. Instead, he had let it all happen and even instigated some of it. What had he been thinking? He wasn't desperate for Jules' or anyone else's attention. He'd always been the quiet kid, preferring to spend his time alone or with a few select friends. He'd never been good in a crowd, and Jules was not someone he should let distract him.

Glancing over, he could see Jules through a gap in the crowd of USA competitors as they all walked down the long track to where the torch burned brightly in the dim light. He was surrounded by people he didn't know: runners, long jumpers, divers, swimmers, wrestlers, volleyball players, people he'd never actually see beyond that night unless he watched them on television.

Georgia walked to his left, smiling and waving at the crowd. She glanced at him. "Smile, Dorian. The cameras are on."

Shaking himself, Dorian tried to forget about Jules. He couldn't let himself get distracted at this point in the game. The Olympics hadn't even officially started and already he was starting to doubt himself.

Looking up at the crowd, he wished he knew where his mother was, but it was impossible to spot anyone in the huge stands that lined the track. Flashes from cameras blinked back at him and large, professional cameras floated over them as they walked, attached to long metal rods. Camera people moved here and there between them, and Dorian smiled into one, waving into the lens.

He should have been concentrating on the feeling of just being there, of walking down that track in the USA uniform, knowing that he was part of something bigger than himself, but something nagged at the back of his mind. He didn't know what it was, though, so he shoved it away, keeping his gaze turned from Jules and trying to take in everything around him.

Years ago, he never would have dreamed he'd be at the Olympics let alone competing in them. He remembered begging his parents to let him take lessons, to send him to camp all summer long. By the time he'd hit high school, he'd been training non-stop and had moved to a gymnastic center across the country. Every spare minute was spent at the gym or practicing, watching videos of former champions on the internet.

His friends had called him obsessed, but he never cared. He was doing what he wanted, what he'd always wanted, and now he'd finally made it. As far as he was concerned, all the sacrifices had been worth it, even if it had meant not having a life outside the gym, seeing his parents only on holidays, and being a complete idiot when it came to social interactions with other people.

The ceremony seemed to go much faster than it did on television, but most of it was a blur to Dorian. All he would remember afterward was walking and listening to speeches but not remembering a single word. It felt almost like high school graduation, the excitement humming in the crowd, knowing something much bigger was on the horizon.

The women's gymnastics team stood beside him as they listened to the speeches, and one of the girls whispered to her teammate, "Did you see Jules this year?"

The other girl stretched back to look at Jules through the crowd. Dorian frowned, determinedly not turning his head to watch her.

"He looks even better than last time. What's the betting he takes all-around?"

It shouldn't have bothered him, but after last night, it made something bubble up inside him—embarrassment, shame, jealousy? He wasn't sure, but he didn't like how it felt. For years, he'd fantasized about what being with Jules might have been like, and after last night, he finally knew, but it hadn't been how he'd imagined it. Of course, when he'd imagined it, he had found Jules charming and romantic. Now he was torn between finding Jules infuriating and feeling stupid about what they'd done. Dorian didn't want to hear any more and stepped up next to Georgia instead. She smiled at him briefly before turning back to the podium.

Jules wasn't his problem. *He* was the only thing standing in his way right now.

"You're going to remember this for the rest of your life," Georgia said as they stood together, two amongst thousands all there for the same thing, all hoping for that same moment.

Dorian didn't doubt it. He would probably always remember the way he happened to look back, eyes locking with Jules' for just a second, the way Jules' mouth curled upward, then the moment was over. His heart sped up and a flush spread over the back of his neck. He blamed the lights blaring down, but he would remember that forever too.

Chapter 4
Sweeping the Floor

The hardest part of competitions wasn't the constant practice, the early wake-up calls, or dealing with other competitors who secretly hoped you'd break your ankle with each dismount. For Dorian, it was being away from home, away from his friends who, even though they barely understood gymnastics, didn't give him too much shit about wearing a leotard. This was the Olympics, though, which for his friends meant it was an excuse to come to a foreign country and drink the bars dry.

"You're allowed to have one drink," Jason said, pushing a glass of something bright blue under Dorian's nose, but he shook his head, pushing it away.

"Can't," he replied even though all he wanted to do was get drunk and stop worrying about Friday when everything would finally start. "I'm not even supposed to be out right now."

"I can't believe you have a curfew." Jason rolled his eyes. "What are you, five?"

Dorian didn't reply. He could only think about practice that day and the horrible time he'd had on the bars, messing up his routine twice and getting chewed out by Brian. He'd deserved it, though. He couldn't lose focus for a second or things went wrong. People got hurt. He was having trouble getting Jules' infuriating smirk out of his head, the way he'd said, "And that's the sound of the all-around going to me."

Around them, the bar was more like a club, and Dorian was sure he'd heard the same five songs over and over again in the past hour. He could barely hear Jason over the noise, and the flashing colored lights were starting to give him a headache.

Dorian still couldn't explain Jules and his constant need to make Dorian feel like an inexperienced athlete at his first competition. He had put in the hours to get there the same as Jules had. His ridiculous crush — okay, it had been an obsession — with Jules prior to the Olympics may have clouded his judgment, and it had hurt when Jules had merely laughed at him and called him "squirt" the first time they'd met.

Jason arched an eyebrow when he didn't reply. "Dor, relax. You're in the fucking Olympics. You're a fucking Olympian. That's awesome."

Dorian nodded after a second, sighing to himself. He hadn't really taken much time to accept it lately, too worried about performing and practicing and trying not to let Jules get under his skin, but Jason was right. "Yeah," he agreed finally, quirking a small smile. "I almost thought it would never happen after the last injury."

"But your ankle is totally healed, right?"

Dorian shrugged. "As much as it'll ever be. Just don't tell anyone on the team that I said that."

"Come on, it was two years ago," Jason said, grabbing his drink. "Since then, you've won, like, a thousand world championships."

"One," Dorian corrected him, but he couldn't help smiling. He'd done a fairly good job after the injury that everyone had thought would put him out of the running. An injured ankle coming off the floor exercise. It had taken him out of that year's World's competition, and hard work and perseverance had been the only thing to bring him back. He was determined not to let that happen again.

"Still," Jason said, tossing him a significant look. "That's more than most people."

Dorian smiled, shaking his head. "It's not like everyone can be a gymnast."

"Yeah, only the uptight workaholics," Jason joked. "And they never do anything else."

Dorian couldn't argue with that. He practically lived in the gym during the school year, always working on harder routines with his teammates. Gymnastics was his whole life, and it had been since his dad had died. He had to prove somehow that it was all worth it, all the work his parents had put into getting him here. Nerves welled up inside him at the thought of letting his mom down. He didn't think he could stand it if he did, seeing her face, knowing what he'd put her through all these years. For a second, his eyes rested on the glass of alcohol sitting before him. One drink surely wouldn't... no. He shook his head, telling himself to get a grip.

"I should get back," he said finally, rising from the table. "Early wake-up tomorrow."

"You have an early wake-up every day," Jason reminded him, but Dorian was already heading for the door. Jason caught up with him, though. "Just one more bar, Dor. Come on."

"I can't," he replied, stepping out into the cool night air. The streets were filled with revelers, people celebrating the Olympics to begin. He was glad he could blend into the crowd here even as he weaved out from in between people, Jason following doggedly.

"Hey," Jason said, catching him by the shoulder and dragging him around. "You should enjoy this. You only live once, Dor."

Dorian rolled his eyes but smiled. "Thanks, but I really should get back before I get in trouble. I'll see you later. You didn't lose the tickets, did you?"

"Your mom has 'em," Jason replied. "She figured it was safest."

Dorian nodded, checking his watch. He had to get the train before it stopped running and he was stuck in the city all night, not that Jason would be opposed to that. He was pretty sure Brian and Georgia would have a fit, though.

"I'll see you on Monday then," he said. "Don't drink too much."

Jason nodded, laughing and shaking his head at Dorian as he turned and disappeared into the crowd.

The metro ride seemed longer than normal, but it may have been because he kept nodding off every second then jerking awake, fearful of missing his stop.

He finally stumbled off the train, walking the long distance to the village and fishing for his room key as he took the elevator up. At his floor, he dragged his feet down the hallway, pausing at his door and sighing. He really needed to get to bed or Brian would have his head tomorrow.

"Breaking curfew?"

Jules' voice startled him, and Dorian glanced over to find Jules leaning in his doorway, the next room over. He had a knowing arch to his eyebrows, and Dorian looked away instead, pushing the card into the slot. He didn't really want to talk to Jules right now. The light clicked green, but he didn't open the door.

"Just went for a walk."

"Yeah, you smell like a walk," Jules drawled.

He probably smelled like bar smoke and beer. He didn't reply, though, and the door locked itself again. He should have gone in, he told himself, but he didn't unlock it again. Down the hall, Jules pushed off the door and meandered closer despite how Dorian's body tensed.

"Hey, I won't tell," Jules said softly, pausing a foot behind Dorian. Dorian kept his eyes on the handle. "Everybody's gotta get out sometime. No use being cooped up like an animal. You should go party with your friends. It might be your only chance."

Dorian turned sharply to face Jules, the key edges pressing into his palm. He nearly knocked into Jules; he was too close now, stepping up to him.

"I'm going to beat you, Jules, and nothing you can say will shake me. Just because you're a douche doesn't mean you're any better than me. I'm gonna win."

Jules didn't react for a minute, his hand coming up to rest against the wall behind Dorian. Dorian swallowed slowly, keeping a close watch on every movement, ready to hit back if he had to, but Jules didn't try to hit him. Instead, his mouth curled into a smile and he tipped his head down to meet Dorian's eyes.

Dorian's heart pounded against his throat, nerves he hadn't felt before coursing through him as he stared up at Jules. The rest of the hallway was deathly still around them.

"You're stronger than you look," Jules said finally, and his smile widened. "But not strong enough to beat me." His body leaned forward, and Dorian had nowhere to go, pressed up against the wall with Jules far too close to him. He couldn't explain the way his breath shook when he exhaled, so close to Jules, close enough to see the stubble on his jaw, the green ring around his irises. "So you celebrate with your friends, but remember that in that gym, you're mine."

Dorian blinked, and in that second, Jules moved back, heading to his room and closing the door behind him. Letting out a shaky breath, he turned back to the door and shoved the card in the slot, jerking the handle open and slipping inside. Leaning up against the door, he closed his eyes for a second, feeling winded though he'd done nothing.

He stood there for a long moment, feeling weak, but he turned finally and locked the door. Jules was just messing with his head.

Mitya was sleeping soundly in his bed, where Dorian had left him hours ago. He probably hadn't stirred at all throughout the whole thing. Dorian tossed the keycard on the table and flopped onto the bed, not bothering to get undressed. He had to be awake in a few hours anyway. As he lay there, staring at the dark ceiling, he couldn't find an explanation for why his limbs felt shaky, why he hadn't shoved Jules away. He didn't like the feeling and rolled over instead, forcing himself to fall into an uneasy sleep.

"Big day tomorrow," Jules commented, grabbing his water from the table and shooting a glance down the table to where Dorian sat. To his slight disappointment, Dorian didn't look up from his plate. "You guys better be nervous."

"You wish," Carey replied, digging his fork into his salad. "What is this, your second Olympics? It's my third."

"And yet you've never won a gold," Jules pointed out, grinning as Carey punched his shoulder lightly. Then again, he hadn't won a gold either. He'd come close four years ago, but he'd had to settle for bronze in the all-around. He hadn't medaled in any individual events and the team had barely missed third place to the Ukrainian team. This was his year, though. He could feel it.

He glanced down the table at Dorian, who seemed intent on his salad. Mitya was quiet as well, but it was Dorian's silence that made Jules want to say something.

"You nervous, kid?"

He enjoyed the way Dorian's eyes flashed to him, annoyance written all over his face. It was like playing with an annoyed kitten, dangling a string just out of his reach. He knew Dorian couldn't resist biting back.

"I'm fine," Dorian muttered finally.

"It's normal to be nervous," he said, taking a swig of his water. Around them, the cafeteria was filled with athletes, the noise of chatter and silverware surrounding them. "My first time, I almost fell off the bars. Hope that doesn't happen to you."

He could tell from the way Dorian's fingers tightened over his fork that he hadn't helped anything. If Dorian wanted to let everything get to him, he wasn't going to get far.

The first time Jules had heard of Dorian Stuart — some up-and-coming gymnast from the south — he'd scoffed. Since when did the south have great gymnasts? But Dorian had trained at a Center. He was a World Champion, and if he could make it on the Olympic team, there was no reason he shouldn't be good enough. It had amused him when Dorian had introduced himself the first time, slightly fumbling, wide-eyed as though he couldn't quite believe it. Of course, the first time Jules had called him "squirt," that had all changed. Jules kind of missed the wide-eyed innocence. The constant scowl didn't improve his looks.

Whenever he looked at Dorian, though, Coach Harper's words came back to him.

"This is your shot at the gold, Jules. Don't let anyone, especially that Stuart kid, take it away from you. You're better than him; remember that. You've gotta let him know you're competition and he should watch out."

Coach Harper was just looking out for him. He'd been Jules' coach for almost eight years now — he knew him better than anyone. He was the whole reason Jules had been able to go to the last Olympics and a big part of him being here now. Without his parents' monetary support, Jules only had Coach Harper to help him through. Harper had a lot of faith in Jules' abilities, and Jules couldn't appreciate it enough. Besides, he was right about Dorian. Had to keep him on his toes. Couldn't make it too easy, after all.

It was too late to go back now, though. It looked like his die was cast as the villain in Dorian's mind, so he figured he might as well live up to it. What other form of entertainment was there when stuck in an Olympic village for a month?

Still, teasing Dorian could only entertain him for so long. At some point, surely Dorian would stop reacting. Most everyone did. Besides, there were other things Jules would prefer to do with Dorian that didn't involve talking. He hadn't told anyone else on the team, and he doubted any of them would care. Who he slept with was no one's business. They all had their own problems to deal with. His dad hadn't even pretended he wanted to come this year. Jules figured he was better off without him anyway. He had been for most of his life.

For a moment, he gazed down the table at Dorian while the others discussed the judges and the odds of favoritism for the Chinese gymnasts. Dorian picked at his dinner, probably as nervous as Jules had been his first time. Dorian was better than Jules had been at that age, though, and he knew it. That was part of the problem. So far, Jules hadn't seen much humility from Dorian.

He didn't blame him. He hadn't exactly been the most humble victor at that age either. The night he'd won the bronze medal four years ago, he had celebrated by taking a hot reporter out for drinks and fucking him outside a club in Athens. Not exactly his smartest move, but it had been a good fuck.

Dorian looked up, meeting his eye. For a second, he looked confused, but then he stood and left, taking his tray with him.

"There goes the entertainment," Jules muttered, and Carey looked over. Mitya raised his head across the table.

"People are not entertainment."

"Oh, come on, Mitya," Jules said with a grin. "You gotta admit it's a little funny."

"You are teammate," Mitya said instead, and Jules sighed.

Mitya would say that. He was very big on loyalty considering his own background. Jules couldn't even imagine what it had been like for Mitya: moving to a different country as a child, not knowing the language, struggling to fit in. Jules had always fit in wherever he went, being loud to cover up the things he wanted to hide. If he could get everyone to like him, they wouldn't ever see the problems behind closed doors. After a while, it had just become a habit. He had never understood people like Dorian who would rather sit alone than talk to people.

"It's just for fun," he said, and Mitya shrugged.

"Not always fun for everyone."

Coach Harper would have told Jules that the Olympics wasn't about being a team, not when a teammate could take the win away from you. Jules didn't know what to say to Mitya, and he grabbed his fork instead.

"All right, listen to me," Georgia said, pulling Dorian's head from where he was staring out at the floor, watching the guy from Ukraine do his routine, the judges scribbling things down on their pads of paper. "You've done this routine a hundred times. Don't think about the people watching. Don't think about the judges. Don't think about your teammates. These are your sixty seconds."

Dorian nodded, telling himself it would all be fine and taking a deep breath. He glanced up at the big screen where the guy had finished and was performing the bow to the judges and the crowd. He was next.

He stepped up out of the pit, shaking out the nerves in his body, loosening his shoulders.

"And, Dorian," Brian called as he stepped towards the large, blue mat to take his place. Dorian looked back. Brian smiled. "Take one step out of bounds and you'll be doing your parallel bars routine for a week."

Dorian smiled impulsively, nodding and stepping onto the floor.

For a moment, all the lights seemed to bear down upon him as he stood on the edge of the mat. He waited, watching the judges input their scores for the last person. He didn't need to see what the scores were. He didn't need to waste his time worrying about that.

The floor manager nodded at him once they were ready and he stepped into the corner of the mat as the announcer called his name to the waiting crowd. Other events were going on—Mitya was on the high bar, and other guys were doing other things—but it only mattered that Dorian was standing there, ready for his first event in the Olympics.

He paid his respects to the judges, closing his mind off from everything else when it came time to perform. The routine came easily, the back flips, forward saltos, the handstands that might have been over a little too soon, but as he stepped into the last corner to perform his last tumble, he was completely focused. The noise of the crowd was gone, just a rush in his ears.

He felt the air whooshing past him as his body moved, twisting gracefully in the air and landing just inches away from the boundaries.

The noise came rushing back, the crowd roaring in his ears as he turned to them and lifted his arm, jerking his head in acknowledgement. He couldn't stop the smile that spread over his face as he trotted down to the pit, grabbing the bottle of water Georgia held out.

"Good boy," Brian said, patting his back, and Dorian smiled, turning around to the camera following him.

He took a moment to wave, taking a drink of water and started to pace. Jules sat behind him, over a few feet, but he didn't say anything, probably because of the camera hovering in Dorian's face as Dorian peered up anxiously at the screen. He hadn't messed up. His handstand may have been a little short, but he hadn't fallen. He hadn't gone out of bounds. He'd stuck all the landings. He had to get a decent score.

He let out a breath of relief as the scores flashed on the screen, all ranging from a 9.5 to 9.8. It was better than he had expected, and he smiled to himself as he finally dropped into a chair and the camera swooped off to record someone else.

"Nice score, munchkin," Jules commented from beside him, flashing him a smirk. "Maybe someday you won't need a boost to the bars."

Dorian turned away from him, determined not to give him the benefit of knowing just how much he distracted him. He tried not to think about the other night, about Jules' hand in his hair, his cock in his mouth, hot and heavy against his tongue. He tried not to think about any of it, the annoyance that always built up in him when he did, the anger at Jules trying to get under his skin, the fact that it seemed to be working. Just because he'd sucked Jules off didn't mean they were friends. It didn't mean they liked each other. It didn't *mean* anything.

Except that he couldn't get it out of his head. A few years ago, it would have been his fantasy night, but now it just made his insides feel all jumbled up and confused. He didn't like it one bit. The most he could do was ignore Jules and hope he didn't make it to the all-around. At least then, Dorian might be rid of him.

Chapter 5

Bottling It Up

"I gasped," his mother babbled as they sat in a small restaurant in a corner of the city, dinners half-eaten but mostly forgotten as they went over the day. "When you were so close to the edge in that last tumble. I thought for sure —"

"I didn't, though," Dorian interrupted, and she nodded fervidly.

"I know." She smiled, reaching for his hand over the table. "You did so good, peaches. And you'll keep doing well."

"Mom, don't call me peaches," he said with an embarrassed wince. He was glad none of the team was around to hear that, especially with his mom's prominent southern drawl.

She shot him a look, taking her hand back. "Don't talk like that to your mother. I can call you whatever I want."

Dorian sighed but didn't argue.

"I promise I won't embarrass you in front of your teammates," she went on, taking a sip of her hot tea. Dorian hadn't understood drinking hot tea in the middle of summer, but it seemed to be the only thing Chinese restaurants served. "Speaking of, how are things going with y'all? Everybody gettin' along?"

Dorian jerked his shoulders in response. He really didn't want to talk about Jules or how every time Dorian looked at him, it just made him angrier. There was no real reason that Jules picked on him except that he was the youngest and shortest on the team. It had never made sense to Dorian.

"Dorian," his mother said knowingly when he didn't respond except to flick a carrot around his plate.

"There's just this one guy who's a complete jerk."

"Well, maybe he likes you."

"Mom!" Dorian shot her a look, a flush rising on the back of his neck at the suggestion. He couldn't even remember the last person he'd liked, and it certainly wouldn't be Jules. That didn't explain why it made him so nervous, her suggestion. She shrugged.

"You're a handsome young man," she said despite the way he buried his face in his hands. He didn't need his mother trying to figure out his love life for him. He didn't want her to try. He'd like to keep her as far away as possible if he could. "There's plenty of folks out there who might like to get to know you."

"Not him," he said sharply. "He's an ass."

"Watch your language," she reprimanded him.

Dorian didn't reply for a minute, frowning at his plate. He was pretty sure that Jules didn't like him, and this wasn't some kindergarten courtship complete with pushing him down on the playground, not that Dorian knew much about that. He'd never had a real boyfriend. Relationships were not any help in winning Olympic gold.

His mother picked up her cup. "Well, you just know that I'm proud of you, and if your dad was still here, he would be too."

Dorian nodded down at his plate. "You guys put a lot into getting me here," he said quietly. "You paid for the coaches, the training, you let me move to Colorado to train. Dad worked two jobs. I don't think I could ever —"

His mother held up a hand to stop him as he looked up. "You stop right there, Dorian. I wouldn't have done it any other way. And when you win that Olympic medal, your dad is gonna be lookin' down from Heaven and I know he wouldn't have changed a thing either."

"Thanks," he said, although he still felt he should say more. He always felt like he didn't say it enough. His dad had died before he got the chance to be a world champion, before he could really prove anything, prove that all the difficulties had been worth it. He hated the guilt that rose up in him even as his mother reached for his hand, squeezing it tightly.

"You're welcome." Sitting back, she finished her drink, looking around the table. "You know, I didn't know how I'd do with all the Chinese food, but it's really not too bad."

Dorian laughed, shaking his head. "I'm sure the locals will be happy to hear that."

"Don't make fun of your mother," she only said as he laughed. "I'm the only one you've got."

"You're the best one I've got."

She smiled, satisfied, and Dorian felt better than he had in days.

It was more nerve-wracking than Dorian had expected, all the cameras, the constant people taking his picture, shoving photos in his hands to sign, interviewers hovering around as if trying to absorb information by watching them sit on the benches. It meant that Dorian really had to watch himself. Normally, it wouldn't be a problem, but with Jules constantly around, he had to work harder to act normal. He shouldn't have even been thinking of Jules, but he couldn't help it when Jules was always there. The moments of peace he got in his room or away from the arena seemed to be few and far between.

The rest of the team got on famously, laughing and joking together, usually at Dorian's expense these days. Only Mitya refrained, but Dorian thought Mitya only cared about the Games. Dorian should too, he told himself firmly as he yanked open his assigned locker in the locker room, surrounded by other gymnasts, all chattering in their native language.

Mitya sat on the bench behind him, pulling off his tee-shirt and exchanging it for his uniform. Dorian stared into his locker for a moment, eyes not taking in the shiny metal, his outfit folded neatly at the bottom. If only he could feel like he belonged. He'd long given up on that, but that didn't mean he didn't still long for it when the guys laughed and joked behind him. After a second, he stirred to life, pulling off his USA jacket and tossing it onto the bench behind him. He reached for his uniform, but paused, hand closing around it, as Jules passed behind him.

"Hey, shrimp, you look a little tense," Jules said, and it wouldn't have been enough to provoke Dorian, but when Jules' hands landed on his shoulders, he snapped.

He turned faster than Jules probably expected, if the way his eyes widened was any indication, and shoved him back against the lockers with a strength deceptive of his size, but he was an Olympics gymnast after all. Jules hit the lockers with a slam that shuddered the entire row, and Dorian's upper arm pressed to his throat in a second.

He didn't get much further than that, though. Within seconds, both Carey and Adrian yanked him back, surprise in their eyes, but Dorian didn't care.

"What the hell are you doing?" Carey demanded, but Dorian ignored him.

"Don't touch me," he snarled at Jules, yanking his arms free from Carey and Adrian's grips.

Mitya glanced up from his place on the bench but didn't comment, arching a thick eyebrow and then returning to his own business. Dorian turned back to his locker as Jules blinked and exchanged a glance with Carey. Both Carey and Adrian were watching him closely, probably thinking he was going off the deep end.

"Relax," Jules said seriously, frowning at him slightly. "I was just trying to help you out."

Dorian didn't reply, glaring at Jules. All he could think of was the other night, Jules kissing him, Jules laughing at him, him sitting alone at the end of the table at lunch. The other guys on the team still watched him.

"What the fuck is your problem, dude?" Carey asked after a second. "You can't just go around hitting teammates."

Dorian knew that. He knew that the stress was getting to him and he had to find a better way to get rid of it. His team probably thought he was going a little crazy. He felt like he was. It was all too much pressure, and with Jules constantly on his last nerve, he wasn't sure he could make it through the rest of the week.

He'd never felt like this before at any of his other competitions. It somehow felt as if all his hopes and dreams were riding on this, on the Olympics, and it would either make or break him. It didn't help that Jules was always around, confusing the hell out of him. What did Jules want with him anyway?

Everyone was still looking at him as he glanced up, feeling like a cornered dog, as if he had done something wrong and not Jules, who had provoked him. There was no way out of it, though.

"Sorry," he muttered a second later. He forced himself up from the bench. "Just trying to get through this week."

Carey and Adrian frowned, exchanging a glance. Jules watched Dorian without a word as he turned his back on them.

"Yeah, well, keep your issues to yourself," Carey said, turning back to his locker.

Dorian didn't speak another word the entire time in the locker room and was the first one to finish getting ready. He strode down the hallway to the arena. He could hear the rumble of the crowd already before he even entered. At the door, he paused, taking the moment to himself.

He hated to admit it, but Jules was right. He was stressed. He was worried. He was just a few events away from something he'd wanted since he was six years old and he'd first watched the Olympics with his parents, hunkered down in their cramped living room with furniture from the seventies. He'd begged them to let him stay up to watch the men's gymnastics, and he hadn't been disappointed. Since then, it had been all he'd dreamt of.

Now it was finally here, and he only felt as though he was about to collapse under all the pressure. He was only nineteen. The urge to cry welled up inside of him unexpectedly as he stood at the double doors. There was so much pressure to do well, to not have wasted the last ten years of his life. The emotions welled up inside him, a lump in his throat as he told himself to stay calm.

His mother would have suggested tea. Jason would have suggested getting wasted, but he wasn't allowed to do the latter, and he hated the former. He'd have to find another way to get rid of his tension, but he didn't have time at the moment.

"You cannot win standing here."

Mitya stepped up beside him and nodded at the arena beyond.

Dorian ran a hand through his hair, swallowing around the lump and blinking back the wetness at the edges of his eyes. He paused, glancing at Mitya. "How come you don't laugh?"

Mitya didn't even spare him a glance, bouncing up and down on his toes. "Not here to laugh."

Dorian smiled at Mitya's comment. It was just what he needed to hear. He nodded after a second. "Let's go."

Dorian could feel it happening before he even hit the mat, feel the way he opened up too late, how his body tilted forward as his feet hit and he stumbled, taking a step too big to catch himself. Pulling himself back sharply, he straightened up, turning to the judges, then the crowd. The crowd cheered, but he could only feel disappointment as he trotted back to the pit. It wasn't a huge thing, but every deduction counted. A step out of place, holding on a second too long before the release at the top of the high bar, moves the judges didn't like.

"You did fine," Georgia commented as he walked past her, wiping the sweat off his brow and flopping into a chair.

He almost didn't want to see his score, but the camera hovered in his face, trying to capture his reaction, and he tried to ignore it. Glancing over, he caught sight of Jules flirting with another interviewer. He frowned for a second before remembering the camera and looked away sharply, reaching for his water bottle as the scores flashed up on the screen.

9.2 | 9.0 | 9.4 | 9.2 | 9.2 | 9.5

Not as bad as it could be, he thought, but definitely not as good as he wanted. Leaning down, he rubbed his ankle for a second. It felt fine, but paranoia always sprung up in big competitions. He forced himself to stop, though. He didn't need Brian or Georgia seeing and getting worried. Georgia would insist on having the medic check him out even more frequently, but there was nothing to check.

He couldn't shake the worry, though. Injuries had a way of coming back at the most inopportune moments in sports. Maybe he'd mention it later to Georgia, despite the extra attention it would cause. Instead, he pulled on his jacket and zipped it halfway up.

His eyes fell on Jules again, smiling and leaning towards the interviewer. They clearly weren't having an interview since there was no cameraman anywhere nearby and the woman appeared to be blushing at something Jules said.

A stab of something too close to jealousy for Dorian's liking hit him as he watched, and he looked away abruptly, hands curling around the edge of the bench. He couldn't be jealous of Jules. What did Jules have that he didn't? Except a bronze medal from the Olympics. Dorian would have his own soon enough, if he kept himself together for the next few days.

"You okay?" Georgia asked as she took the seat next to him, stretching out her legs and looking at him.

He nodded quickly. He needed to stop thinking about Jules.

Georgia seemed to take his silence as him being upset and patted his knee twice. "It was just one step on one event. Vault is tomorrow. It's your best. I wouldn't be surprised if you took gold on it."

Dorian nodded again. "Thanks, Georgie."

"You should relax tonight," she advised him, glancing at the floor, the other competitors doing their events. "Watch a movie, go to bed early."

"Yeah," he said slowly, glancing over again, but the newsgirl had finally left, and Jules was stretching, adjusting the grips on his hands. "I'll be fine if Jules isn't around."

Georgia smiled, gripping his knee for a second before letting go. "Good boy."

She rose from her chair, but Dorian didn't follow, taking a gulp of his water bottle and ignoring Jules down the row.

Chapter 6

Foreign Hospitality

The book he was reading wasn't very interesting, and Dorian couldn't stop his attention from drifting away from it as he sat on his small bed in the cramped hotel room. Mitya wasn't there, out with the other guys from the team, Dorian assumed. He hadn't been invited along, and even if he had, he would have said no. There were better ways to spend his evening than being made fun of.

The book couldn't hold his attention, though, and when the door opened, his head shot up. Mitya entered along with Carey, who laughed at something, and grinned when he caught sight of Dorian on the bed.

"Catching up on your reading?" he asked, and Dorian hoisted up the book. Carey sat down on the end of Mitya's bed as Mitya turned on the television. So much for a relaxing evening. "Don't know how you have time. Jules said you snuck into the gym the other night."

"I didn't sneak." Dorian knew he shouldn't reply, but he couldn't help it.

"You could get kicked out for that," Carey commented, but Dorian knew Carey wouldn't say anything, not unless he wanted an alternate to come in at the last minute and ruin all their chances.

"Well, then you better not tell anyone," he snapped back, trying to focus on the book, but the words blurred before his eyes.

Even when he wasn't there, Jules could annoy him. Georgia's words came back to him, though, and he reminded himself that there was no point in rising to Carey's words. He couldn't get in trouble again or it could jeopardize the whole Games.

Carey shrugged as though he didn't care one way or the other. "I guess you need all the practice you can get."

Dorian bristled, and the book came down from in front of his face. "Did Jules say that?"

Carey shrugged. "You are the least experienced."

"I have two world champion golds," he replied, arching an eyebrow. "I've competed in more international competitions than you have."

"Just saying your bars routine needs work if you want to get all-around. Jules is definitely the favorite."

Dorian looked away, glaring at the small dent in the wall. This wasn't helping him to relax at all. He already knew that. He knew all of that already. No matter how hard he tried, the bars had always been his worst event. His first few years at the Center, he'd fallen so many times, they'd started to keep a tally. He could never figure out why he was perfectly fine on the rings but not two stationary bars.

Mitya changed the channel. Carey leaned back against the wall. "I'd put my money on Jules if I were you."

Dorian rolled his eyes, trying to concentrate on his book again, but he could only see blurred words as he tried not to think over Carey's words. He didn't need his teammates constantly pointing out his weaknesses. It just made him feel useless, like he didn't deserve to be there. He said nothing in reply to Carey, then, trying to ignore the unsettled pressure on his chest.

Carey brought his knees up. "How's the stress management going? Hit any other teammates lately? Sometimes I think they should test for mental stability before picking teams."

"I am not crazy, I—" Dorian huffed. "That's it!" He threw his book to the side. It hit the wall, pages splaying awkwardly as it plummeted to the floor and he jumped over it on his way to the door.

He didn't heed Carey's dubious look as he slammed the door behind him and strode the few feet that separated his room and Jules. He didn't care if Jules was sleeping. He didn't care what he was doing. He was going to fix this.

Pounding on the door, he was probably waking up the entire floor, but he didn't care. "Jules!" he called through the thin door.

"Jules!"

The door opened a second later as he went to pound again, and he was met with a half-dressed Jules, only in his boxers, eyebrows in the air.

"Yes?" he drawled, blocking the doorway, and Dorian glared, forcing his brain from stopping and staring at Jules' muscular chest. He'd seen it before. Now was no different.

"I need to talk to you."

Jules paused, then smiled a different smile than Dorian had seen yet, a little too cocky mixed with something Dorian was supposed to understand but didn't.

"You picked kind of a bad time, shortstack."

"I don't care what time it is," Dorian snapped. "And stop calling me that."

He willed himself to stay calm, although it wasn't easy. He'd promised Georgia, though, and she was right after all. Hitting Jules wasn't going to make anything better. If anything, it would only get him in more trouble, and he certainly couldn't afford that.

"Shut up for a second," Jules interrupted, glancing over his shoulder into the room. Dorian finally stretched up to see, and he understood as he caught sight of the news reporter from earlier sitting on his bed, her shirt only half buttoned.

Shaking his head, his stomach curled as he realized what he'd interrupted. "Didn't mean to interrupt your company. Does she want an interview? I can give her one."

He took a step forward, but Jules grabbed him before he could get much further, shoving him out into the hall with an urgent look.

"I'll just be a few minutes," he said to the girl before he closed the door behind him.

"She doesn't want my side of the competition?" Dorian asked as the door shut, and Jules shot him a look.

"You're really annoying for someone so small," he said, and grabbed Dorian's arm as Dorian opened his mouth to get louder. "If you're gonna make a scene, do it where no one can see you."

Dorian tried to pull away as Jules dragged him down the hall, yanking open the supply closet at the end of the corridor. Inside smelled like cleaning products, but Jules shoved Dorian in. He stumbled over a broom, turning to face Jules as he clicked on the dim light and shut the door.

"You better stop calling me names and teasing me and everything else you've been doing," he ordered him. "It's not funny, and it's not fun. You're making me look insane."

"You do that all on your own," Jules said. "Where would I be without you, Dorian?"

Dorian's eyes narrowed and he shoved aside the fallen broom and stepped past the shelf filled with boxes of complimentary-sized shampoos and conditioners.

"You'd probably be back in your room fucking away what's left of your dignity with some airhead reporter who'll give you a little more screen time tomorrow in exchange for a night with an Olympian. What a great image the US team is presenting this year. What a boost to your ego to screw some overeager girl in a foreign country. That sure makes you seem like a much better perso—"

Jules cut him off abruptly by shoving him back against the shelf, which rattled as he hit it, and biting Dorian's bottom lip, Dorian's head knocking back into the shelf at the force of the kiss.

He blinked, surprised for barely a second before he got his hands in between them and pushed Jules back.

Jules smiled, tilting his head to the side. "How would I get off without you?"

"No," Dorian said when Jules moved forward again, body pressing him against the shelf, warm and hard against him. "We're not—doing this—again." The words came out stuttered as he forced himself to keep control of his body, even with Jules grinding up against him too hard. He had to keep his head this time.

He shook his head sharply, trying to get his hands between them again, but the moment they touched Jules' skin, he seemed to forget any resolution he may have had.

"Fuck," he cursed loudly a second before Jules' mouth covered his own in a hot, open-mouthed kiss, more tongue than anything.

He couldn't explain why this was happening, why it was happening with Jules, why in a supply closet, why now. He didn't stop Jules from kissing him, though, from pinning his wrists back against the shelf as he gasped and cursed himself. Instead, he bit down on Jules' bottom lip hard, drawing a surprised noise, muffled against his mouth, but Jules barely reacted except to push up against him harder and faster.

Dorian broke away with a pitiful moan, hating himself, hating Jules, hating the whole situation, but it felt so good. Jules' body, muscled and strong, warm, pressed into him, and all he wanted to do was get lost in the feeling of him. It had been so long since he'd been with anyone, and a part of him ached to stay here, to pretend that Jules was something else, something more than a competitor doing this to get under his skin. He could pretend if he wanted. He could kiss Jules like he had kissed the first boy he ever liked. That first boy had been a long time ago, before he'd really understood what any of it meant, before he had told anyone. It had been stolen kisses behind stores, hidden behind trees in the park, until his coach had taken him aside and told him that whatever was distracting him had to go. Dorian hadn't seen that boy since.

Some days, he couldn't believe he had actually looked up to Jules, thought he was a decent person, but it was moments like this that he remembered why he'd spent many a night in the years before, jerking off to Jules in the darkness of his own room.

He couldn't escape Jules, though, as Jules kept his wrists back against the shelf and stared at him through darkened eyes, the corner of his mouth curling slowly as Dorian panted for breath and licked his swollen lips. The shelf jutted out uncomfortably against his back and he tried to shift, but it did nothing more than make his predicament with Jules more obvious.

He couldn't hide that he was hard, cock pressing against his jeans. He didn't want Jules, but the thrill of getting off with someone he disliked so much, of finally relieving some of his stress was too much to deny.

"Are you gonna tell me to stop?" Jules asked as the moment passed between them.

Dorian knew Jules could feel his erection, could feel the way he sucked in a sharp breath when he shifted, how his eyelashes fluttered and his mouth fell open at the friction between them, not just the sparks of annoyance and anger that brimmed in the air around them. He was annoyed at Jules now, not for starting this, but for taking so long. They didn't need to talk.

"Not unless you keep talking," he snapped, ignoring how Jules' eyes seemed to sparkle at his words, as though he'd somehow won an argument.

"Good," Jules replied, twisting Dorian's arm behind his back and flipping him around.

Dorian's cheek hit the shelf and he let out a pained hiss, eyes narrowing as he twisted to look back at Jules. "Watch it!"

The hiss turned into a squeak a second later as Jules slid in behind him, his cock pressing against his lower back, already wet through his boxers. He squeezed his eyes shut for half a second, feeling the blood throbbing in his cock.

Georgia had been right. He did need to relieve his stress, and this would do just fine. He almost didn't care that it was Jules two seconds away from fucking him. He would have taken anyone right then.

Jules' mouth hovered over his ear, breath hot against his skin, and Dorian forced his eyes open despite the desire just to sit back and enjoy this. Jules' hands slid underneath his tee-shirt, fingers grazing up his sides as he skimmed it up and over his head. Dorian said nothing until Jules reached for his jeans, pulling them open and sliding them down. As they dropped over his ass, he glanced back.

"You have a nice ass," Jules commented before he could say anything.

"Too bad you're so much of one," Dorian shot back, and Jules laughed, twisting his arm in close to his back. Dorian winced at the sudden movement, stretching his neck back. "*Ow*."

"Toughen up," Jules only replied, leaning into Dorian's neck and licking up to his chin. Dorian wanted to protest, but his body reacted on its own, and he let out a soft noise at the touch. He bit his tongue in retaliation, but it was too late.

A rustle of fabric met his ears, Jules' boxers dropping to the floor, then Jules' fingers slid along his mouth. Jules' chest covered Dorian's back, warm and hard, and Dorian swore he could feel Jules' heartbeat.

Dorian bit down on Jules' fingers as he coaxed his mouth open, but Jules didn't say anything, shuffling him closer to the shelf. The little bottles rattled again, and Dorian cast them a brief glance, finally opening his mouth and sucking Jules' fingers without too much protest.

"Mmm, good boy," Jules hummed in his ear, a hand sliding down his chest, grazing over his hip.

Dorian only bit down in reply, but he couldn't help gasping seconds later when Jules' hand wrapped around his cock and tugged.

Of all the things he'd never thought he'd do, fucking a teammate, one he didn't even get along with, in a hotel closet was one of them. He'd never expected to moan breathily as Jules stroked his cock to full hardness, fingers still in his mouth, wet and slippery as he pulled them out.

His whole body tensed the second Jules pushed a finger deep inside him, already too dry as he bit his lower lip and tried not to whimper, a combination of pain and desire, wanting more than just Jules' fingers inside of him but hating the idea of it.

"Ah! Shit!" he cursed sharply at the second, nearly dry finger Jules pressed inside him. "Use something else."

"Like my dick?"

Dorian didn't smile, only glowered at the shelf pressing into his forehead. "Like lube, you asshole."

Jules glanced around for a second, a skeptical eyebrow arched, then espied the tub of little bottles. He grabbed a bottle of conditioner and unscrewed the top. "It'll do," he muttered, pouring some into his hand and spreading it on his cock.

"Wait," Dorian said sharply, twisting around in Jules' grip. "What about a condom?"

"They're in my room," Jules replied simply. "You want me to go get them?"

Scowling, Dorian turned back, a moment of indecision spasming through his body. "No," he replied darkly. That would take even longer and would be nearly impossible to explain to anyone.

"We all got tested before we came here," Jules reminded him, sliding his slicked-up finger back inside Dorian instead, dragging it against the inside of his body.

Dorian tried to focus on his words and not the ripple of heat echoing up his spine at Jules' touch.

"And how many newscasters have you banged since then?" he bit out through clenched teeth, reaching for his own prick and giving it a hard squeeze to release the pressure.

"None... yet." Jules smirked, rubbing his fingers deep inside Dorian, and Dorian bit back his moan.

"I hate you," he breathed instead, bowing his head against the shelf, and he knew Jules smiled at that, his finger disappearing from his ass and his hands moving to his hips instead.

Jules pulled Dorian up, then spread his own legs to meet his height. "Yeah," he replied.

Dorian gasped too loudly as the head of Jules' cock, slick with conditioner, pressed inside him.

His body tensed, legs trembling as Jules sunk inside him, hard and thick. His toes curled and heat flooded his cheeks as he tried to keep his breathing even. His fingers curled around the wobbly shelf as Jules thrust in once, then twice, not bothering to build up to a rhythm, but Dorian didn't want him to.

Dorian just wanted to get off, to come from the feeling of someone else behind him, someone moving inside him in a way that made his chest seize up, stomach turning itself over in knots, blood thudding in his cock as he reached down and jerked himself off along with Jules' uneven thrusts. He felt comfortably full, the pressure deep inside him spreading heat through his body as he moaned.

Jules made little noise, just a soft exhale every once in a while, every time he pushed in harder than before. Dorian could feel each puff of breath hot against the back of his neck, fluttering his hair.

"Ah, shit," Jules muttered a few minutes later.

Dorian ignored him, biting his bottom lip and squeezing his eyes shut. He was so close, so close to the release he needed, and he didn't care what Jules was doing. He felt Jules moving behind him, the burning heat rising on his skin as they moved together, fucking like they didn't care about who might be beyond the door, what was waiting for them down in the arena.

The feeling of Jules coming, hot and wet, dripping down the back of his leg, brought Dorian to the edge, and he came moments later, eyes shut tightly and mouth dropping open to gasp for breath as come covered his hand and he jerked until he could barely breathe. His hand dropped uselessly to his side.

Jules moved away first, grabbing a towel from one of the many stacked on the shelf. He wiped himself off and dropped it on the floor.

Opening his eyes, Dorian let out a shaky breath and rolled away to lean on his side, reaching for a towel as well. "Could you have made more of a mess?" he asked as he wiped the come off his ass and leg. For a second, he wanted to stay there with Jules. Maybe they could have a real conversation. Maybe they could get past this. He glanced back at Jules, not sure what he was hoping to see, but Jules was searching the floor for his clothes.

"Gentlemen pull out," Jules quipped, reaching for his boxers.

Dorian rolled his eyes, hope dying in his chest. That was it. It was over. They were back to normal, and Dorian didn't feel nearly as relieved of stress as he should have. Instead, he just felt confused and annoyed as Jules flicked a piece of his hair and grinned.

"Gotta get back."

Jealousy curled in Dorian's stomach. "Wouldn't want to miss that."

Jules laughed, pulling open the door while Dorian grabbed his jeans off the floor and hopped into them quickly.

"Don't worry. I'm sure she doesn't give head nearly as well as you do."

He stepped out before the bottle of shampoo Dorian hurtled at him could hit him. It bounced off the frame instead and fell to the floor. Turning away, Dorian snatched up his shirt and kicked away the dirty towel.

Chapter 7

Late-Night Conversations

It was nearly four in the morning when his phone went off, and Dorian rolled over on his tiny mattress, groping on the table in between his and Mitya's bed. Mitya didn't even stir, and Dorian cracked open his eyes, wincing at the light from the phone's screen. He was half-asleep as he answered, not even reading the name on the caller ID.

"Hello?" he asked, rubbing his face and jerking awake suddenly, unsure how he'd gotten there. He blinked, sitting up and looking over at Mitya, but Mitya snored softly and turned over.

"Hey, man!" Dorian recognized the voice as Ryan, one of his teammates back at school. Ryan's voice woke him up even further. "How's it going?"

"Ryan?"

"Yeah, what's up? Were you sleeping? What time is it over there?"

Dorian slipped out of bed, grabbing the key card and padding to the door. He stepped into the hall and shut the door behind him. In the hall, everything was utterly silent.

Yawning, he rubbed his forehead. "I don't know, like four in the morning."

"Oh." Ryan laughed. "Sorry."

Dorian smiled slightly. "No, it's okay."

It was nice to hear from someone back home, someone who didn't know everything that was going on. He hadn't really thought about it much, but he missed his old teammates. They always seemed to know exactly what to say when he was nervous before meets.

"Well?" Ryan asked excitedly. "How's everything going? I'm so sad I couldn't go, but it's so freaking expensive. But don't worry. We're recording everything, so when you get back, we're gonna throw an awesome party and rewatch it all."

Dorian laughed slightly, sinking back against the wall. "How's everybody?"

Ryan made an undefined noise. "Same as usual. Coach keeps telling everyone he knows that he trained you." He laughed, and Dorian couldn't help smiling too.

"Did you remind him that I have a professional coach in Colorado?"

"He doesn't care about that," Ryan said, and Dorian could practically see him shrugging. "It's just so awesome that you're in the Olympics. Tomorrow's the vault, right?"

"Yeah," Dorian agreed, nodding. "I'm trying not to think about it."

"Oh, please," Ryan scoffed. "You own the vault. It's your bitch, Dor. And everybody's gonna know it tomorrow."

Dorian laughed, shaking his head. Ryan could always make him feel better.

"You're so sure."

"Of course I am," Ryan said obviously. "We trained together all last year. I've seen you own that thing. You have nothing to worry about."

"I wish you guys were here," Dorian said, sighing slightly. He wished his team here could be like the one at home. The guys at home were supportive and his friends and they didn't tease him about his height. They included him and didn't care about his social awkwardness. He wasn't good at talking to new people. He usually said the wrong thing or said nothing. He should probably look into getting a publicist so he would never make a bad impression again. Somehow, he wasn't sure even the best publicist could stop that from happening.

"We'd just drag you down," Ryan said. "Wyatt never gets his dismounts right, you know that."

"That's not what I meant."

Ryan laughed. "I know. I'm just saying. You're there because you're awesome and ten million times better than us."

"You guys are just as good as these guys."

"That's nice of you to say," Ryan said, laughing, "but it's total bullshit and you know it. You're the only one dedicated enough to actually do it."

Dorian smiled. His heart felt lighter than it had in a while. He'd forgotten how much he missed his team. They were so completely different from the Olympic team. He actually had fun with them.

"I tried to get you to come to tryouts," he said, shrugging. "You didn't want to."

"Right," Ryan said, sounding amused at the idea. "Us at Olympic tryouts, against you and Jules Gardner and whoever else. They wouldn't let me in the building."

"That's because you wear ridiculous outfits."

"Hey, the girls like the see-through look. Gets them hot under the collar. Not that you'd care about that."

Dorian knew he wasn't like the others guys on his college team. He'd never been concerned with getting laid or appealing to anyone beyond a judge's panel.

"Speaking of," Ryan said slyly, and Dorian knew it was coming, the question he'd prayed would never come up. "Jules Gardner, the hero, the idol, the object of your lustful affections, what's he like? Did you fanboy all over him?"

Dorian felt his face burning in embarrassment, and he was glad that he was on the phone and Ryan couldn't see. "Can you just never mention any of that ever again?"

"Why? Did you make a fool of yourself?"

Dorian laughed, but it was quick and embarrassed. At least someone could make light of the situation. "No. He's just not... what I expected." That was the understatement of the century, but he really didn't feel talking about Jules, not when Jules was what he thought of most of the time anyway.

"Most people aren't," Ryan said dismissively. "That's just how life goes."

Dorian made a noise of agreement.

"Well," Ryan said a second later. "It's probably late, and you need to sleep before tomorrow. What are you doing up anyway?"

"Ryan," Dorian said obviously, and he could practically hear Ryan's grin through the phone.

"I'm just kidding. Go to sleep, man, and I will be watching later on."

Dorian smiled. "Have a drink for me."

"Oh, I'll have plenty," Ryan assured him. "Good luck."

"Thanks," Dorian replied, hanging up the phone a minute later. He stood in the silent hallway and sighed to himself.

Dorian sat on the bench, watching Adrian on the pommel horse, following each movement of his legs, each deduction when he missed a placing with his hand. He didn't pay attention to the crowd above him or the cameras swooping around on their big black metal arms. He didn't listen to the television in the corner airing live coverage of everything he could see in front of him.

His mind was focused for the first time in days. He had to be focused. He couldn't be thinking of Jules talking to Brian as they watched Adrian's performance. He couldn't be thinking of Jules' hands on him or they way his body had felt pressed against his...

Dorian blinked quickly, giving his head a small shake. There was only one thing to focus on.

"Nervous, munchkin?" Jules asked as he passed by a minute later.

Dorian shook his head firmly at the ground. "Don't talk to me."

"Come on," Jules said, dropping into the chair next to him. "You weren't that bad. I've had worse."

Dorian shot him a disbelieving glare. Jules knew just how to make things worse. "Do you ever think of anyone but yourself?"

Jules shrugged. "Not like you're any different, kiddo. Why do you want that gold medal so badly?"

Dorian didn't reply, turning back to staring at the ground and focusing on his breathing instead.

"That's what I thought," Jules said, kicking his feet out and putting his hands behind his head as the camera swooped over them.

"You're up, Dorian," Brian called a minute later, and Dorian got to his feet, shaking out the nerves in his fingers and climbing up the stairs slowly, his feet seeming to drag as he reached the mat and headed to his place.

He knew the crowd could be watching any of the different events going on simultaneously, but he always felt as if all eyes were on him when he stepped up to the mat. The floor manager nodded at him, and Dorian stepped onto the mat behind the white line, turning to the judges first then focusing on the long, blue mat that stretched before him to the springboard and vault at the far end.

The moment before he moved, those few seconds when he prepared himself, told himself that he could do this, and any mistakes he'd made in practice were just practice, in those moments, he knew he would make it.

As he ran down the mat and launched himself off the vault, he could see the arena spinning, feel his body twisting the way it was supposed to, three turns, then release. He landed squarely on the mat, feet planted firmly beneath himself and rose to an explosion of cheers from people in the stands.

He couldn't congratulate himself yet, though. He had one more vault left. He watched the judges scribble down notes and scores as he walked back to the beginning. Bracing himself for his second vault, he took a deep breath and glanced up at the big version of himself on the screen. He looked mostly calm on the outside, just a little jumpy as he bounced up on his toes and waited for the signal.

He finally got it, and he knew before he even left the springboard that everything was perfect. The air rushed past his body, those few seconds a complete blur as he landed, barely wobbling as he straightened up and turned to the judges.

He broke into a smile as he returned to the pit and Brian clapped him on the back, as close to affection as they would get for a job well done.

Georgia said nothing, staring at the screen for the scores. Dorian grabbed his water bottle and pointedly ignored Jules watching him from the bench. If he was staring at his ass, he'd get caught on camera and Dorian would have nothing to do with it.

As the scores came up, Georgia let out a short squeal that she quickly concealed as she turned to Dorian. "You're in first place," she said as calmly as she could. "Now let's hope everyone else messes up their vaults."

Dorian grinned, his heart feeling light. He could do this. "That's good sportsmanship."

"That's competition." She shrugged but punched his shoulder lightly. "Good job."

"Thanks, Georgie."

He turned around only to find that Jules was still watching him. Jules did nothing, and Dorian smiled to himself as he sunk down on the bench. He could definitely do this.

"Have a beer!" Jason insisted, shoving it into Dorian's hands. "Have a beer, dude! You're a fucking gold medalist!"

"On vault," Dorian corrected him.

Whatever it was, Jason didn't care. Mostly he was surprised he'd managed to talk Dorian into coming out with him. He'd thought the Olympics were all about enjoying the local culture, after all. He certainly had so far. He was pretty sure he could get used to eating Chinese food every single day and paying twenty bucks a night for a great hotel. No one had ever told him that China was so cheap. So far, he'd already stocked up on a ton of bootlegged DVDs, snagged a fake Prada bag for his mom, and picked up a fake Rolex for his brother. He should come to China for all his gifts throughout the year.

"Still a medal."

Though Jason didn't understand much about the Olympics—Dorian had already explained three times about the medals (one for team, one for all-around, and as many for individual events as he qualified for)—he was there to support Dorian. Dorian at least knew what he wanted to do with his life, even if he was sometimes way too overzealous, whereas Jason still hadn't declared a major in school. He admired that about Dorian. Compared to his Ph.D. brother, Jason was starting to look like the dunce of the family if he didn't choose something soon and graduate on time. For now, though, he was content to watch Dorian live out his dream and score with the hot Asian chicks who seemed to flock around the foreigners.

"So what's left?" All Jason knew was that the competition wasn't over. There were plenty more days to go.

"They haven't finished individual events yet," Dorian explained. "And after that, they'll announce the team placements. Then it's the all-around competition, if I make it."

"You'll make it. If you don't, you'll scratch somebody's eyes out." He took a swig of his beer. The one thing he wasn't sure he liked about China was the beer. Tsingtao beer just didn't taste like normal beer to him. At least here, though, they never carded.

When Dorian pushed back the beer, Jason shook his head. "When will you know about the all-around?" he asked. He hated to think if Dorian didn't make it. He would probably go off the deep-end. Jason had been there for his first injury, and he only remembered Dorian being a handful the entire recovery process. He'd barely rested, just long enough that he could get back on his feet and back to training.

"In a couple days," Dorian muttered, turning back and setting his elbows on the table.

Jason nodded, though he knew less about how it worked than anything else in his life. All he knew was that it was his job as the best friend to make sure Dorian didn't get stuck in his head the whole time. The first time he'd met Dorian, right after his thirteenth birthday and the summer before Dorian had shipped off to the training center in Colorado, Dorian had barreled him over in the park. Dorian hadn't even noticed, too focused on what he was doing. Six years later, he hadn't changed much.

"Then you'll relax?"

Dorian shot him a look across the table. "If I make it to all-around, I have to work harder than I ever have if I want to win."

Jason rolled his eyes. He was pretty sure Dorian wouldn't know how to relax unless someone injected him with drugs, not that Dorian would ever let that happen. He refused to even be in the same room with smokers, so getting him to take drugs unless he was grievously injured would be a task. "Well, I'll be rooting for you."

He grabbed the bottle and took a drink. He'd never been out of the country before, and China wouldn't have been his first choice, but so far, it had gone well. Granted, he had mostly hung out with Dorian's mother, but Sherry was pretty easy-going. Jason suspected that Dorian's drive came from his dad, along with his stubbornness. He'd only met Dorian's dad once before he died, but Dorian's tunnel-vision had certainly worsened after the fact. Before, he'd only mentioned the Olympics a few times to Jason, but after that, it seemed to be the only thing he talked about. Jason's comments about girls and video games had gone in one ear and out the other.

It had taken Jason a long time to figure out that Dorian's disinterest in women wasn't only due to his focus on gymnastics. Dorian had officially come out to him a year earlier on the anniversary of his dad's death, of all days. As coming out went, it hadn't been spectacular, and Dorian had even looked a little insulted when Jason had laughed and said he already knew.

"Oh no," Dorian muttered, and Jason twisted around as Dorian stared at the door.

"What?"

Dorian ducked his head, and Jason watched three guys come in. They looked vaguely familiar.

"Hey, kitten," one greeted Dorian, rounding the table. "Celebrating your win?" He glanced at Jason. "Enjoy it while you can. I'll see you on the bars in all-around."

The other two guys laughed as they walked away, and Dorian's face flushed as he stared at the table. Jason frowned at their retreating backs. As they left, he realized where he knew them from.

"Isn't that Jules Gardner? Aren't you on the same team?"

"Yeah," Dorian muttered, glancing up at the beer in front of Jason.

"What a little bitch," Jason commented, finishing off the beer. "You did beat him, right?"

"On vault. Not that it really matters since Jules is the favorite on pommel horse anyway and he'll probably at least medal there."

"Give yourself some credit, man. You're an Olympian too. You just gotta put him in his place," Jason said obviously, twisting the bottle in his hands. "Show him you can dish out as much as you can take."

Jason wasn't surprised that Dorian had no idea what to do when it came to Jules. He'd spent most of his life in a training facility where competition was high and beating someone else was the only way to win the hierarchy. This wasn't training, though.

To say that Dorian's social skills were zero was giving him the benefit of the doubt. Jason had witnessed several moments over the years of Dorian's inability to socialize with normal people who understood nothing of gymnastics. Dorian usually came off as weird and entirely too serious. Since his dad died, it had gotten worse. All Jason remembered of the summer Dorian's dad had died was Dorian spending the whole time in the gym when he wasn't shut up in his room talking to no one. Jason tried his best to keep him light. Competition always got to him, though, and it didn't seem like his teammates were helping.

"Yeah," Dorian muttered, turning away from where Jules and the other two had settled.

It wasn't exactly enthusiastic, but you had to take what you could get with Dorian, so Jason grinned, pushing the drink towards him, but Dorian didn't take it. "Enjoy it while you can. Soon you'll be back at school with another four years to wait."

To his relief, Dorian smiled and didn't look back at the guys. "I'm still not having any beer."

"Oh, come on!"

Chapter 8

Trust Is a Two Way Street

Dorian closed his eyes as the hot water cascaded over his body, washing away the sweat of the day, the tenseness in his shoulders, the strain on his body from a hard day. Jason was long gone back to his own hotel room in the city.

Dorian just wanted to forget about the day, although the gold medal now tucked away safely amongst his things wouldn't be forgotten. But tomorrow was another day and one more step closer to winning that all-around.

The shower was nice and relaxing, and Dorian just let the water run over his body. He planned on making it an early night, or as early as Jason would have allowed, having kept him out later than he should have.

Mitya wasn't in the room, but Dorian had no desire to find out where he'd gone. As long as he kept quiet when he came back, he wouldn't care.

The water scalded his skin, too hot, but he didn't turn it down, standing under the stream and sighing long and slow. His body felt heavy, sleepy and warm. He kept his eyes closed and concentrated on his breathing instead.

"Hey, halfpint!"

A voice just outside the curtain startled his eyes open and his heart jumped as he stepped back, slipping on the tub. He didn't fall, though, and ripped aside the top half of the curtain.

Jules glanced back from where he rummaged in the counter drawers. "Where are the playing cards?"

Dorian stared. "How did you get in here?" he demanded, reaching behind him for the water and turning it off.

Jules held up a keycard. "Mitya. Are they in your suitcase?"

"Hey," Dorian said as Jules reached for the bathroom door. Stumbling out of the tub, he grabbed the towel before Jules could get a good look at anything.

"Relax, it's nothing I haven't seen before." Jules grinned, pulling the door back, but Dorian slammed it shut, catching Jules' attention. "What?"

"You can't just barge in here unannounced looking for stupid playing cards."

Jules quirked an eyebrow. "Why? Were you hoping I was looking for something else?"

"Because it's a private room and there are such things as manners," Dorian snapped, crossing his arms over his chest, still dripping water onto the floor. The mirrors had fogged up completely, obscuring their reflections, and the fan whirred above them.

Jules laughed shortly. "You southern belles are all about manners, aren't you? Well, sometimes you just gotta take what you want."

"You're right," Dorian said, hand sliding down and twisting the lock on the door. "I think it's about time you paid me back for all the shit you've been giving me since I got here."

Jules didn't react when he locked the door except to arch an expectant eyebrow. "Princess wants payback, huh?"

"Might be your last chance," he said, ignoring the nickname, his cool tone deceptive of the annoyance and desire he felt as he stared into Jules' deep brown eyes. "After tomorrow, we'll know who made all-around. You'll regret not taking the opportunity before you get sent home without a medal."

Jules eyed him for a moment, then smiled, licking his lips and pushing Dorian's shoulder back against the bathroom door. "So it's my turn?" he drawled, but Dorian wasn't going to go through this with Jules. He knew what he wanted, and Jules had all but told him to go for it.

Reaching for Jules' shoulder, he forced Jules down onto his knees in the steamy bathroom.

"Yeah, it is," he replied sharply, pulling the towel apart and letting it slither to the ground near his feet.

He wasn't hard yet, but he knew he could get there. Already, the thought of finally getting one over on Jules caused an arousing rush in his body. He gazed down at Jules, hand still tight on his shoulder in case Jules decided to wriggle away.

Jules didn't look defeated. In fact, a knowing sparkle lit up his eyes as he met Dorian's, a smirk curling his lips as he paused and his eyes flicked to Dorian's prick in front of him.

Dorian had thought Jules might fight him a little more, so he was surprised when Jules reached for his cock instead, stroking slowly, pausing to lick the palm of his hand, then return. Dorian kept a close watch on him for the first few minutes, sure it was just a trap, but Jules didn't speak, shifting on his knees and jerking him until he was hard. It took a surprisingly short amount of time, but Dorian didn't care.

"You think this proves something?" Jules asked finally, licking up Dorian's cock, and Dorian blinked, mouth falling open slightly.

"*This* isn't about proving anything," Dorian replied, keeping his voice steady despite the way Jules moved his mouth in, hot over his skin, tight and wet around his prick. Jules was as good at this as anything else, and that thought pissed Dorian off a little. "This is about getting off, like you said before."

Jules hummed in agreement around Dorian's cock, sucking and licking all around it as Dorian closed his eyes and focused on the feel of Jules' mouth, the lick of heat curling in his stomach as Jules moved faster, mouth opened in an obscene way when he finally forced himself to open his eyes and look down. After a minute, Jules pulled back, using his hand to jerk Dorian off again as he licked around his fist.

"Everything is about winning," he replied, taking Dorian back in, and Dorian nearly choked on his breath.

Jules' mouth and tongue slid all around his cock, a tight heat crawling up his spine as he squeezed his eyes shut, fingers digging into Jules' shoulder. He opened his eyes when Jules reached up and pried his hand off.

"No marks for competition," he murmured around his cock then went back to sucking as Dorian curled his hand into a fist instead.

Jules had a point.

"Jesus," Dorian breathed, head falling back against the door with a clunk. He felt hot all over, and his hips pushed up into Jules' mouth as Jules tongued the head of his prick and sucked, cheeks going hollow.

Dorian made an embarrassing noise and cursed under his breath a second later, hand scrabbling for Jules' shoulder again despite his earlier words. He couldn't help it, couldn't help when he came, stomach unraveling as his hips pushed into Jules' mouth, his pink lips stretched across Dorian's cock.

"Mmm," Jules hummed, leaning back and wiping the side of his mouth.

Dorian sighed, grabbing his towel off the floor and cleaning up. He didn't say anything as Jules climbed to his feet and turned to the mirror, examining his shoulder in the reflection. He shrugged after a second and turned back to Dorian.

"Anything else, short stuff?"

Dorian rolled his eyes and unlocked the door. "The cards are on the bedside table."

Jules rubbed a hand over his head as he headed out the door, completely unfazed by the turn of events. Grabbing the pack of cards off the table, he glanced back at Dorian, who pulled on his boxers.

"See you on the podium."

Dorian flopped onto his bed as Jules shut the door behind him. A part of him felt better and a part of him felt worse. Instead of doing anything about it, he sighed and lay down, hands on his stomach and eyes on the ceiling.

Dorian lay in bed, on top of the covers, staring up at the ceiling. He glanced down, though, at the sound of a key card in the lock. The door swung open a second later and Mitya came in, shutting the door behind him and tossing his key on the tiny table by the bed. Pushing himself up, Dorian watched Mitya pull off his shirt and get ready for bed. Mitya barely glanced at him, rummaging in his suitcase.

"Why'd you give Jules a key?" he asked finally as Mitya straightened up and headed for the tiny bathroom. He couldn't say he was mad at Mitya, but he wasn't sure if what he'd done with Jules helped or hindered anything. If it hadn't been for Mitya, though, it might not have happened at all.

Mitya shrugged as he stepped inside. "We needed cards."

"Why didn't you come get them then?"

The sound of the sink turning on met his ears, and Dorian could only see Mitya's back as he brushed his teeth.

"Jules is teammate," Mitya grunted around his toothbrush. "You're supposed to trust teammate."

Dorian scoffed. "I don't trust him."

"You don't like him," Mitya corrected. "Because he is good."

"Because he's an asshole."

"Still teammate," Mitya replied.

"So because he's my teammate, I should just forget about how mean he's been? I should just let it all go?" Dorian frowned. That was not going to happen as far as he was concerned. Jules had picked on him since the moment they'd been put on the team together. So he was the youngest. So he was the shortest. If being a team meant working together, Jules wasn't doing a good job of it.

Mitya came out of the bathroom, wiping his mouth and climbing into bed. "Being teammate means supporting other," he said, "not hating."

Maybe Mitya trusted Jules, but Dorian had his doubts. Mitya, for all the times he kept his mouth shut, was friends with Jules and Carey and Adrian. He had no reason to be worried. They all had their good points, and Mitya was the best on the parallel bars on the team. The rest of the team respected Mitya, even though he was barely a year older than Dorian. Coming from Russia, he'd had great training and even better discipline.

"But they haven't supported me," Dorian pointed out. "What am I supposed to do?"

Mitya shrugged. "Let go or support."

Dorian paused. "Why do you think my parallel bars are so bad?" He hadn't asked Mitya before, but alone in the semi-darkness, he felt safer to ask. They all knew he was terrible on them.

Mitya grunted, pulling the covers up. His dark hair fell over his forehead and Dorian could see the outline of his large nose in the darkness. "You don't trust yourself."

Dorian didn't know what to say, and Mitya leaned over and clicked off the lamp, throwing the room into darkness. Dorian sat up for a long moment, contemplating Mitya's words, unsure quite how to interpret it, and in the end, he lay down, a sick feeling in his stomach that he hoped was due to something he'd eaten and not Mitya's words.

Dorian leaned down as the man placed the silver medal over his head and they shook hands. The woman handed him a bouquet of red roses. Beside him, the man had moved on to Mitya, who bent over as well.

A gold medal in vault and a silver for the team finals. All in all, Dorian couldn't say this Olympics hadn't gone well so far, aside from the whole Jules thing.

The crowd screamed their approval as they held up their flowers to them. The Russian gold medal team got louder cheers, but Dorian didn't care. Glancing down at his medal, he smiled. He was one step closer to competing for all-around. After the ceremony, they would know for sure, although he was fairly certain he was in. Only twenty-four people would make it, and he had to. He *had* to.

His mother was somewhere in the crowd, probably crying as the Russian national anthem began to play and Dorian looked over to the side where Brian and Georgia stood, beaming at them. He couldn't let them down, the only two people on the team who really believed in him, just like his mom, just like Jason, just like his dad who'd died still working hard to pay for his training.

Down the row, Jules smiled up at the crowd, and Dorian looked away from him. He couldn't explain Jules, who lived to get under his skin, who had used every short joke in the book, who still didn't see him as competition despite that Dorian had proved himself time and time again. Jules who made something stir in Dorian's chest whenever he thought about those moments behind locked doors, no matter how much he despised him.

He thought of what Mitya had said, about being a teammate. Dorian had never had this much trouble before. Back at school, his teammates were all his friends, but none of them had Olympic dreams, not like he did. They did it because they loved the sport, and that was why he had started in the first place. After twelve years of competitive gymnastics, though, Dorian had forgotten what it was like just to have fun doing gymnastics. It hadn't been about fun in a while.

Shaking the thoughts from his mind, he focused on the unfamiliar music swelling around him, trying to ignore the cameras flashing down at him from every direction. He wasn't really looking forward to seeing his face on every internet news site, every news program, maybe even a Wheaties box. Maybe that was what Jules wanted, but Dorian wasn't in it for the fame.

The anthem ended and the crowd exploded in cheers. More people came forward to shake his hand, and he didn't know most of them, but he smiled anyway and thanked them all for their congratulations.

"Good job, boys," Brian said as they finally escaped the crowd and the journalists swarmed instead. Dorian stepped out of the way of the reporters, especially as the woman from Jules' room the other night, hurried forward. "Should know the all-around results any minute now. Dorian, go give an interview." He pushed Dorian back towards the reporters despite Dorian's reluctance.

He ended up in front of a young woman, probably not much older than he was. Shifting awkwardly, he hated the way the camera hovered right before him. If he never had to see another camera in his life, he would be happy. It just made him uncomfortable.

"Dorian," she said excitedly. "How does it feel to have won silver with the US team and gold in vault at your first Olympics?"

"It's awesome," he replied, remembering that press was half the battle. If he could make a good impression, they would leave him alone. "I'm really, uh, proud of everyone on the team. They did a great job." It was clichéd and short but at least it wasn't something stupid.

"And how do you feel about competing against your teammate,

Jules Gardner, in the all-around?"

"What?" Dorian frowned, glancing over her shoulder at Jules, who was grinning and laughing with his reporter.

"The all-around competitors have just been announced," the woman said, and Dorian searched for Brian instead, for a confirmation. He found Brian talking with one of the officials, and Brian caught his eye and grinned. "You and Jules will be competing together. How do you feel about that?"

Dorian blinked and forced a smile. "Well, I think Jules is a fierce competitor, but I'm not worried." Honestly, at the moment, he just wanted to get out from under the microscope of the camera. Press had always been his least favorite part, though Georgia constantly reminded him of its importance. Without it, he wouldn't get any endorsement deals, and therefore, not get any money to pay for all the training. It was a vicious cycle that he tried his best to avoid.

The girl smiled and nodded at the cameraman, who shut it off and turned away.

"Well, good luck," she said before following the camera to the next person. He let out a breath of relief as she disappeared, the nerves in his throat dying down now that he didn't have to talk anymore.

"You're in the all-around!" Georgia cried when Dorian made his way over, and she grabbed him into a hug. "You better nail your parallel bars."

"I know," he agreed, an elated feeling welling up inside him like a giant balloon. He grinned, though. "I can't believe it."

"Believe it," she said firmly. "It's what we've all been working for. Now, go put that medal with your other and meet Brian and me in the gym in half an hour. You and Jules have work to do."

Dorian glanced over to where Jules was still smooth-talking the reporters. "I'll be there."

"I'll get Jules," Brian said, and Dorian turned, smiling at the people still congratulating him, but he wasn't thinking about the medal around his neck, only the one he would hopefully have tomorrow.

Chapter 9

Vaulted

"Looks like it's just the two of us, shorty," Jules said as he stepped up next to where Dorian was doing crunches.

Dorian cast him an unimpressed look. He sat up.

"And twenty-two other people," he pointed out, grabbing the towel and wiping his forehead. Dorian took a swig from his water bottle and glanced around the room at the other people still training hard as their coaches looked on.

Brian and Georgia stood off to the side, having a discussion about something, but Dorian couldn't hear what they were saying. His attention was on Jules instead who shrugged nonchalantly as though those other twenty-two people didn't matter at all. Maybe they didn't to him, but they did to Dorian.

"Shouldn't you be training?" Dorian asked when Jules didn't respond.

Jules looked down at him and smiled. "I was just enjoying watching you freak out."

"I'm not freaking out." Dorian lay back down. His mind flitted back to what Mitya had said the night before and he paused. How was he supposed to support Jules when Jules had done nothing but tear him down from the start?

"Maybe not yet, but you'll get there when the pressure mounts and you're so close to that medal you can taste it. See, no one remembers what team won or who won individual events. They only remember who won all-around."

"It's men's gymnastics," Dorian grunted, doing another sit-up. "No one remembers anything. They only remember the women's."

"The public, but that's not who counts and you know it, kid."

Dorian knew it. The public didn't matter except for endorsement deals. The people who mattered were already in the sport. They would remember your name and your wins. And your losses.

"What do you want?" he asked finally, setting the weights down again and puffing out a breath of air.

Jules laughed slightly. "I want that gold medal, same as you. I just know how to get it."

"Sleeping with reporters and being an unsupportive teammate," Dorian deadpanned, arching an eyebrow. "Way to go."

"You're still upset about her?" Jules asked curiously, and Dorian rolled his eyes.

He wasn't upset about the reporter. He'd never been upset or jealous or whatever else Jules was going to suggest.

"You can fuck whoever you want," he said instead, rising from the mat and taking his towel with him.

Jules caught his wrist as he stepped past, though, and Dorian turned sharply. Jules stepped in closer, his mouth hovering somewhere near Dorian's ear. Dorian's whole body stiffened, unable to force himself to move away. His heart beat faster at Jules' touch. Maybe he was a little jealous of that annoying reporter.

"Yeah, I can," he whispered, and Dorian swallowed, lowering his eyes to the mat and hoping no one around was looking. "Good luck tomorrow."

Jules released his wrist and stepped away. He felt shaky, confused at the way Jules' voice had softened. It didn't make any sense. He had never felt this way before with anyone, not a competitor or a friend. The only time he'd ever felt remotely similar had been at parties back at college, all nervous when guys would smile at him and take his hand and lead him somewhere secluded so they could make out and no one would see.

He took a breath instead and returned to where Georgia stood with Brian, arms crossed over her chest as she watched Jules do chin-ups. She glanced at him as he stepped up.

"Everything okay?"

"Fine." He shrugged, rubbing at his hair and wishing there was more truth to that statement than there was.

Mitya snored in the bed next to him as Dorian lay awake, staring at the dark ceiling, unable to shake the feeling that he should be doing something else. The clock told him it was nearly two in the morning. He should be asleep, getting his rest for tomorrow, the day that would decide his fate for the next four years. A gold in the all-around could mean endorsements, sponsorships, commercials. It meant respect from fellow athletes. It meant another four years planning for the next Olympics.

He couldn't, though. Every time he closed his eyes and told himself to go to sleep, images of parallel bars and vaults and Jules invaded his thoughts. Huffing, he opened his eyes again and looked at the clock. Still two AM.

He felt jittery, as though he'd drunk too much coffee when he hadn't had any in days. No caffeine, no extra sugar that wasn't written into his diet. Sitting up, he glanced over at Mitya's sleeping form, but Mitya didn't stir. Dorian really envied his ability to sleep through everything. What he wouldn't give just to go to sleep right now.

It clearly wasn't happening, though, so he threw off his covers and padded to the door, keycard in hand.

The hallway was dim and silent as Dorian stepped out. He didn't really know where he was going, but he shut the door quietly behind him. Maybe Georgia would be awake, but he somehow doubted it. Most normal people were asleep at two in the morning.

He wandered the halls for a while, unsure what to do, and he wasn't really surprised when he ended up down in the empty lobby, settling into one of the chairs and staring at the blank television in the corner. The light was on behind the counter, but there was no attendant anywhere.

Tomorrow would be the biggest day of his life. He couldn't afford to make any mistakes this time.

He knew there would be other chances. Plenty of people made it to the Olympics more than once, but what if he didn't? What if this was his only shot and he wasted it? He couldn't bear the thought of disappointing his mom. She'd always been there to support this crazy dream, even when both she and his dad had been working two jobs just to pay for it.

This was the only way he could really pay her back for all those years of struggle, of living in a rundown house built in the seventies and not updated since, of the strain of letting him move all the way to Colorado to keep training, not being able to visit on holidays.

He sighed at the blank TV. It all came down to tomorrow.

Jules couldn't sleep. It wasn't a normal thing, and he didn't really appreciate the intense quiet that always came with this time of night. Even with Carey in the next bed, rustling his sheets, it was too quiet. Of course, there was nothing to do this late at night and he knew exactly why he was awake in the first place.

Four years ago, he had been a ball of jittery nerves the night before the all-around competition. He'd spent the whole night tossing and turning, and in the end, he hadn't gotten the gold anyway. This time, at least he knew what was coming tomorrow. At least he was prepared.

That didn't prevent his body from feeling restless and completely awake and unable to do anything other than lie there. For a moment, he considered waking Carey up, but Carey would just grumble at him and tell him to shut up. He couldn't stand this. He had to get up. He had to get out of this room.

The hallways were silent as he padded down to the lobby, thinking of turning on the television and getting lost in some mindless entertainment, if there was any at this hour. So far, what he'd seen of Chinese television made very little sense to him. Little kids dressed in lamb costumes and singing songs could only hold his attention for so long.

He wasn't expecting to find Dorian sitting on the couch, although it didn't surprise him. Dorian seemed the type to stay up all night and stress about things he couldn't control. Jules had learned long ago that worrying over things you couldn't change didn't help. He smiled to himself as he hovered in the doorway. From here, he could see Dorian's profile, brows furrowed and mouth pressed together, deep in thought.

Jules bet he knew exactly what he was thinking too. He'd been there before. Dorian would probably never lighten up, and as much as that annoyed Jules, he found the stubbornness endearing. Perhaps there was something wrong with him too.

Moving over, he slid his hands over Dorian's chest, feeling the way he jerked beneath him, surprised, already pulling away before he could lean down. Dorian's chest was warm, firm, worn tee-shirt soft to the touch.

"What are you doing up at this hour?" he asked, voice low.

Dorian jerked forward out of his grip and whipped around to face him. "Jules, what are you doing?"

Jules let Dorian pull away, dropping his hands and rounding the couch. He plopped down next to Dorian, ignoring the way Dorian stiffened. Just once, he wished Dorian would let his guard down. "Contemplating life," he replied. Truthfully, he couldn't stand to pretend to sleep anymore. He glanced at Dorian, smiling slightly at how Dorian's eyebrows came together, evaluating him.

"Shouldn't you be sleeping?"

"Shouldn't you?" Jules countered. "Or were you thinking of sneaking into the gym again?"

He probably shouldn't have said it when Dorian shrank slightly. If he wanted anything to happen here, he probably shouldn't have reminded Dorian of the monumental jerk he'd been. It went both ways, though, and he wasn't sure Dorian was the one who should be mad. Yes, he'd started it, but Dorian had taken everything so personally. He could hear Coach Harper's voice in his head, telling him to say something, something that would bring Dorian's confidence down the night before the finals. It was the perfect opportunity to insult him or casually mention how bad his parallel bars routine was, but he just couldn't bring himself to do it.

If he was honest, he found Dorian fascinating, as much as his teammates found Dorian annoying and mouthy. That was also true, Jules admitted as he watched Dorian next to him on the couch. Instead of arguing with Dorian, there were many other things he'd rather be doing. Of all the people he'd been with in his life, none had fought him quite like Dorian; none had given it back just as good. He enjoyed the push and the pull.

"I was just... thinking about tomorrow," Dorian admitted finally, and Jules nodded. Dorian looked tired as he said it.

"Scary, isn't it?" he asked. "All that pressure. But think of it this way, tomorrow you'll know what kind of person you are."

"And what kind of person are you?"

Jules smiled. He still hadn't figured that out, even after all this time, but he didn't say it out loud. One medal didn't solve any problems. He still had money issues. He still had parents who didn't care. Coach Harper was the only reliable one in his life. He still had Dorian shying away from him, barely opening up. Jules supposed that was his fault. He hadn't exactly been the most accommodating to start off with, but the sex was good and that had to count for something.

He liked the way Dorian's eyes flicked to him when he thought no one was looking, how he let the kisses linger. Maybe Jules was making something out of nothing, but he could swear Dorian liked him just a little, or at least didn't hate him as much as he pretended.

"We'll find out tomorrow," he said finally, reaching out and brushing Dorian's hair from his eyes. Dorian didn't flinch at the touch, and Jules couldn't help it as his gaze dropped to Dorian's mouth, soft pouted lips so inviting.

It was probably the wrong time for anything so open, but he didn't care as he drew Dorian's mouth to his. To his surprise, Dorian didn't fight him, mouth opening to his, and Jules felt Dorian's hand grip his knee for half a second before it was gone and Dorian pulled back.

"No," he said, staring up at Jules.

Fuck it. Jules wanted it. He wanted Dorian to stop being the stuck-up brat and just enjoy something. He didn't understand why it was so hard, why Dorian had to make everything so hard. Jules got it. It was a competition, sure, but it wasn't the end of the world if one of them didn't win the gold tomorrow. Life would still go on, and he would have liked it if Dorian would at least entertain the idea that Jules wasn't some psycho out to crush him constantly because he wasn't. If he was half as competitive as Dorian, he would have given himself a heart attack by now. There was more to life than a shiny metal disc. It wasn't even real gold anyway.

Behind them, a shadow crossed the light behind the desk. Dorian said nothing more, pulling away and rising from the couch. As he left, though, he glanced back, and Jules watched him go. Flopping back on the couch, Jules sighed loudly. Now he didn't even have Dorian to distract him and only hours to go until the end.

Dorian ignored Jules, or tried to, unable to when Jules did his routines and Georgia and Brian muttered under their breaths with every deduction or triumph. Dorian tried not to look at his scores or listen to the commentary on the little TV in the pit.

He had his own events to worry about. He'd spotted his mother earlier in one of the close seats. She'd grinned and waved excitedly at him. He'd waved back, but all it had done was sent a wave of nerves through his stomach. He couldn't think about her anymore. He had to just focus on the events. He shouldn't have been paying attention to anyone else's events really. This wasn't about them. It was only about him.

Jules was in the back of his mind, though, as he always was these days. Dorian didn't like the way he felt around Jules, unsure of himself, like a teenager with hormones he couldn't control, the desire to push Jules up against a wall and kiss until his lips were swollen and he couldn't breathe. It wasn't something he'd ever felt before and he wasn't sure how to deal with it. Jules was not someone he should feel this way about, not after everything that had happened with them.

Now was not the time to think about it, though. Now was the time to focus. The rings went well, probably his best ever, and he knew it the moment his feet hit the mat perfectly, sticking the landing, and the crowd went wild. He'd ignored Jules' eyes on him as he returned to the pit, grinning at Brian's congratulations.

There were still more events to go, and he made it through the pommel horse fine, then the floor, but the parallel bars came next, and he had to admit he was nervous. They'd never been his best event, never, and he knew they never would be. He could practice forever, but he'd never be a champion on them.

Sitting on the bench, he reached down to rub his ankle. It felt fine, but nerves were starting to get the best of him.

"You're going to be fine," Georgia assured him as he watched the French competitor do his routine. He nodded, though he didn't feel completely confident yet.

"Get it, ducky," Jules called as Dorian stepped up onto the mat and headed for the bars.

Dorian ignored him, chalking up his hands and trying not to think about the next two minutes. They would be over soon enough. Then he could move on to better things like vault and high bar.

He heard the announcer say his name as he stepped up to the mat and acknowledged the judges as usual. The bars stood before him, innocent, although he knew better. They'd bested him before.

The mount went fine, and he concentrated on following his routine, the routine he'd been working on for months. He repeated their advice as he went into the long handstand. Keep tight, know where the bar was, don't be afraid of it.

He tried to relax through every move, in every instance where he tensed. It was just one event, and as long as nothing major happened, he would be fine.

The two minutes always seemed excruciatingly long while he was on the bars but the moment his hands left the bars for the dismount, it seemed short. His body moved upward, a triple salto as he released and came down. He landed, pausing as his landing shook and he took a step forward, but he managed to catch himself and straightened up to applause from the crowd.

A wave of relief crashed over him as he turned to the judges, then the crowd. Swallowing down the nerves that finally started to dissipate, he returned to the pit to gulp down some water and force a half-smile at Georgia's encouraging words.

He didn't want to look at his scores. There were only two events left now, two events before he could have that gold around his neck, and he didn't want to screw it up by psyching himself up. He could do vault and high bar in his sleep.

He watched Jules do his bars, more confident than him, moving through his routine easier, smoother. He didn't congratulate him when he finished and dropped onto the bench next to him.

Jules glanced over. "Good luck," he only said as Dorian rose to prepare for vault.

Frowning, Dorian left without a word. Jules had never wished him luck before, not seriously anyway. That, if anything, made him more confused than before.

In a few minutes, he would be doing his best event in front of the whole world. He would finally prove to everyone that he could do it. He could go from being a scrawny kid from a small town to an Olympic gold medalist.

"Kill it," Brian said as Dorian stepped onto the mat and headed for his place as the scores for the previous person came up on the screen.

It was just him and the vault, just the long stretch of blue mat between him and his destiny. For the first time all day, he wasn't nervous.

The launch went perfectly, his body twisting around, two and a half twists as he came down, body opening up at just the right time and his feet came down on the mat.

He knew it was wrong the minute his foot touched the ground, and the excruciating pain that followed made him damn sure. He crumpled to the ground, struggling to pull himself up, but any pressure he put on his ankle ripped through him. He knew it was bad— it was the same ankle from before, the injury everyone had feared would impede him.

Georgia and Brian were there in a second, and the crowd seemed to hush as they hauled him up, an arm over either of their shoulders. Dorian glanced down at his ankle, already starting to swell, too painful to put any pressure on it as he limped off the mat. As Brian lowered him onto the bench and the medic examined him, Dorian looked up, seeing his dream fade away before his very eyes.

"I'm fine," he insisted, trying to get up, but Brian shoved him back down. The medic pressed on his ankle and he gasped in pain, gritting his teeth. He forced himself to unscrew his face. "I can do the second vault."

"No way," Brian said firmly. "You are not pulling a Kerri Strug."

"I'm fine," he repeated vehemently. This couldn't be the end. He couldn't let it. He had to finish. He had to.

He looked at his ankle, though, turning purple and swelling even as he watched. The medic was shouting for ice, examining him, but every touch sent a sharp piercing pain through him, and he bit his bottom lip against the pain, the pressure settling on his chest as he tried to breathe.

"Torn ligament, probably a fracture," the medic said as he stood up. "You're lucky it didn't break completely."

"No, but—" He couldn't argue it, not with the medic shaking his head and Brian's strong hand forcing him to stay down on the bench.

He had to get up. He had to finish. There was no way he could let it all go. He didn't care about the pain in his ankle, although the moment he put any weight on it, he winced at the feeling of a knife shooting up his leg.

Dorian looked away. A camera swooped over him and he grimaced, the fight draining out of him.

All that work and one landing messed up everything. He couldn't look at anyone as they wrapped his ankle and applied a cold compress. He'd failed. He'd failed himself and everyone he knew. Now Jules would win. Jules would get to gloat and the whole team would be right about him.

He caught sight of Jules watching him once the medic had finally finished and Brian hauled him up, helping him limp off where the cameras wouldn't be flashing in his face. He looked away from Jules, the unmistakable pity that made his stomach curl into a ball, as they passed and cringed at the pain in his ankle. His life was over.

Chapter 10

Sweet as Peaches

His mother was the first to visit, tears in her eyes as she hurried into medical area.

"Dorian, are you all right?" she asked, feeling his forehead, and he pushed her hand away. "Do you need surgery? How bad is it?"

"Mom," he said, frowning. He didn't have a fever. "It's okay."

He lay on the uncomfortable exam table, foot propped up, and he just wanted to go back to his room. He wasn't sick. His ankle was just swollen up to the size of a watermelon and hurt like hell to walk on.

"I'm sorry," he said finally when his mom settled down and pulled up the lone chair in the room.

"What for?" she asked, shaking her head and grabbing his hand.

He looked away, emotions welling up inside him, emotions he usually tried to quash rather than think about.

"I didn't win, and now I'll probably never be able to compete again."

He wasn't expecting his mom to slap him upside the head, but she did, and he stared at her.

"You idiot," she said as his mouth fell open. "You think I care about gold medals?"

He winced, immediately feeling bad. "Well, no, but, I mean, you've put so much into this and all I did was fail."

"You worked your heart and soul to get here, and so did your daddy and I," she said seriously, tears brimming in her eyes, hands on her hips. "And don't you think for a minute that I'm disappointed you didn't get some little circle of metal. All I care about is that you're alive and healthy, and you are. You did your best, and you've got a gold and a silver to prove it. Who cares about the all-around? You're already an Olympian, and I wouldn't have done a damn thing differently."

Dorian felt the tears well up before he could stop them, all the stress of the last few weeks, the tension, the pain, trying so hard to ignore everything came to the surface, and he covered his face, taking a shaky breath.

His mother dragged him into a sideways hug, squeezing him tightly as he tried to bite back the emotions threatening to choke him. A tear escaped, sliding down his cheek as his mother held on tightly. She pulled back after a second, wiping away the wetness from his face and planting a kiss on his cheek.

"Now you rest up, peaches," she said, smoothing down his jacket and nodding uselessly. "I'll come visit you later."

"They were just doing x-rays. I'll get to leave soon," he said, "go back to my room."

"Good." She nodded again, smiling at him. She grabbed his arm tightly, staring into his eyes. "I am so proud of you."

"I know," he said, and she kissed him again then wiped lipstick off his cheek.

"You take care, sweetie. Have someone find me if you need anything."

"Thanks, Mom."

Dorian smiled as she left the room, then sat back with a shaky sigh. His ankle twinged as he tried to move it, so he stopped bothering and just lay back, hoping someone would give him some pain pills soon.

At long last, they gave Dorian a pair of crutches and ordered him to bed rest, which meant Brian rolled him to the Village in a wheelchair and took him up to the room.

"Now, bed rest means no walking except to use the bathroom, no getting up for anything unless it's life or death. If you step on that ankle, you might damage it for life. I'll put the crutches next to the bed. Call me if you need something. Don't be stupid."

"Thanks," Dorian replied, pursing his mouth. He wasn't an idiot.

He was glad when Brian left and he had the room to himself, although there was nothing to do there. Mitya wasn't there, but Dorian was glad. He reached for his book, paging through it half-heartedly before sighing and closing it.

He didn't want to turn on the tiny TV perched in the corner. He didn't want to know what he'd see on it. With his luck, he'd see Jules winning the gold in all-around. He could sleep, he thought vaguely, a tempting idea considering how he hadn't slept at all the night before. He didn't feel tired, though, only in pain and annoyed at himself. Hopefully the pain meds would kick in sooner rather than later.

He looked up sharply at the door unlocking. Jules stepped in, and Dorian looked away. Jules was just about the last person he wanted to see right now.

"Hey, peaches," Jules greeted him, shutting the door behind him.

Dorian immediately groaned. "Were you spying on my mom and me?"

Jules shrugged. "Hospital curtains aren't soundproofed." He tossed the keycard onto the table between the beds and sat down on Mitya's bed, facing Dorian. "You're all over the news."

"Great," Dorian deadpanned. That was exactly what he needed. "Are you here because I stole all your press? Or did you just come here to gloat?"

"Surprisingly, neither," Jules replied, setting his elbows on his knees.

Dorian arched an eyebrow in surprise. What other reason could he possibly have for visiting?

"I thought you'd be thrilled," he said finally. "Isn't it what you wanted?"

Even as the words came out of his mouth and Jules' eyes flicked down, an admission of a sort, Dorian remembered the look on his face back in the gym. It had been pity, something Dorian hadn't thought Jules felt for anyone, let alone him. He didn't deserve anyone's pity.

"Well, not *really*," Jules admitted. "What is the fun of competing with a gimp? Takes all the fun out."

"Well, I'm sorry I took your fun away," Dorian muttered. "It'll be my small comfort when I can never do gymnastics again."

Jules shook his head as though Dorian was being a complete idiot. "Competition is only fun if there's someone to compete with. If you're better than everyone, what's the point?"

Dorian frowned. "So you've been picking on me because…."

"Because you're the youngest." Jules shrugged. "It's your first time. It's fun to watch you wind up like a clock. Because you take it so seriously, man. But there's always going to be another competition. There's always going to be another Olympics."

"Not for me," Dorian muttered, trying to shift his ankle, but he winced in pain instead, a wave of nausea flowing over him, and he ceased trying. "And you treat me like I've never done anything. I'm a world champion."

"Do you really think we'd care at all about you if you weren't good?" Jules arched an eyebrow. "It was just joking."

"Well, it didn't feel like it to me." Hearing it didn't make Dorian feel much better. Competition was over. Someone had already won the all-around and he was out of the running. Why couldn't Jules just tell him? At least then he could be left alone, unless, that was, that Jules wanted to stay. The thought made Dorian slightly uneasy, though he wasn't sure why. "I didn't come here to feel like high school all over again. You have no idea how hard I worked to get here, for this, for it all to be wasted."

"It wasn't wasted," Jules replied, shaking his head. "You got a gold medal and a silver, and people are gonna remember you."

"As the guy who broke his ankle on national television, whose teammates hated him, who couldn't even do his best event."

"We don't hate you." Jules rolled his eyes. "You just take everything so seriously."

"Sorry," Dorian snapped. It was all too little too late now. "But I didn't want to waste what apparently was my only chance."

"You've got your whole life ahead of you," Jules said finally, rising to his feet. "This was just two weeks."

Dorian shook his head. All he felt right now was empty. He didn't feel angry at Jules. He didn't feel unhappy. He just felt empty. And a little nauseous, but he blamed the pain pills for that. He looked away from Jules. "It was supposed to be the best two weeks of my life and it's turned into the worst."

Out of the corner of his eye, he saw Jules shift. It was strange, he thought, Jules coming to visit him. Since they'd started this Olympic thing, he hadn't felt much more than annoyance at his teammates, worry over the competition, and confusion about Jules. Now that Jules was here, sitting across from him while he waited for the pain meds to take effect, he wasn't sure what to say.

Why was Jules being nice to him? After everything? Could Dorian have gotten it wrong? It wouldn't have been the first time he'd made an incorrect assumption and regretted it later.

"I was just trying to loosen you up, Dor, but you're wound so tight, it's impossible. You gotta learn how to relax. That's why your bars routine is so bad. You're so afraid of falling that you cause yourself to do it. You think you can't, so you don't."

Dorian frowned. "I've worked my ass off to get where I am," he said, but Jules cut him off with a shake of his head.

"And so has every other guy out there. Mitya's dad moved the whole family from Russia just so they could have a better life. My parents got divorced when I was ten and my dad refused to pay for anything. I had to work ten times harder to get what I wanted. You just need to accept who you are and stop trying to be better than that."

A wave of guilt hit him, jumbling with the nausea from the meds in his stomach. Jules was right. Of course he was right. Dorian wasn't the only one who'd struggled to get there. Most athletes' path to the Olympics wasn't smooth. He felt bad as he thought it, glancing at Jules' face and trying to force the words to come out.

"I know," he managed finally. When Jules' mouth curved into a smile, Dorian didn't know what to do.

He shifted his leg instead, a strange feeling filling him, a lightness that wasn't connected to anything that Jules was saying. The pain in his ankle was receding, leaving a tingling numbness when he tried to move it. His head felt lighter too, and he tried to shake away the fog creeping in, but the meds were starting to take effect and there was nothing he could do now.

Instead of feeling angry or sad, he actually laughed, surprising Jules.

"You know what's funny?" he said, and Jules looked confused, eyeing him. Dorian glanced away from him, sliding his fingers down the sheets. He marveled at the slightly rough texture under his hands, smiling to himself at it. Those meds must have been really strong. "I really liked you. You know, four years ago when you were at the Olympics and I was just sitting in training, wishing I was there. I really wanted to be like you. 'Cause you had everything I wanted."

Jules still eyed him closely, but then he smiled. "The meds are kicking in, huh?"

Dorian didn't reply to the question, smiling over at Jules. For once in his life, he didn't feel like he had to hold everything in. He could say whatever he wanted right now and no one could hold it against him. Even if he made a fool of himself, it wouldn't matter.

"I thought you were so cool," he said, things coming out of his mouth that he'd vowed never to say to Jules' face. "And you were so talented."

"And now?"

Dorian smiled, stretching out his arm to touch Jules, but he stopped an inch away and laughed instead.

"You're still talented and you're really hot, and you really annoy me, and all I wanted was for you to think I was cool too. But..." He sighed. "But I'm not and I never will be."

"Dorian," Jules said slowly, but Dorian smiled, shaking his head.

He didn't care what he was saying. He didn't know half of it, and he wouldn't remember it tomorrow. He was already starting to feel tired, the medication dragging him down to a sea of unconsciousness, but he had to tell Jules how he felt first. He had to get it out, everything he'd been keeping in since this whole thing had started.

"I don't know why I let you kiss me or why I'm such a bitch, but I liked it. It was like you were the person I wanted you to be for a second, the person I'd built up in my head, but you're not. You're different." He smiled slightly, meeting Jules' eyes.

Jules looked amused now, and he reached for Dorian, smoothing back his hair. "You're different than I thought too. You can smile."

Dorian pushed away Jules' hand, but his fingers curled into it instead. He felt tired now, more tired than before, and it was a struggle to keep his eyes open, but he stared at Jules for a second, feeling the warmth of his palm against his.

"I think you're the most annoying, hottest guy who's ever actually wanted me, and I kinda like you again, but if you tell anyone that, I'll kill you."

Jules laughed, pulling his hand away from Dorian's as Dorian slumped back in the bed, sighing slowly, trying to stay awake, but the medication made everything blurry and soft.

"You're not gonna remember any of this tomorrow, are you?"

Dorian forced his eyes up to Jules' and he smiled. "No."

"Go to sleep, Dorian," Jules said instead, rising from the bed and heading for the door.

"I could have won today," Dorian mumbled as Jules pulled it open.

Jules glanced back, almost smiling. "Goodnight."

The door shut behind him, and Dorian closed his eyes, slipping into a blissfully painless sleep.

Chapter 11

A Medal Isn't Everything

"Oh, look, look!" Jason said, hitting Dorian's shoulder, and Dorian merely frowned, but Jason wasn't looking at him from where they were both squished onto his bed. Instead, he pointed at the tiny television screen where Dorian saw himself, moving in slow motion, twist around in the air and come down. "Right there. You can just *see* it happening."

Reluctantly, Dorian watched as his feet touched the ground followed by an immediate echo of pain in his face as he tried to stay up, but his ankle collapsed and he hit the mat. The crowd gasped as one and the announcer babbled on.

"It's too bad this isn't Tivo," Jason commented, squinting up at the screen.

"Not like it matters," Dorian muttered. "They replay it every five minutes."

True to his word, the television flashed to a reporter for a moment, then back to replay the moment, over and over, until Dorian could feel the pain each time he watched it.

"Can you turn that off?" he asked finally. He was sick of seeing himself being injured on international television.

"And here's afterward," Jason said instead, not listening at all, and waving at the screen where Brian was helping a pale-faced Dorian off the mat and into the pit. "Dude, you should have heard your mom during this. She was freaking out."

Dorian wasn't listening. He was watching the TV, but not at himself being mobbed by people, the medic examining his ankle as he tried to insist he could still compete. Instead, he was watching

Jules, who stood off to the side, a look of concern and disbelief on his face.

He remembered that moment—well, he remembered every moment of that day—and now Jules' face stared at him on the television screen, looking worried as Brian helped Dorian hobble to the bench. He'd never seen Jules look like that before. It made him think of what Jules had said, that night before the all-around, about what kind of person he was.

He looked away after a minute, glancing at Jason beside him. "Do you think I'm a bad person?"

Jason frowned. "What? What are you talking about?"

Dorian sighed, glancing down at his still-swollen ankle. It would probably be like this for weeks, then he'd have to go through physical therapy to even get back to normal, let alone able to do gymnastics anymore.

"Do I only care about winning? Should I have stopped after the first injury? Was I just asking for this?"

"What are you talking about?" Jason asked again, frowning at him. "Everybody knows you're competitive. It's just how you are. You don't give up. It's a good quality to have. Besides, if you'd stopped, you wouldn't have gone to the Olympics, which in my opinion, was totally worth it. Even if you will have to walk on crutches for the next year."

Dorian didn't reply, looking at the TV again where the announcers were discussing his injury.

"You're *not* a bad person," Jason repeated firmly, nudging his shoulder. "You just have bad luck."

"It wasn't luck that got me here." Dorian shrugged. "Who won all-around anyway? No one will tell me."

He was afraid it was Jules and Brian and Georgia just didn't want to upset him any further, but no one seemed to be talking about it.

Jason shrugged. "Some Chinese guy. I didn't really care once you weren't there. That Jules guy got bronze again, but who cares about bronze?"

Dorian nodded slowly. He wasn't upset that Jules had medaled. A medal was really just a small thing in comparison to keeping himself healthy and able to walk. At least Jules had that.

"Look, they're playing it again," Jason said a second later, jolting Dorian out of his thoughts. On the screen, Dorian watched again as his ankle twisted in an unnatural angle. Jason watched excitedly. "And your face, right there! Right there you know it's bad."

Dorian wasn't listening as Jason rambled on about getting a screenshot of that when they got home and putting it up in the dorm.

Brian helped Dorian up onto the platform while cameras flashed in his face, and the rest of his teammates watched him from where they were already seated behind their microphones. Dorian's two medals clinked over his USA jacket, and he hobbled on his crutches into the closest chair, Brian lowering him down slowly. Dorian pushed a hand through his hair and prayed that this press conference would be over soon. The sooner it was over, the sooner he could get on that plane to go home.

"Dorian!" The first reporter spoke, and Dorian recognized her as the woman from Jules' hotel room. He bit back any unpleasant feelings he had towards her and tried to put on a smile. "How is your ankle?"

"Painful," he replied simply, "but the doctors say there's a good chance of recovery, although I don't know about any more competitions."

The reporters clamored to ask a question at the same time and one in the back won out.

"This was your first Olympic games," he said, holding up his microphone. "How do you feel things went overall?"

Dorian paused, then glanced down the table at the rest of his teammates. Mitya sat next to him, scribbling nonsense on his piece of paper. Beside him, Jules was watching him, no hint of amusement this time. Dorian looked back at the reporter.

"I'm glad I got to come and compete, but to tell you the truth, I'll probably remember my team the most. Although if they don't stop playing my injury on TV, I'll never forget that moment either."

The reporters laughed, and Dorian sat back, relieved as they moved on to Jules instead, asking about his medals in the all-around. Off to the side, Georgia caught Dorian's eye and smiled.

It hadn't turned out like he'd thought his first Olympics would, and he may not ever come back, but he certainly wouldn't forget it.

Dorian struggled to put his jacket back on as he stood near the security conveyor belt, trying to stay upright on one crutch. His bag rolled out and he sighed, one arm in his jacket. He hated having crutches.

"I got it," someone said from behind him, grabbing his bag off the belt before he could finish putting on his jacket.

Turning, he saw Jules throwing the bag over his shoulder along with his own. He didn't say thanks, but turned and limped down the hallway, Jules alongside him.

People milled around the airport, browsing in the duty free shops or sitting at the small cafés, sipping coffee and chatting as they waited for their flights.

"That was a nice speech at the press conference," Jules commented as they walked slowly, Dorian moving jerkily on his crutches still.

"It wasn't a speech," he replied, not looking at Jules.

He didn't know how he felt about Jules, if he was angry with him or just tired of fighting. A part of him just wanted to forget this whole week, but he doubted he would ever be able to.

He hesitated as they walked down the hallway, surrounded by duty-free shopping on either side. He felt as though he had to say something, something to make up for how he'd acted, how much of a jerk he had been in his own right to Jules, to all of his teammates.

"Jules," he said finally, pausing and leaning on his crutches as he looked at Jules, hating the way his heart began to thud against his throat, a mixture of fear and apprehension. "I'm... I shouldn't have..."

He didn't know exactly what to say. He hadn't thought about it beforehand. It wasn't rehearsed like a press speech was. It was much harder to get out considering he still didn't know what any of it meant.

Jules merely arched an expectant eyebrow as he hesitated.

"I wasn't a very good teammate," he said at length. "And I wish I could just redo this whole thing."

He jerked slightly as Jules caught his arm, crowding him out of the way of the people in the hallway and into a small space between a phone booth and a wall. Dorian stumbled over his crutches, but Jules held him up as he found his footing again.

"What are you doing?"

Jules smiled slowly. "I'm accepting your apology, however vague it was. I wasn't exactly the best teammate ever either."

Dorian flushed slightly, biting his lip and wishing they really could just redo everything. Maybe he and Jules would have gotten along. Maybe he wouldn't have been standing there, perched on crutches and wincing at the pain in his ankle. Maybe he would have been able to kiss Jules without feeling as though he was losing to him.

"Look, I just want to forget about this whole last month," he muttered, looking away from Jules. "All it proved was that I'm a jerk, and you're a jerk, and we're both too competitive to actually get along."

Jules laughed, much to Dorian's surprise. "You can pretend all you want that you hate me, but we both know the truth, and the truth is what you'll remember most about the past two weeks isn't that moment when you knew it was over. It was the moment you knew you wanted me."

Dorian's eyes widened, but he didn't have a reply.

"We have to get to the plane," he said instead, pushing at Jules' shoulder, but Jules didn't move.

"You don't have to say it out loud," Jules went on, reaching for Dorian's face and pulling his chin around to face him. "But you're gonna have to admit it someday."

Jules kissed him then, stuffed in the tiny space between the wall and the phone, people passing by blindly beyond them. Their lips met and Dorian's eyes closed, mouth opening up to Jules.

Something stirred deep in his chest as Jules kissed him, something he'd tried to ignore this whole time, since the first time Jules had pinned him to the mat in the arena. He couldn't deny it now, though, not when Jules kissed him deeply, tongue sweeping into his mouth, and he didn't even try to resist.

He wasn't sure what it meant, or what Jules meant exactly, but Jules was right. He would have to admit it someday, but it didn't really matter if Jules knew already.

"Hey."

A voice behind them broke them apart, and Dorian looked over sharply, eyes wide in embarrassment as Mitya stood there, arms crossed over his chest.

"Plane is boarding," he only said, turning and walking back to the gate.

Dorian rubbed at his flushed cheeks, half in embarrassment, half from Jules' kiss. Jules stepped back from him finally, and together they walked towards the gate in silence.

The attendant checked their tickets and wished them a good flight back. Dorian hobbled down the sloped runway to the plane, Jules behind him. As they waited for the queue at the door to clear, Jules paused thoughtfully.

"You know, I've never been to the south," he said after a minute, and Dorian glanced at him. "I hear they have good peaches."

Dorian smiled to himself after a second. "They do."

"Maybe I should visit," Jules said, hoisting up the bags as the line moved forward a few feet.

Dorian watched him for a minute before turning back to the line. "Maybe you should."

The Olympics hadn't turned out like he'd thought, Dorian would admit as he stepped onto the plane and greeted the cheery flight attendant, but it hadn't turned out all bad either. He took his seat, stretching out his leg carefully, and Jules sat down next to him, their arms brushing together on the armrest. Dorian merely smiled and looked away. Not bad at all.

Chapter 12
Unexpected Travels

Dorian sat on the lowest bleacher step, arms on his knees, his left ankle extended onto the gym floor to prevent any spasms of pain that always seemed to flare up when he kept it in the same position too long. He sighed as he watched Ryan land his double back flip off the high bar.

His ankle twinged as he pulled it back, and he frowned at it. In three months, he was still just able to walk on it, and not for long distances or stand on it for a prolonged amount of time. His physical therapist said he was lucky he hadn't needed surgery, and that he wouldn't so long as he was careful.

That didn't make him feel any better, though, and he left her office each week a little less convinced that he'd ever be able to compete in gymnastics again. It was a pipe dream, he knew, to think that in four years, he might have been ready to compete for the Olympic team again, but it wasn't one he was quite ready to give up.

The coach shouted at Wyatt as he came off the rings and stumbled on his landing. Dorian could see what he was doing wrong—he opened up too late out of his tumble—but he merely looked away. He couldn't even do the rings anymore.

"There you are." A voice beside him made him scowl and avoid Jason's eyes as Jason walked up to him. "What are you doing in here?"

"Nothing," Dorian replied, pushing himself up and ignoring how his ankle protested at the weight without his cane to help him, but Dorian hated always having the cane. He felt like a grandpa hobbling around with it.

"Why do you insist on torturing yourself?" Jason asked as Dorian turned towards the door.

Dorian resented that and shoved the gym doors open. "I'm not allowed to even watch the sport now?" he snapped back, stepping out into the warm afternoon sun and heading down one of the tree-lined paths that filled campus.

Tulane was a nice university, as far as schools went. Dorian had chosen it for its location (only three hours from his mother's house in Cherry Grove), plus they'd given him a scholarship for gymnastics.

Dorian walked as fast as he could manage, but it wasn't nearly fast enough to lose Jason, who sauntered along beside him.

"You were watching practice," Jason pointed out.

"It's my team!"

The look on Jason's face told him that Jason knew exactly why he went to practice, and it wasn't out of loyalty. Instead of elaborating, he pursed his lips and looked away. "Dude," Jason said as they walked, Dorian's limp starting to come back as they went. He really shouldn't have been putting so much pressure on his injury. "It's okay."

"No, it's not okay!" Dorian exploded, spinning around, and the few people walking past them on the path jumped and skirted around them. "Don't you understand? This has been my life ever since I can remember, and now, now I can't *do* anything! I feel like my whole world has just, ugh!"

He covered his face with his hands and huffed out a sigh. He couldn't explain it, not to Jason, who, even though he tried so hard to understand gymnastics, couldn't understand this. Shaking his head, he turned around and kept walking. He didn't know where he was going. There was nowhere to go other than back to his apartment, except that Jason was his roommate and there was no way to escape him.

Sometimes he felt bad about taking out his frustrations on Jason, but there wasn't much he could do about all the tension that seemed to fill his body at every moment of the day, ready to snap at the wrong word from one person.

Jason caught up to him a moment later, falling into step but not speaking as they crossed the campus.

The trees were still green despite the onset of winter. Dorian could feel it in the air, from the cool mornings to the way the afternoons were still bathed in the warmth of the southern sun. Autumn had flown by in stuffy heat waves and he was glad for the change. It was his favorite time of year, but this year, it just seemed to mock him when he thought of all the meets he wasn't getting to compete in, the people he wasn't getting to see, wasn't going to see ever again probably.

As they reached the edge of campus, Dorian had to pause, pulling his ankle up and rubbing it softly. Jason glanced at him.

"Sorry," Dorian muttered a second later, feeling guilty about his earlier outburst. It wasn't Jason's fault.

Jason shrugged. "It's been a long couple months."

That didn't excuse Dorian's behavior, but Dorian wasn't going to argue. He straightened up, testing his weight on his ankle. He really shouldn't have walked so far without his cane, but he'd purposefully left it at home today. His physical therapist would give him hell at the next appointment, he knew.

"Maybe you need a break," Jason suggested as they finally crossed the street. "Take a vacation or something."

"And where would I go?" Dorian asked doubtfully. All his friends lived within a ten mile radius of campus and his mom was a good three hours away. He didn't want to see her anyway. She would just fuss over his ankle and force him to sit down the entire time he was there.

"I don't know." Jason shrugged again. "You know tons of people."

"Gymnastic people," Dorian pointed out. "And I thought the point of this was to get away from it?"

"Do something fun, then. Pick your favorite gymnastic person and go visit them. Maybe they'll take your mind off it."

Dorian doubted there was anyone who could take his mind off his predicament. These days, it was all that he thought about. He fell asleep thinking about it and he woke up thinking about it.

"What about Jules?" Jason asked as they walked down the sidewalk towards their apartment. Their apartment was one of the many crappy ones close to campus, with stains on the carpet from previous tenants and a hole in the wall that had been there since they moved in, but it was cheap and it was an apartment which offered a tiny bit more privacy than the dorms.

Dorian paused as Jason mentioned Jules. "What about him?"

"You guys are sort of, well, something, right? You talk."

"We've talked to each other a couple times since coming back."

He didn't mention that he stalked Jules through social networking and thought too much about calling him late at night, but he never did because they didn't have that kind of relationship. They didn't have much of a relationship at all, or at least not one that Dorian could define anyway.

He kicked a leaf as he walked, hating the pulse in his ankle as it reminded him angrily that he wasn't supposed to do that. He just wanted things to go back to normal.

"You could go see him," Jason went on as if Dorian hadn't spoken. "I bet it's snowing up in Connecticut this time of year."

"Yeah, lots of ice," Dorian muttered unenthusiastically. Ice would be hell on his ankle. He wasn't sure Jules would want to see him anyway, and dropping in unannounced at Jules' training wasn't something he was sure he was ready for.

"Stop making excuses, dude," Jason said, punching his shoulder as they came upon their apartment building. "Just go somewhere. Get out of here."

Dorian scoffed. "That won't help."

Jason rolled his eyes. "You need a lay."

"No, I don't," he replied, heading for the stairs, but Jason grabbed his arm and steered him towards the elevator.

"Stop acting tough and take the elevator. You know you're not allowed to do so many stairs."

"You're not my physical therapist," Dorian muttered as Jason kept a hold of his arm while they waited for the elevator, as though he might make a run for it.

"I'm your friend," Jason replied. "And I need you to pay the other half of the rent, so we're taking the elevator, and you are going somewhere this weekend."

Dorian sighed, but he just didn't have the energy to argue the point with Jason, and he stepped into the elevator when it arrived a minute later.

Campus was entirely too big, Ryan had always thought so, but New Orleans made up for it with its penchant for huge parties and delicious southern cuisine. He was late for Italian, but he was less interested in learning the subjunctive tense as he came up on Dorian crossing the lawn. "Dorian!" he called, watching how Dorian paused, leaning against his cane. It had to be a bitch, hobbling around like that all the time.

Jogging up behind Dorian, he saw Dorian's shoulders sag. At least Dorian could pretend to want to talk to him. It wasn't like he tried to get him to talk about his feelings which he totally could have done. They'd gone over avoidance in his psych class last week, and Dorian showed all the symptoms. Since the Olympics, he'd just been distant. Still, he didn't have to be a dick about it.

He slapped Dorian on the shoulder as he arrived. "Hey, where you going?"

"Chem. It's across campus."

"I've got Italian," Ryan said brightly, falling into step beside him. Dorian looked like shit, if he did say so himself. He had bags under his eyes and dragged himself along as they walked. Did he even sleep anymore? It wasn't like he had anything else to do. He didn't ask, though, because Dorian wouldn't tell him the truth even if he did. Dorian kept things close to the vest most of the time.

Ryan knew he didn't look like Dorian at least. He ran a hand through his tousled brown hair, nodding at a passing girl, who only rolled her eyes and hurried past. He looked damn good.

"You left practice before I could ask you yesterday," he said as they walked, and Dorian glanced up.

"What?"

"Coach says I'm not holding my handstands long enough."

"You aren't."

Ryan scoffed. Trust Dorian to tell the harsh truth. "I just wanted a second opinion, and I figured I'd ask the master."

"I'm not the master."

"You know more than Coach. And you love to nit-pick." It was true. Ryan didn't know anyone else quite as blunt as Dorian.

"Are you trying to make me feel better?"

Ryan laughed. "If I was doing that, I'd just get you a hooker."

He doubted whether Dorian would ever allow that—he was so uptight about his love life. Maybe that would lighten him up. Or maybe it would just make things worse, and Ryan did *not* want things to get any worse. Dorian was already a huge pain in the ass since coming back from the Olympics. He wasn't sure he could take any more moping. If it went on much longer, the whole team was going to have to stage an intervention.

Dorian had been the star of the team, even after he'd stopped competing with them last year to focus entirely on training. Ryan had no idea how he'd managed to juggle school and training.

In all honesty, Ryan was glad Dorian couldn't compete anymore. It gave more of a chance for the rest of the guys, plus he'd been a little worried about what might happen to Dorian if he competed for too long. He was so competitive sometimes. It was ridiculous. Maybe this was just fate's way of telling him to slow down.

As much as Ryan tried to stay positive, he wasn't sure there was anything anyone could do to get Dorian out of this. Sometimes he just wanted to give up. It would have been a lot easier. He could have just gone on with his life and his plan to become a European bum, backpacking all over Europe and becoming the grizzled old man still staying in hostels far past a respectable age, telling stories to new travelers and drinking too much foreign beer.

"I don't think a hooker would help," Dorian said, and Ryan nodded.

"Probably not," he agreed. "But it might take your mind off things, and not all distractions are bad. I've got a very pretty distraction this semester. She's tall, blonde, can do this thing with her tongue where she—"

"Okay," Dorian interrupted. "I don't need to know all the details."

"I wouldn't want to offend your delicate sensibilities," Ryan said with a grin, shaking Dorian's shoulder as they walked. "You southern gentlemen are so upstanding."

Dorian rolled his eyes. "I'm no different than anyone else."

"Sure you are," Ryan said convincingly. "You're an Olympian, and you've never had a real relationship. I thought southern gentlemen were all about romance and wooing and shit. Flowers and candy and balls and whatever."

Dorian snorted. "Is that what they teach you up North?"

Ryan shrugged. He winked at Dorian, nudging him in the side. "Come on, man, where's your southern romance?"

Aside from the eternal stubbornness, the constant scowl, and the ridiculous competitiveness, Dorian wasn't all bad. He had a good eye for gymnastics. He was smart. There had to be someone he wouldn't scare away. His only option couldn't be hookers no matter how much they joked about it. Maybe if he could get Dorian laid, he would stop being so depressing.

Then again, Dorian never talked much about his personal life. He never brought dates anywhere, but then, he never *went* anywhere either. He was practically a shut-in. The only time Ryan had seen him with anyone was a party last year when Dorian had allowed Ryan to set him up (okay, Ryan had basically forced him to go with his friend, Jon). He'd just wanted Dorian to loosen up. Maybe it was the southern values thing, but in Chicago, it wasn't such a big deal, being gay. Or maybe he just never paid attention. He had plenty of gay friends back home.

"I don't want to date anyone here."

Ryan knew absolutely nothing about dating guys, but it couldn't be that much different than dating girls, right? You saw someone you liked, you hung out, you slept together. It wasn't rocket science. "What about somewhere else, then? There's gotta be somebody out there who floats your boat." Dear God, there had to be someone who could make Dorian stop moping.

When Dorian paused, Ryan grinned. There was someone.

"Look," he said. "Don't wait around for someone to come to you. You've got money from your medal, right? Hop on a plane and get out of here. Maybe you'll discover the world isn't such an evil place."

If Ryan couldn't help, someone else had to. He wanted his friend back, the one who would actually laugh and smile, the one he'd met last year at the first team meeting and who'd showed him how to stick his vault landings. Sometimes it seemed so long ago that Dorian had dragged his drunk ass home after a party and stopped him from calling up his ex-girlfriend and making a fool of himself.

"Maybe," Dorian said finally, and Ryan grabbed his shoulder.

"I'd really appreciate the old Dorian back, man," he said sincerely. "I'm in serious danger of drunk dialing again and you're my only savior."

Dorian laughed slightly. "Glad to know I'm needed."

"You are. You saved me from getting back together with Katie last year. Plus you improved my vaulting skills, like, twenty percent."

"Only twenty?"

"Hey, I wasn't that bad to begin with." He grinned at Dorian. Maybe there was hope after all, he thought, as Dorian laughed. "So, you know, maybe a weekend away would do you good. You'll feel better and I'll have my party buddy back. Who knows, this time, you can even drink with us."

On Dorian's look, he rolled his eyes. Dorian would probably never drink anything in his entire life, but just once, Ryan would like to get him drunk and see what came out of his mouth. He was definitely an enabler, as his mother liked to say.

Enabler or not, he wanted the old Dorian back, and one way or another, there had to be a way to get it.

Chapter 13
Slippery Paths

Honestly, Dorian wasn't sure how he had talked himself into this, but he found himself bundled up in a coat from his training days and standing outside a pair of big blue double doors. The frigid winter air blasted down his neck, and he shivered, grip tightening on his cane. Jason had made sure he'd taken it with him to the airport.

Although, with all the ice and piles of snow that lay scattered around him, it was probably a good idea. He'd never been particularly graceful on ice, which was why he hadn't tried to be a figure skater or hockey player.

The wind got colder the longer he stood outside the doors, and he knew he should go in. He just couldn't force himself to do it.

It wasn't as if he and Jules had ever seriously discussed anything about their relationship, and him just showing up might be kind of weird. Then again, Jules had said the last time they'd talked that he missed seeing him, and Dorian thought he'd hinted that they were more than friends. Obviously they were, or had been, but since the Olympics, Dorian hadn't gotten anything clarified.

A tree branch cracked and fell a few feet to his right and Dorian jumped at the sound. He didn't wait much longer to pull open the doors to the gym and step inside.

Inside was like every other gym Dorian had ever been in, a little bigger than most, but basically the same. He did a sweep of the inside, over the training equipment, and before his eyes fell on the couple of people standing together on the opposite side, a voice rang out.

"Hey, peaches!"

Dorian could feel his cheeks flushing as Jules broke away from the group and hurried over to him. Dorian wasn't sure what to do, but Jules had grabbed him into a warm, tight hug. He was slightly surprised, but the hug didn't last long, and Jules pulled back to grin at him.

"What are you doing here?" he asked, but Dorian was staring at Jules' head.

"You have hair," he said dumbly, and Jules laughed, running a hand over the very short brown hair on top of his head.

"Gets cold in the winter, short stuff," he replied, throwing an arm around Dorian's shoulders. "Come meet the guys."

Dorian let Jules lead him to the guys, noticing the way Jules' arm dropped the minute they got close.

"Guys, this is Dorian." Jules introduced him to the couple of guys standing around in their workout clothes. "A fellow Olympian. Dorian, this is Steve, Russell, and Pete. They train here during the season. Coach Harper is around here somewhere too. He'll want to meet you for sure."

Dorian nodded at each guy as Jules introduced them. He wasn't very good at small-talk. He never had been. He especially didn't want to answer questions as Steve nodded at his cane.

"How's the injury? Saw that on TV." He shook his head. "Major suckage."

"It's... coming along," Dorian muttered. He'd rather not tell the guys that even three months after the fact, he couldn't climb more than a flight of stairs without it getting sore and wobbly.

Jules was watching him as he answered, but Dorian didn't meet his eyes. He glanced down at his ankle instead, careful not to put his weight on it.

"Didn't you win gold on vault?" Pete asked a second later when the silence lasted a beat too long.

Jules smiled, patting Dorian's shoulder. "He's the world champion."

"Not anymore," Dorian added, though, forcing a smile as he glanced up. All three guys frowned slightly, and Dorian knew he should stop talking, but he couldn't help it when all he could think of was how his future was ruined.

"Yeah," Jules said a minute later. "Well, I don't know why you're here or for how long, but I'm starving. We should get dinner."

"It was nice meeting you guys," Dorian said as he turned with Jules, but they didn't get far before an older man with graying hair approached them. Jules smiled.

"Dorian, this is Coach Harper."

Dorian had heard a lot about Coach Harper in the past, though most of it was about the numerous gold medalists he had coached. He was older than Dorian had expected, shorter as well, with salt-and-pepper hair and a thick mustache. The smile stretching his lips wasn't exactly warm, and Dorian felt an urge to move closer to Jules as they were introduced. He stubbornly didn't, though, and shook Coach Harper's hand.

"Dorian Stuart," Coach Harper said knowingly, as though he knew him very well. "Good to finally meet you. Jules didn't mention you were coming to visit." He glanced sideways to Jules. "Shame about that ankle. You could have been great."

"Uh, thank you," Dorian replied slowly, unsure if he should take it as a compliment or not. Something about the way he said it made him pause, as though Harper was glad he'd been injured. That was stupid, though, he told himself. He really shouldn't be so paranoid.

"We're gonna grab some dinner," Jules interjected when Dorian shifted awkwardly, unable to think of anything to say as Harper's cool blue eyes grazed over him. It made him uneasy, though he couldn't say why. He tried to shake it off when Jules' hand landed on his arm, steering him away. "See you tomorrow, Coach."

Dorian didn't look back as they headed for the locker room.

"So why are you here?" Jules asked once they were inside and he swapped out his jersey for a tee shirt and jeans. Dorian sat on the bench, glancing around at the rows of lockers.

"I don't know," he admitted, tapping his cane against the floor, feeling like an old man. "I just had to get out of my apartment, out of that town."

"I thought New Orleans was awesome," Jules said, zipping up his sweatshirt and tugging on his shoes.

Dorian shrugged. "It's not the town really, it's..." He trailed away, thinking it would sound far too depressing to say 'me.' He shook his head. "So that's Coach Harper, huh? I hear he's a slave driver."

Jules arched an eyebrow but let him change the subject. Dorian pushed himself to his feet, still not putting too much weight on his ankle. He wanted to last as long as possible without having to really use the cane.

"He's the best coach I've ever had," Jules said, leaving the locker room and heading for the parking lot. "He's really the only one that's been there for me the past few years, and he's coached me to two Olympics, so I'd say that even if he is hardcore in training, it's well worth it."

Jules didn't talk about his past much, and Dorian got the feeling he didn't want to. When they stepped outside into the snow and ice, Dorian knew his hopes not to use his cane was an impossible dream.

"Maybe you should have rethought coming here," Jules said as they walked down the concrete path towards the parking lot.

"Why?" Dorian asked sharply, frowning as he looked at Jules, a momentary pinch of panic taking hold of his chest.

"Ice," Jules replied simply, steering him out of the way of a patch.

"Oh." Dorian gave himself a mental shake. "I'm fine." He was panicking over nothing. So what if they hadn't discussed anything? They liked each other, he was pretty sure.

"I'm sure you are," Jules said, releasing his arm.

Dorian didn't reply to that but kept a closer watch on the ground from that point forward. Jules stopped at a beat-up looking pick-up truck, a grey-blue color as though the paint had been stripped off, faded in places with a few rust spots on the door handles.

"Your chariot," Jules said, pulling open the door for Dorian. It squeaked on its hinges, and Dorian frowned, not at the car but at Jules holding the door open. He was perfectly capable of opening a door.

He didn't mention it, though, instead climbing in awkwardly and letting Jules shut the door behind him. Jules climbed in the driver's side and shoved the keys in the ignition. The engine rumbled to life, loud beneath Dorian.

"What are you in the mood for?" Jules asked as he backed out of the spot and paused at the entrance to the lot.

Dorian shrugged. He was beginning to wonder why he'd come here at all. He didn't feel any better seeing Jules, and he couldn't explain how it felt weird to be in the same room with him and not be arguing. He'd thought seeing Jules would make him feel good, and it had for a second, when Jules had hugged him. For a moment, his problems had disappeared, but the hug had ended and his problems had come rushing back. It couldn't be like that all the time.

"You're a regular chatty Cathy," Jules commented, finally turning left out the lot.

Dorian looked away from the window and the glittering, snowy landscape rushing past. "Sorry."

"And you're apologizing to me," Jules said, arching an eyebrow as he glanced over briefly. "Something is definitely wrong with you."

Dorian didn't know what to say. A lot of things had been wrong in the last few months, and he didn't see how this trip was going to make any difference.

"Fine, don't tell me," Jules went on, peering out the windshield at the buildings they passed.

Dorian didn't recognize anything, but he hadn't been to Connecticut for a while, not since one summer back in middle school for gymnastics camp. He'd done most of his training in Colorado, far away from home.

They pulled up to a small shack of a restaurant a few minutes later, and Jules hopped out, slamming the door behind him. Dorian was at least glad that he didn't open the door for him and instead let him struggle out on his own, lowering himself carefully to the ground and shutting the door.

"Hope you like greasy burgers," Jules said, flashing a smile at Dorian as he headed for the door, skirting the pile of snow near the door and holding the door open as Dorian caught up.

Inside looked just as cramped as it did from the outside, but it smelled amazing. Jules didn't bother to wait for a server and just took one of the booths next to the window. Dorian slid in across from him, wishing he had something to say. He'd never felt so out of place before, as if he just didn't know what to do or say. He'd never felt like this around Jules before, at the very least.

Jules slid a menu under his nose a second later, and Dorian looked up. Jules was already reading his menu, though.

"The burgers are really good here," he said, and Dorian opened his menu slowly. "And the pulled pork sandwiches."

"Isn't this off your diet?" Dorian asked skeptically, eyeing the pictures of mouth-watering foods that were surely full of way too many calories.

Jules shot him a look. "There's four years until the next Olympics. Don't tell me you've been sticking to the diet? You can't even do routines anymore."

Dorian didn't like the stab of disappointment as Jules said it even though he knew it was true. It just hurt to admit it. He didn't want to admit it quite yet. There was still a chance he could compete, if he just worked hard at the therapy and didn't give up.

Jules paused as Dorian's face twitched and he lowered his eyes to the menu.

"I mean..."

"No, you're right," Dorian interrupted. "I don't have to stick to a diet anymore. Why should I?"

He didn't look up to see Jules' frown. Instead, he concentrated on the menu. Why had he even come? It had been stupid.

It wasn't that Dorian had grand ideas about their relationship going beyond occasional sex and teasing, but maybe in the back of his mind, he'd thought about it. Sure, he'd thought about it, of what it might be like to actually date Jules, but it was a stupid idea. Clearly.

"Afternoon, Jules," the waitress greeted them when she stepped up to the table a few minutes later. "Surprised to see you back so soon."

Jules smiled at the young woman, and Dorian had a momentary thought that she was pretty, and he tried not to wonder if she was like the reporter back at the Olympics, one of those girls.

"Yeah, well, a friend came into town," Jules said, nodding at Dorian, who forced yet another smile. He didn't feel much like smiling these days, but he'd grown up with southern manners and his mother would have his head if he wasn't at least polite.

The girl paused for a second, staring at him and waving her pen at him. "Wait, I know you. You're the guy who got injured! That was just awful!"

Dorian hated talking about it. He never knew what to say, and people brought it up constantly, as if he needed to hear about it. He lived every day of his life with it. He didn't want to relive it anymore.

"How's the recovery coming?" she asked, and Dorian could feel his smile slipping.

"Fine," he said, and she seemed to get the message, turning back to Jules.

"You want the usual?" she asked, and Jules smiled at her, his smile genuine at least.

"You know me, Case. And Dorian'll have the club sandwich. No cheese." Jules' smile directed towards Dorian, and despite Dorian's annoyance, something knotted up in his stomach at the sight. He almost smiled, handing his menu over to the girl instead.

The girl smiled at him. "Coming right up."

As she left, Jules turned to Dorian, leaning across the table and fixing him with a questioning look. "She was just being nice."

Dorian sighed, rolling his eyes. "I know, but I'm sick of talking about it. Everyone always wants to know how it's healing, if I'm ever gonna compete again, how awful it was to watch my entire career go up in smoke on international television." He glared at the table. "If any of those answers were good news, I might feel better about it."

A lump rose in his throat as he spoke, and he huffed. He didn't like talking about it. Talking about it made it real. It made him feel useless and like crying.

Jules paused instead of replying, and Dorian looked out the window. A light flutter of snow had begun falling since they'd been sitting there, dusting the cleared walkways. It was already getting dark at barely five in the evening and the yellow street lamps flickered on. It looked almost magical outside, but Dorian felt far from festive.

"At least people are talking about you," Jules said finally.

Dorian shot him an unimpressed look. That was exactly what he didn't want to be known for. That wasn't why he'd worked so hard to make it to the Olympics.

"Lighten up," Jules told him, reaching for his chin, but Dorian pulled away. Jules arched an eyebrow but sat back instead. "This isn't competition, peaches."

"Stop calling me that," Dorian replied, turning his fork over in his fingers.

"What do you want me to call you then?"

Dorian glanced at him slowly, unsure if he was being serious or not. Jules appeared to be waiting for his answer, though, and he shifted in his chair, stretching his leg out to stop his ankle from getting sore.

"I don't know," he answered. "Just not that."

Jules smiled, back to his usual self as he stretched back in the booth, his foot brushing up against Dorian's. "I'll think of something."

Chapter 14
Off the Diet

The snow had thickened by the time they finished, a blur of large flakes that floated past the window and settled in the grass, quickly obscuring any remaining green. Dorian watched one flake flutter down and disappear into the mass of white on the ground.

Jules watched him for a minute, then leaned forward over the table. "You have time to come back to my place for a while?"

Dorian shrugged. "Yeah. I don't have anywhere else to—" He stopped himself as he caught Jules' eye. "Yeah, for a little bit."

After all, Jules didn't know why Dorian had come, that he had absolutely no plans except to see him. He didn't even have a hotel room anywhere. In retrospect, he hadn't really thought this through. He'd shown up with absolutely no warning. Jules could have a boyfriend, or even girlfriend, for all he knew, and here he was showing up with misconceptions about him.

Jules didn't comment on it, though, much to Dorian's relief, and slid out of the booth, dropping a few bills on the check and not bothering to let Dorian offer to pay.

Dorian pulled on his jacket, grabbing his cane as he stood up, his ankle protesting from the prolonged inactivity of sitting. He ignored it, though, following Jules past the cashier.

The girl smiled and waved at them as they left and Jules turned to her.

"Tell Janey I say hey," he said as Dorian pulled open the door to a blast of swirling snow.

"Will do!" she replied cheerfully.

Dorian glanced over as Jules stepped out behind him. "Do you go there a lot?"

Jules shrugged, shivered in the cold with only his sweatshirt on. "Not too much. After all, it is *off the diet.*" He nudged Dorian with a knowing smile and pulled out his car keys. "Just don't tell my coach."

Dorian was glad when Jules didn't open his door this time and just went around the front to his own.

Snow settled in his hair and on his jacket as he pulled the door open and climbed in. Jules hopped in the other side, immediately turning the heater up.

"Shit, it's freezing," he said, starting the car. "It's not cold down where you are, right?"

"It's like seventy, maybe," Dorian replied. "Sixty at night."

"Fuck, I need to move down there," Jules said, shaking his head. "Is there a Center down there?"

"Not really. I used to train at school with the team."

Jules nodded vaguely, not really listening as he pulled out of the lot and into the snow. Dorian contented himself with looking out the window, glad he wasn't the one driving. He hated driving in the rain let alone snow.

He wasn't sure what he'd expected coming up here, that Jules would greet him with a kiss and tell him how much he'd missed him, that Jules wouldn't flirt with the waitresses. He should have known better, but a tiny part of him, the part he'd never admit to anyone, had hoped it might happen.

Then again, he'd never been in a real relationship. He'd never had the time what with all the training and traveling. His coach had said that relationships only distracted athletes. Dorian had never had a problem with it until now when he realized just how much he'd sacrificed to be an Olympic champion, and now he couldn't even do that. Relationships hadn't been important then.

It hadn't seemed like sacrifice at the time, but now he wondered just what he'd missed out on by being so focused on winning all the time. Now that he didn't have that drive, he felt lost, as though every day was just going through the motions, trying to figure out what he was supposed to do with his life.

He supposed he should just take the fact that he and Jules could at least have a normal conversation now as a good sign. Four months ago, Dorian couldn't even look at him without scowling, and now when he looked at Jules, all he wanted to do was kiss him.

He was ridiculous.

Jules' apartment wasn't too far away from the training center. The tall, white building towered over the street, almost invisible in the swirling snow, and Jules parked his truck along the curb.

"How do you pay for this?" he asked as they got out of the truck. Dorian hardly had any money. Most athletes didn't make any money unless they had endorsement deals to foot the bills. He couldn't count the number of years his parents had had to scrape to make ends meet.

"Us Olympic medalists get something for winning," Jules replied obviously. "What'd you do with your gold medal bump?"

Dorian shrugged. "Paid for school." He wouldn't have been able to otherwise considering he couldn't be on scholarship for gymnastics anymore, and he didn't want to put any more pressure on his mom than he had for the past twelve years. It wasn't her responsibility to get him anywhere in life now. She'd done her part. He just had to figure out exactly where it was he was trying to go.

Snow blew Dorian along the sidewalk until they reached the front door and Jules let him go in first, pulling the door shut against the wind. He brushed the snow off Dorian's jacket and headed for the stairs. He paused, though, as he reached the first step.

"Do you need to take the elevator?"

Dorian shook his head firmly. "I'm fine."

He saw the way Jules paused, a hesitant look as though he didn't believe Dorian, but he didn't argue with him, starting up the stairs. Dorian followed, determined that he could make it. He hadn't been going to therapy for three months so he couldn't climb a few flights of stairs. By the time they rounded the first landing, though, he could feel it in his ankle, the slow ache that meant he should stop straining himself. He didn't stop, though, forcing himself up after Jules.

Luckily for him, Jules stopped at the third floor, digging for his keys again and unlocking the door on the end. Dorian leaned heavily on his cane as he waited, rolling his ankle around to stretch it out and loosen the tension. He knew Jules noticed, though, as he glanced down for half a second before pushing the door open.

"Sit down," Jules said, nodding at the grey couch facing the television.

Dorian wanted to scowl and say he was fine, but his limp said otherwise as he moved to the couch and sunk into the cushions. He pulled off his shoe, stretching his foot and grimacing at the pain. He should know better.

"Want a beer?" Jules asked, returning from where he'd been rummaging in the small kitchen, and holding out a bottle to Dorian. Dorian took it with an arched eyebrow, shrugging out of his jacket, but he set it down a minute later without drinking.

"Beer and burgers?"

"Hey, no judgment, pipsqueak," Jules said, taking a swig of his and collapsing on the couch. "Come here," he said, gesturing at Dorian's foot.

Dorian paused but then lifted his foot and Jules pulled it into his lap, massaging his ankle the way the medics always did during training. He sighed, disappointed in himself. He couldn't even make it three flights.

"You're not supposed to do stairs, are you?" Jules asked, smoothing his thumb over Dorian's skin, and Dorian frowned.

He knew his own limits. He'd known them for years. He didn't like that they'd changed.

"My physical therapist says I should limit my physical activity to walking on flat surfaces and doing stretches whenever I sit for too long." He rolled his eyes.

Jules hummed softly, fingers rubbing along Dorian's ankle, softer now. Dorian settled into a more comfortable position on the couch, an arm draped over the arm rest.

"You should listen to her."

Dorian made a face, watching the way Jules' hands moved against his ankle. It felt nice, better than when the therapist did it, but Jules moved slower, taking his time to smooth out the muscles, unknot the tension. He winced a few times as Jules' fingers moved over certain spots.

"It's taking so long, though," he said, voicing something he hadn't said to anyone. The therapy seemed to be taking forever. It wasn't as if he'd thought he would be miraculously cured after a few sessions, but it was going much slower than he'd expected to even get back to normal. It worried him, the time it was taking.

"Healing takes time. How long did the first injury take?"

Dorian frowned slightly. "That was different. I could still compete after that. After this…"

He didn't like to think about this either, the fact that this might be it for him, for good. It only made him depressed. He shook his head instead, and it was only then that he noticed that Jules wasn't massaging his ankle anymore. Instead, Jules slid it off his lap gently, placing it on the floor, then moved up over Dorian.

"The Dorian I know," Jules said once he was leaning over Dorian, close enough that Dorian could see the creases when he smiled, "would never have doubted his ability to come back. One way or another."

Dorian paused, unsure what to say, how he could respond to that, but Jules saved him the trouble, closing the distance between them, and their lips met for the first kiss in months.

Jules' mouth was warm and soft pressed against his, and Dorian fell into it. His arms wrapped around Jules' neck and he kissed back, opening his mouth to Jules and sighing as Jules licked into his mouth slowly, tracing his lips and swallowing any noises he made.

"Mmm," Jules hummed as Dorian's leg hooked around his thigh, urging him forward, sliding in against his body.

Dorian didn't question the action, how Jules sucked on his lower lip, one hand on the back of his neck, the other sliding under his shirt. Instead, he closed his eyes and let himself drown in the feeling of Jules all around him.

His heart tightened as Jules' kisses turned softer, hand pushing up his shirt as their bodies melded together.

"Ah!" Dorian's eyes opened as their hips met and he felt Jules' cock against his own, half hard already. Jules didn't go faster, but seemed to slow each movement of his hips down to a glacial pace as Dorian sucked in a breath and concentrated on the pulse of blood in his prick, each rock of Jules' hips.

"Tell me why you really came," Jules said, rolling his hips up and staring down at Dorian's face as Dorian gasped and bit his lip.

"You're a—jerk," Dorian gasped, fingers curling into Jules' sweatshirt, hips pushing up for more friction, but Jules didn't go any faster.

Heat rose in his cheeks, a dull flush that he didn't bother trying to suppress. He knew Jules was just asking to torture him. He could tell from the quirk at the corner of his mouth, but when Jules leaned in, mouthing at his neck, it was all Dorian could do not to admit it.

It was going too slowly, Jules' body against his, Jules' mouth sucking on the patch of skin behind his ear that made his knees go weak and his resolve all but crumble.

"You came for this, didn't you?" Jules murmured against his skin, lips brushing against his jaw.

Dorian closed his eyes, letting out a shaky breath, fingers still curled into Jules' sweatshirt. He didn't know why Jules still had it on when his own shirt was pushed halfway up his stomach. There was way too much fabric in between them as Jules rocked his hips down, and Dorian felt a hot rush on his skin.

"No," he replied finally, swallowing hard against the tightening in his stomach.

This wasn't why he'd come, not exactly. He wasn't sure why he'd come at all, but he was there, and Jules was taking too long to do anything that he wanted.

He reached for Jules' sweatshirt instead, tugging it over his head, jerking it off finally and dropping it over the armrest behind him. He looked back to find Jules' eyes on him, his hips stilled against him, despite how he shifted.

"What?" he asked finally, and the corners of Jules' mouth quirked softly.

"Did you miss me?" he asked, and Dorian merely rolled his eyes.

"Jules," he complained, arching up for a long kiss, harder than before, a little more desperate. If he said yes, it would mean that he actually cared about Jules, but maybe that was obvious already. After all, he was here, wasn't he?

"Dorian," Jules repeated in the same tone, and Dorian felt a hot flush on his face unrelated to Jules' hands. He swallowed thickly against the pounding of his heart.

"Yes, okay?" he said finally, staring at Jules and licking his lips. A pressure deep inside him seemed lifted as he said it. "Yes."

Jules didn't ask again, a smile lighting up his face, hands skimming Dorian's shirt up and off, catching on his elbow for a second. A thrill ran through his stomach at Jules' smile, so soft and sweet, something he hadn't seen before from him. Dorian shivered slightly in the cool apartment, the heater not turned up quite as much as he would have liked.

He didn't have to worry about the heat a second later, though, when Jules leaned down, pressing kisses down his throat and to his chest, tongue sliding along his collarbone as Dorian's toes curled from the heat rising on his skin.

Groaning, Dorian arched his body up, hips rocking into Jules'. They were still going too slow considering how long it had been, for him at least. For all he knew, Jules had been sleeping with everyone in town.

"Jules," he breathed a moment later, fingers digging into Jules' shoulder as their hips met and blood throbbed in his cock.

Jules glanced up from where his mouth closed around Dorian's nipple, licking the skin once before pulling back.

His hands went for Dorian's jeans, getting them open and taking a little too much care to get them off, but Dorian wasn't going to ruin this over a couple seconds pause on his ankle. Instead, his eyes followed Jules' movements, Jules' hands as he took off his own jeans, sliding them down over his hips until the dark line of hair leading under his boxers became visible and then the jeans were on the floor as well.

Dorian licked his lips slightly, not taking his eyes off the tented boxers until Jules had crawled over him again, nose brushing against his as he leaned in.

"Guess what I've got this time?" he asked, mouth grazing against Dorian's. Dorian only followed the movement instead of replying. Jules smiled. "Condoms."

Dorian echoed his smile without thinking and dragged Jules back to his mouth. "Good."

He could feel Jules' smile against his lips, but he didn't pause to let him gloat at their predicament. Four months ago, Dorian would never have thought this would happen. He would never have wanted this to happen, but here he was in Jules' apartment, minutes away from being fucked in a way that he'd remember and want to relive for months to come.

Dorian almost didn't want to let Jules go get them, didn't want to let go of him as they pressed together on the couch, squished into the small space. He just wanted to kiss Jules and pretend he didn't have to go back on Sunday, that Jules already knew exactly why he was there and he wouldn't have to explain it.

"I'll be right back," Jules said a second later, pushing himself off of Dorian and climbing off the couch.

Dorian let him go, sighing and swallowing as he watched Jules head to one of the rooms, probably the bedroom. His head fell back against the armrest, and he tried to sigh around the weight that had settled on his chest. He couldn't pretend that nothing was wrong forever.

Jules reappeared a moment later, stripping off his shirt as he returned to the couch and shedding his boxers before he climbed back on top of Dorian, taking a second to admire his body, his sculpted muscles from so many years of training.

Dorian never felt embarrassed by his body, and he didn't squirm under Jules' gaze, only nudged his leg with a knee when it went on a beat too long.

"Hey," he said, and Jules met his eyes, smiling slowly.

"Your injury doesn't seem to have affected anything else," he commented, tearing open the condom wrapper.

"I still work out," Dorian replied, watching Jules roll the condom on, an expectant thrill running over him as he shifted.

Jules nodded slowly, pulling down Dorian's boxers finally and pushing them aside. He flipped open the lube without a word, pushing Dorian's legs up.

Dorian closed his eyes at the first digit that Jules slid in, unused to the strain, the pressure as Jules added a second finger and moved them in and out, stretching him. It felt good, though, and he bit his lip against the sharp breath he took.

Jules didn't take too long prepping him, just enough that Dorian cursed under his breath and reached blindly for him.

"Are you gonna say it?" Jules asked, and Dorian felt the tip of his cock pressed against his entrance, the first painful push as Jules filled him.

"Say what?" he asked breathlessly, opening his eyes finally and looking up at Jules. He gasped as Jules thrust in and heat rippled across his skin, overtaking the slight chill on his arms.

"That you came here to see me?"

"I—" Dorian sucked in a sharp breath, not finishing his sentence, although he wasn't sure what he was going to say anyway.

He couldn't think outside of Jules' cock in his body, the way their bodies moved together, a push and slide that made his toes curl, cheeks hot, and he bit his lip against the tight squeeze in his stomach.

"Just admit it," Jules grunted, reaching for Dorian's cock and jerking him off, fist tight around his throbbing prick.

Dorian stretched back, neck exposed as he tried not to whine at the heat building in his body, the tingle on his skin as Jules' hand moved fast, thumb catching the head of his cock.

"I, fuck, *Jules*," he said instead, all but a moan as he couldn't hold on, couldn't stop himself from coming.

His chest moved with each stuttered breath he took as he came down, opening his eyes to stare up at Jules. Jules hadn't come, still pushing deep inside him, a slow rocking motion, as if Jules was content to go at that pace forever.

Dorian saw the question in Jules' eyes. He leaned up into Jules' mouth, kissing him hard and fast, running his hand over Jules' short hair. "Yes," he breathed, barely audible over their panting breath. "Yes, I wanted to see you."

He felt Jules finally lose it, the sharp breath he took against his lips as he came.

"Shit," Jules cursed a minute later as he pushed himself back, sliding Dorian's legs down to the couch. He glanced at Dorian, though, and smiled halfway, as though he knew exactly what Dorian was doing. Grabbing his boxers from the floor, he used them to wipe off his stomach and then tossed them aside.

Jules grabbed his beer off the table and took a long swig, finally glancing at Dorian. "You don't have anywhere else to go, do you?"

he asked, and Dorian frowned. Jules set down the bottle and moved over, turning Dorian's chin to face him. "That's good. It'll give us plenty of time to catch up."

Dorian almost wanted to argue, but there was really nothing to argue as Jules pulled him into a soft kiss and he shivered against the cool air that swirled around them.

Chapter 15

Nighttime Rewind

Sighing contently, Jules smiled to himself and glanced over at Dorian. It had been a while since he'd had anyone in bed beside him, and he'd never had Dorian there. It was a bit of a surprise, but not necessarily a bad one.

"So you came to see me?" he asked, pushing Dorian's shoulders onto the bed and tilting his head to the side as he gazed down at him.

Their naked bodies pressed together in the cool bedroom, but the heater kicked on somewhere above them. The lamp on the bedside table cast a low yellow glow over the room, reflecting off the framed photos on the walls; there was a picture of the team at the Olympics with their medals, one of them with Brian and Georgia, and one of Jules receiving his bronze medal. It might have seemed a bit over the top to put them in the bedroom, but the rest of his apartment wasn't very impressive considering he rented it from a little old lady who hadn't raised the rates in years. Mostly he was just glad it had a working heater considering the foot of snow outside.

Dorian didn't reply right away, and Jules wasn't really in the mood to wait. After all, Dorian had just shown up at his door with no warning and no explanation. If it had been anyone else, he might have understood, but Dorian... Dorian did nothing without extensive forethought. After all, it had taken Jules a whole month to convince him that he wasn't evil. So Dorian showing up out of nowhere wasn't exactly run of the mill.

Leaning in, he brushed his mouth against Dorian's jaw. "I'm glad you did," he murmured.

"I came to see you," Dorian said again, smiling slowly as Jules grinned back at him.

"That wasn't so hard, was it?" He had never understood why Dorian had to be so stubborn. It wasn't like it was a declaration of love. They hadn't seen each other in months, and when Dorian did show up, he spent most of the time commenting on his eating habits and giving the waitresses the evil eye.

"And why did you come to see me?" he asked, brushing back Dorian's hair.

"Well, you didn't come to visit me."

Jules arched an eyebrow. They had barely talked since getting back from the Olympics except a few late-night phone calls that, if Jules hadn't known better, he might have thought they were the result of some liquid courage on Dorian's part. If Dorian had expected him to fly all the way to Louisiana for what could have been an entirely useless gesture, he was wrong. Dorian hadn't asked him to come, and if anyone had to do the asking, it was Dorian.

"You didn't even call," he pointed out. "It was pretty presumptuous of you. I could have been out of town. It is nearly the holidays."

"Nearly," Dorian replied. "I took a wild guess."

"A wild guess?" Jules repeated, and he slid his hands down Dorian's chest. He felt Dorian take a deep, relaxed breath, and he couldn't help smiling. A few months ago, he hadn't thought they'd ever reach this point. In fact, he still couldn't quite believe it. "We haven't talked much. I thought maybe you'd died after going home."

Dorian scoffed. "I couldn't die. How would they get all the interviews?"

Jules shook his head. Sometimes, he just didn't understand Dorian. Press was the best part of being an Olympian. It was what paid for his apartment, what paid for his training, and what got him all those fans. He couldn't say that having people scream his name was a downfall. He got free trips and free tours and he got to sign autographs for little kids with gymnastic aspirations. "Hate to break it to you, pumpkin, but that's part of being an Olympian."

"Not when you can't even walk up a flight of stairs without having to rest," Dorian replied with a sigh. He looked up at Jules. "You don't understand."

"I don't understand?" Jules laughed, though it wasn't really funny. Of anyone, he should have understood the most. "We've all had injuries, Dor."

"Not like this." Dorian sat up, pushing Jules back. Jules frowned. "I'm never gonna be able to compete again. I'm not even allowed to do it for fun. And everyone keeps telling me I should let it go and move on with my life, find something else to do, but how could I possibly find something else? Gymnastics has been my entire life. I don't know how to do anything else. I don't *want* to do anything else."

Jules watched Dorian for a long moment, eyebrows furrowed. He knew exactly what Dorian was talking about. Every professional did. Gymnastics was his whole life and had been for years. Anything he did outside of it was rare. He lived at a training center for fuck's sake. His days off were usually spent watching movies on TV or playing video games. As much as he would have liked to go out and party, he lived in a small Connecticut town where the biggest entertainment was a two-screen movie theater with a broken popcorn machine.

He wasn't stupid like Dorian seemed to think. He understood, and it pissed him off that Dorian thought he didn't or couldn't. Who else could, really? That wasn't the point, though. The point was that Dorian didn't seem to trust him still. What had he done to deserve that? Nothing he could think of. The least Dorian could do was think of someone other than himself.

Snow piled up outside the window, cold air leaking inside as Dorian sighed.

Annoyed, Jules moved back, leaving Dorian pressed against the bed. "You know the answer, right?" he asked finally. "Stop taking out your anger on people who can't do a damn thing about it."

"I'm not—"

"Yeah, you are," Jules interrupted. He'd had plenty of Dorian's complaining for one night. Why had he come if he was only going to whine about how horrible his life was? Everyone had problems. Jules couldn't even get his dad on the phone to talk about gymnastics let alone get him to show up at a competition. "So shut up for two seconds and stop thinking only about yourself."

The level of selfishness Dorian could achieve was astonishing. Jules had never quite seen anything like it, and he'd witnessed his father walking out without so much as a goodbye to him or his mother. He needed a break and moved off the bed.

"I'm gonna get another beer. You want one?"

"No," Dorian muttered as Jules stepped out the door, rubbing his forehead and pausing before he headed to the kitchen.

The lamp cast a soft, yellow circle on the ceiling as Jules lay there, hands on his stomach, still not dressed, but neither was Dorian beside him. They'd been silent for more than ten minutes and Jules thought that Dorian might be asleep.

"It's so hard," Dorian said abruptly, his voice loud in the otherwise quiet room.

"What is?" Jules asked with a heavy sigh, stretching his arms and rubbing the bridge of his nose. He had almost been asleep. It had been a very long day so far. He wasn't really in the mood to keep talking either. There wasn't much Dorian could say to make the situation better.

"Everything." Jules heard Dorian sigh, breath shaky, and Dorian's arm pressed against his, a little cold. He considered pulling up the covers, but he couldn't muster up the strength. "Getting up, going to class, *not* going to the gym. I feel like my whole world just fell apart."

Jules glanced over at him, but Dorian didn't meet his eyes.

It wasn't easy, Jules knew that. He'd had his fair share of injuries, close calls that put him out of the running for different things, times when he had thought he would have to give it all up and become a dimwitted but charming interviewer or commentator. He hadn't taken it out on everyone around him, though.

"Put it together again," he murmured, rolling over into the pillow and closing his eyes.

For a moment Dorian was silent. Perhaps he'd decided to let it go and go to sleep.

"Maybe I should go," Dorian said instead, already rolling off the bed.

For a moment, Jules considered letting him go, letting Dorian hobble down the stairs, stubborn to the last and wander around in the snow. Even through his annoyance, it was a sad picture. Jules' hand closed around Dorian's arm and pulled him back before his feet hit the ground. He opened his eyes, shaking his head at Dorian and his stupidity.

"Go where exactly?" he asked tiredly, pulling Dorian back. Dorian had showed up without even a suitcase, so he sincerely doubted Dorian had anything planned beyond the 'hello' he'd gotten out back at the gym. It wasn't like Dorian to do something like this, and there was probably more to it than just his ankle or Jules not calling enough or whatever excuse he seemed to have for everything.

Dorian hesitated at the question, and Jules knew he was right. Dorian had flown fifteen hundred miles just to see him. The thought almost made him smile. Maybe the weekend could be salvaged. If he could just get Dorian to stop thinking and talking. The talking always ruined it.

"I've got a better idea," Jules said when Dorian didn't respond, rolling them over so that Dorian was on top, pressed against his chest. "How about you make up for all this moodiness and put your mouth to good use?"

The first time Jules had said something like that to Dorian, back during the last Olympics in the gym the night before the opening ceremonies, he hadn't actually expected anything in return. This time, though, he had much higher expectations of Dorian's reaction, and he wasn't disappointed.

Dorian pressed upward into the kiss. He didn't resist Jules' fingers sliding into his hair, angling his jaw down. Meeting no resistance, Jules kissed him harder. This was the kind of Dorian he liked—one who didn't fight for every little inch, one who let him take control and guide things.

Dorian didn't waste too much time, pushing Jules onto his back and sliding down his body, running his hands over his skin, down to his hips as his mouth followed.

This was what he needed, Jules thought, his eyes closing as he felt the warm press of Dorian's mouth against his stomach. All the stress of practice melted away, and he concentrated on the feeling of Dorian against him. He'd thought about this, about having Dorian here, though he'd never really mentioned it to Dorian. After all, what would Dorian have said about that? He probably would have freaked out with Jules' luck. He was so hard to read sometimes.

Jules sighed softly as Dorian reached his prick, licking up the length and pausing to lick the palm of his hand before wrapping it around the base. Opening his eyes, Jules glanced down, meeting Dorian's gaze and the way Dorian bit his lip nervously.

"Jules," Dorian said after a second, hesitating. "Did you miss me?"

For a second, Jules didn't reply. He liked the way Dorian asked, nervous and quiet, as though he wasn't sure which answer he wanted. It turned out Dorian wasn't as confident as he pretended, and Jules was glad he finally said something. Otherwise, he might have thought Dorian was a robot, incapable of any human emotion other than annoyance.

"Of course I did, peaches."

Dorian blinked at the nickname, but then his mouth quirked into a smile and he moved back in.

"That is *much* better," Jules murmured as Dorian slid in, mouth covering his cock and sucking.

Fuck, Dorian was good at this, although Jules had known that for months now. He'd had the memory of Dorian's mouth on him in his head for a while now, whenever he needed to get off quickly. He groaned as Dorian's tongue slid down the entire length, then his mouth was there, hot and wet, around him.

Jules' fingers slid into Dorian's hair, tightening as he pushed his hips up. Dorian jerked back a second, but then his hands forced Jules' hips down. He forgot about the chill coming in the window when Dorian sucked harder, sliding his head back and forth. The pressure deep in his stomach tightened as his cock hardened in Dorian's mouth.

"You have such a pretty mouth," Jules breathed, stroking Dorian's face, tracing under his bottom lip as Dorian increased his

speed. When he wasn't talking or complaining, Dorian was beauti-
ful, and Jules wondered if there was a chance he could get Dorian
to smile all the time. Maybe after the ankle healed. Maybe after they
figured something out. It wasn't long until Jules felt the inevitable
tightening in his stomach, the flare of heat racing along his skin as he
cursed and grabbed Dorian's shoulder. His grip was too tight, but
he couldn't help it as the pressure wound up and exploded.

His hips jerked up, into Dorian's mouth, and he felt Dorian pull
away. His release was warm and wet, hitting Dorian's chin, and he
didn't even care that Dorian wiped it off a second later. "Ah, shit!"
Breathing heavily, head against the pillow, he only sighed as Dorian
flopped down beside him. After a minute, though, he rolled onto his
side to face Dorian.

"Much better use for your mouth," he said, kissing Dorian deeply. Dorian snuggled into his side and Jules smiled, wrapping an arm
around him. If only they could stay like this and pretend nothing
else existed. It wouldn't have been perfect, but it would have been
good.

Dorian didn't know what time it was when he rolled over, eyes
opening to the darkened room, snuggled deep into the warm covers.
The air outside them felt chilly against his nose, and he burrowed
deeper. He could see the pack of snow built up on the window, just
the outline against the black sky outside.

He didn't know why he'd woken up, all comfortable and warm,
and rolled over to look at the clock on Jules' bedside table. Jules' side
of the bed was empty, though, and Dorian paused. The clock blared
red, telling him it was nearly three in the morning. He'd barely fall-
en asleep two hours ago.

For a moment, he hesitated, unwilling to leave the warmth of
the bed, but finally, he forced himself up, shivering as he grabbed a
sweatshirt that hung off the dresser and pulled it on, padding into
the living room.

He found Jules sitting on the couch, a blanket pulled over him
as he watched a video playing on the television, the volume down

low. Dorian didn't even need to ask to know what it was, not when he caught sight of the Olympics logo in the corner of the screen.

"Why are you watching that?" he asked, stopping by the arm of the couch.

Jules looked up, taking in the sweatshirt he wore. He smiled. "You're wearing my shirt."

"It's cold." Dorian shrugged, looking back to the TV. It was playing Mitya's turn on the high bar. "Do you do this a lot?"

Jules shrugged, and Dorian sat down next to him, surprised when Jules tossed half of the blanket over him. He didn't protest, though, since he only had on a pair of boxers and the sweatshirt. Jules' body was warm against his, and he thought for a moment that he could sit here forever, especially when Jules' arm slid over his shoulder, fingers carding through his hair. He'd never had anyone like this before, anyone like Jules to sit up with in the middle of the night. It was different than with his friends and he liked it.

"Sometimes I'm just in the mood to see it again. It's a good reminder."

"I don't want to be reminded," Dorian muttered, tucking his foot under him and sighing. He'd much rather forget everything that had happened since the Olympics.

"You don't want to remember this?" Jules asked, nodding at the television where it was replaying his gold medal vault, the one where everything just seemed to work perfectly, from the launch to the triple salto to the landing.

Dorian stared at the TV. He remembered that moment, the moment after when he'd known how well it had gone, what it could mean. He'd never forget it.

"I just want things to go back to the way they were," he said finally. "I want to be able to do gymnastics again, to compete."

"Is that all you want to do?" Jules asked, looking at him. "Compete? There are plenty of other things to do."

"Imagine you couldn't do gymnastics anymore," Dorian replied sharply. "How would you feel?"

Jules paused, and Dorian immediately cringed. Why did he have to be so mean? How did Jules even put up with him?

"I'd probably feel useless," Jules admitted finally, raising his fingers to brush under Dorian's ear. "But that's what I'd have you for."

Dorian wasn't sure what Jules meant by that. They hadn't exactly discussed their relationship yet, and it made Dorian a little nervous. So he didn't say anything and merely sighed, leaning into Jules' side and watching himself being presented with a gold medal.

Dorian poked at the eggs on his plate, wincing in the sunlight bouncing off the snow piled up on the windowsill and hanging on to the tree branches outside. He wasn't really hungry, and he'd woken up this morning to a sore ankle that he couldn't explain.

Jules finished his orange juice and dumped his plate in the sink, turning to face where Dorian sat at the counter. "I'm guessing you don't have any important plans for the day?"

Dorian's eyebrows furrowed and he looked up at Jules, who merely laughed.

"You really didn't think this through, did you?"

He really hadn't, Dorian admitted to himself. He'd come on a whim and Jules might not have even been there for all he knew.

"You can come to practice with me," Jules said instead of waiting for Dorian's answer, pulling his uneaten plate out from under him and ignoring the half-noise of protest Dorian made.

"I'll just stay here," he said, but Jules scoffed.

"There's nothing to do here."

"There's nothing to do there," Dorian pointed out, but Jules swung around the counter to ruffle his hair.

"Watch."

Dorian shot him an unimpressed look, ignoring the way his heart beat faster when Jules smiled at him, eyes crinkling.

"That's exactly what I want to do," he deadpanned, but Jules merely laughed.

"Stop feeling sorry for yourself. It's not doing anyone any good," he replied, breezing away to change.

He had a point, Dorian thought, looking out at the snow floating past the window.

It was as bad as Dorian had expected, sitting on the bleachers watching Jules and the others practice. He could only see what they were doing wrong and think how much better he could have done it if he'd just had the chance.

The worst part, perhaps, was when Coach Harper dropped down onto the bench next to him and nodded at Jules on the floor. "Miss it, don't you?"

Dorian glanced at him, unsure about the way he smiled: too friendly considering they barely knew each other. "Yeah," he agreed simply.

"You had a real shot at that medal," Harper went on, either ignoring or not noticing Dorian's discomfort. "I was watching you, you know. You were a real up and comer. Serious competition for Jules." He grinned, teeth bearing. "But he beat you in the end, didn't he?" Dorian didn't say that technically Jules' hadn't. Technically, he'd been out of the running due to his injury. Harper laughed loudly, though. "I was worried for a while there when you medaled on the vault. It looked like you might take the whole thing away from Jules. Between you and me, Jules wants it as much as anyone; he just laughs it off sometimes. I've gotta crack the whip when Olympics come around. Got to keep everyone in line, you know?"

Dorian frowned, unsure what to say. "He's competitive," he said instead.

"I told him, 'Jules, you can't let other people dictate your successes. You're in charge of whether you win or lose. Although, it doesn't hurt to give yourself a leg up.'" He winked at Dorian, and Dorian prayed Harper would leave soon. For being one of the best coaches in the country, he didn't make Dorian feel at ease. He didn't know how Jules stood it. It made Dorian miss his own coach, who never hinted at 'leg ups,' whatever that entailed. Something told Dorian he didn't want to know. Luckily, he was saved from replying when Jules came over, wiping sweat off his brow.

"So what'd you think?" Jules asked, sitting down next to Dorian. Coach Harper patted Dorian's knee, a painful thump, and rose. He ambled off, leaving them alone.

Dorian watched him go, the unease not leaving with him. Jules waited for his answer, though, so he sighed. "You're opening up too late on your tucks," he said. "And Pete doesn't hold his handstands long enough."

"Aren't you just a ray of sunshine?" Jules grabbed his water bottle and took a swig. Dorian didn't have anything to say, Harper's words about a leg up still fresh in his mind, as Steven came over to join them.

"So what'd you guys do last night?" he asked, wiping the sweat off his face with the towel around his neck.

Dorian glanced at Jules, but Jules just smiled and shrugged at Steven. "Hung out, you know."

Steven nodded as if he did know, although his gaze wasn't suspicious at all as he looked between them. It should have comforted Dorian, but instead he just felt confused. Had Jules told his teammates nothing? What did they think he was? Just a friend?

"Did you meet Shelby?" Steven asked.

"Who?" Dorian looked at Jules immediately, and Jules shook his head.

"Man, Shelby was nothing. Two dates' worth. Not even that."

A sharp curl of jealousy sparked in Dorian's stomach as he listened to Jules talking dismissively about some girl. He didn't say anything, though, frowning down at his hands. He guessed he should have expected it. After all, they hadn't ever talked about what they were, if anything. Jules could see other people.

"I thought... well, whatever," Steven said. "I can't keep 'em straight. Dorian, how long are you staying for?"

"I have to get back tomorrow," he said easily. "School and everything."

"You're lucky you have time for that," Steven said, taking a swig of water. "We don't even have time for movies."

Just then, Coach Harper blew his whistle, staring over at the three of them.

Steven sighed. "Back to work." He shot Dorian a smile before turning and trotting back across the mat.

Jules was watching Dorian, but he didn't comment on it as he rose to his feet. "It shouldn't be too much longer," he said, returning

129

to the mat.

Dorian extended his leg, stretching his ankle slowly and avoiding meeting Harper's eyes as Jules left.

Chapter 16

Figuring It Out

"Your friend doesn't seem to be enjoying himself much," Russell commented, clapping chalk on his hands as Jules looked over.

On the bench, Dorian hadn't moved for a while, and Jules was starting to think it had been a bad suggestion. Leaving Dorian alone in his crappy apartment hadn't seemed any better of an idea at the time either, though. It wasn't his fault Dorian had showed up out of the blue. Jules had practice. He always had practice.

"He's not the sunniest," he said instead. That was the understatement of the century.

Russell laughed. "And what's he doing here exactly?"

"I'm not really sure." Jules frowned, watching Dorian on the bench. He still hadn't quite figured it out, although he was fairly sure Dorian wasn't in any trouble. The last time they'd talked on the phone, almost three weeks ago, Dorian had only mentioned school starting and term papers he needed to get started on. Their conversations hadn't exactly gone in depth about anything.

"Maybe he's got a crush on you."

Jules didn't reply. He'd known Russell as long as any of the guys he'd trained with. Most of them were perfectly content pegging him as the guy who slept with whoever caught his fancy, whether true or not. Sure, he enjoyed messing around with people he found interesting, but he wasn't a giant whore like everyone seemed to think. Dorian wasn't 'one of many.'

"Oh, shit, you didn't," Russell said a second later, staring at Jules.

"Didn't what?"

"Shit, you did!" Russell shook his head as Jules tried to work out what he meant. "So how long are you going to string him on for?"

Insulted, Jules turned away from Dorian. "I'm not. I don't do that."

Russell shrugged. "Well, you do kind of. Shelby was, what, two dates? And before that, Frank..."

"Dorian wasn't a date," Jules interrupted, feeling ruffled.

"Hookup, whatever. Same thing," Russell said dismissively.

Jules couldn't believe him. Of all his friends, Russell was the one who understood him best, who never commented on how many dates he had or who he went out with. Russell had his own girlfriend to worry about so he didn't need to pry into Jules' love life. "What's it to you what Dorian is?" he asked defensively. Dorian definitely wasn't just a hookup, and he wasn't some stranger he'd picked up in a bar somewhere. Yes, Dorian got on his nerves, but he put up with it. Why did he put up with it?

There were plenty of other people he could have dated, could have hooked up with. He was an Olympian for Christ's sake. If he wanted a date, he could get one, but instead, he found himself going out of his way for Dorian, the guy who seemed to be barely able to stand him. What kind of masochist was he?

Russell held up his hands in defeat. "Nothing. Just seems like he's had a bad few months, and if he likes you, he's got some more bad times in store."

"What the fuck does that mean?"

"You know. When you get tired, you'll just dump him. It's what you do, Jules. No judgment, just saying."

Jules stared, annoyance bubbling up inside him. "I'm not going to dump him, I—" Oh fuck, he realized as he said it. He was falling for Dorian. Stubborn, annoying, perfectionist Dorian. He almost laughed as he thought it, but Russell was already giving him a strange look, so he stopped himself. Well, he'd certainly gotten into it this time, he thought. "It's none of your business, Russell," he said instead, drawing himself up. He'd have to deal with his feelings for Dorian on his own and Russell certainly couldn't help.

"Jules, get back on the mat; this isn't break time!" Coach Harper snapped, effectively ending the conversation, and Jules was glad for that. Harper shooed Russell over to the rings and grabbed Jules around the shoulders, steering him towards the mat. "Listen, Jules," he said, lowering his voice. "A friend shows up, that's fine, but don't let it get in the way of your training. You remember what I said to you before the Olympics?"

"I don't get distracted — I do the distracting?"

"Exactly." Harper flashed him a grim smile. "You don't win by being nice. You're not competing for Miss Congeniality. Olympics are over, but your career isn't. I told you before that Stuart could be trouble. You did a good job keeping him down in the Olympics, but even though he can't compete, he could still be a hindrance. Don't let it distract you."

Jules paused, glancing over at Dorian. He'd done some stupid things during the Olympics, but it had all worked out so far. He wasn't particularly worried, and after all, Coach had his best interests at heart. There were only so many ways to win the Olympics aside from talent. Coach just wanted him to do well.

"I won't," Jules assured him, and Harper squeezed his shoulder.

"Good."

Finding Dorian again, he smiled to himself. Maybe it hadn't been such a bad thing, Dorian showing up unexpectedly. He'd just have to see if they could make it through the rest of the weekend.

By the time Jules got out of practice, Dorian was bored out of his mind. He'd spent the past hour analyzing all the faults in Jules' teammates, wondering who exactly Shelby was, and what Harper had meant.

"Are you hungry?" Jules asked as they stepped outside into the frigid cold.

Dorian shivered and didn't reply, gripping his cane tightly as they walked to the car.

"Dorian?" Jules asked when they reached it and he still hadn't replied.

"Sure," he muttered, hand on the door handle.

Jules paused, and Dorian knew it was coming. He just wished they could get through one conversation without someone starting something. Granted, it was usually his fault, but he was starting to get tired.

"Now what? Did someone else ask about the ankle?"

"Not everything is about that." Dorian could see his breath puffing before him, feel the chilly wind down his back. He pulled his coat closer and leaned on the cane. The ground was slippery and he grabbed onto the door handle to keep steady.

Not everything was about his ankle, as much as he thought about it. He wasn't sure he should even bother mentioning it since Jules would just assume he was jealous and stupid. Maybe he was. He was jealous of some girl he didn't even know, some girl Jules had gone out with and not even deemed important enough to mention.

Jules seemed to huff, as though Dorian tired him. "Well, I just figured. You've been so moody since you got here. I thought that was just reserved for competitions."

He shouldn't say anything, Dorian knew. He should just forget it and not start something else. He should have, but he didn't. "Who's Shelby?" he asked instead.

Jules' expression changed to understanding almost immediately. "Shelby is no one."

As much as Dorian wanted to be angry, he just felt stupid. "She's someone you went out with. I mean, I thought we were kind of — I don't know."

He waited for Jules to say something, and when he only frowned, Dorian nodded. "And Coach Harper said something strange about the Olympics. He said you had to get a leg up. What does that mean?"

Jules shrugged "He likes to talk big."

"Didn't sound like it."

Sighing, Jules paused by the car. "Why do you have to take everything so personally?"

"I guess I shouldn't," Dorian replied finally. "Maybe coming here was a bad idea after all."

He never should have listened to Ryan or Jason. What did they know about this stuff? Neither of them had had a real relationship lately. As much as it pained him to admit it, he had really hoped this trip would explain some things. That was his fault for assuming.

"No, it wasn't," Jules interrupted him. "I'm just confused."

"Yeah, well, so am I."

"What was this trip supposed to do for you anyway?"

Dorian shook his head. "It was supposed to make me feel better about losing the only thing I've ever wanted. And instead, I feel worse than before."

"You know why that is?"

"Because I assumed something I shouldn't have." Dorian shook his head. "I should have called. I should have checked if you even wanted to see me."

He should have, but he hadn't. That was what he got for going without any notice. They should have talked about this beforehand, but Dorian wasn't very good at talking, or emotions, or really anything involving guys.

Jules frowned at Dorian. "You are an idiot, peaches."

"Stop calling me that," Dorian snapped. How could Jules just brush this off? "This was obviously a mistake."

He turned away from the car, heading the opposite way down the sidewalk. He didn't know where he was going, but he had to get away. Hadn't that been the whole point of this? He wasn't sure what he had expected.

This whole trip had been a disaster. He should have just stayed home and saved himself the plane ride. All that was left now was to go home, forget about Jules, and try to work out what to do with the rest of his life.

The sidewalk stretched on before him, icy in patches, snow piled up, crushed into a thick pack under his feet. His cane slipped a few times, but he didn't slow down or stop. Luck had never been on his side, and a particularly slippery patch of snow sent him falling backwards, landing in a pile of snow next to a tree.

"Dorian."

Jules jogged up to him, reaching for his arm, but Dorian shied away.

"I'm fine," he said trying to push himself up, but his ankle protested as he tried to put his weight on it.

He ended up sitting in the snow, lips pursed together as snow began to fall from the sky again and Jules stood back a few feet, waiting for him to give up.

It was useless. He was useless. He couldn't even walk normally anymore. It was time to face the facts. This really was the end. There'd be no more tumbling, no more vault. Everything he'd worked for was gone forever and he'd have to find something else to fill his life with.

The thought was heartbreaking, and he thought that this had to be the lowest point of his life, sitting in a pile of snow, unable to get up on his own, with Jules standing over him waiting for him to admit it.

Instead, he laughed, not because it was funny, but because he couldn't think of anything else to do, not when the emotions started to choke his throat and he rolled a bit of snow in between his fingers. He shook his head, huffing against the tears pricking his eyes.

"I never expected to be here," he said quietly. "I never expected my career to end right when it started. I was supposed to go on for years, go to more Olympics, get my picture on a Wheaties box. I never expected to like a guy who cares more about how often he gets to eat burgers than how often I get to see him. I am an idiot."

"Yeah, you are," Jules agreed, grabbing Dorian's arm and hauling him up despite Dorian's reluctance.

"Great, then I'll just go."

Jules rolled his eyes, grabbing Dorian under the shoulders and supporting his weight as his ankle wobbled. "We both are. Come on," he said, tugging Dorian towards the truck.

Dorian sat at the counter, feeling stupid, as Jules cooked dinner, a measured amount of chicken and vegetables. "So is this some sadistic form of amusement?" he asked as Jules rummaged in the cupboard for something. "Keeping me here when you clearly don't want to?"

Jules tapped out the pepper onto the chicken. "I'm keeping you here so you don't injure yourself anymore," he replied, poking the chicken with the spatula. "And I do want you here."

Dorian didn't relax, setting his elbows on the counter. "So am I crazy?" Jules arched an eyebrow, flipping the chicken over and stirring up the vegetables. "Harper thought I was competition so he told you to do whatever it took to win?"

"Of course not," Jules scoffed. "Competition is competition. Everyone does things differently."

Dorian wasn't sure how to take that. "And what have you told your teammates about me?"

Jules shrugged. "Nothing."

Dorian nodded, sitting back. "Because we're nothing." It made sense. They *hadn't* talked about anything. He shouldn't have assumed.

Jules sighed, shaking his head. "Because I haven't seen you in three months, and nobody made any promises."

"Right," he agreed softly. Jules was right, after all. Dorian hadn't made any efforts to figure anything out either. It was just as much his fault.

"Shelby was just a girl a month ago."

"And I'm just a guy now," Dorian pointed out. "What's the difference?"

"There isn't," Jules said simply, setting down the spatula as Dorian frowned and looked away. "Except that I've known you longer and I like you better. And when you're not complaining, you're nice to be around. If you wanted a promise, well, I'd need one in return."

Looking up, Dorian paused. "What kind of promise?"

Jules rounded the counter, stepping up to where Dorian sat on his stool, cupping his face. "Find something that makes you happy."

"Gymnastics makes me happy." Dorian blinked up at Jules. He didn't have anything else. He couldn't ever remember having anything else. He'd driven his parents crazy watching old VHS tapes over and over again until he had the routines of champions memorized.

It hadn't always been about competitions. He'd done it because he loved it, and that, perhaps, was why he felt so utterly lost without it. Sure, he could still do bits and pieces, things that didn't require running or jumping, but without that, it all seemed a bit pointless.

"So do it."

"I can't. I can't compete." Dorian's eyes flickered down to his ankle, but Jules pulled his attention back up.

"Figure it out."

"And then what?" Dorian asked. "What about us?"

"What about us?"

Dorian paused. He didn't know exactly how to say this. He'd never asked anyone before. He'd never even felt like this before.

"What are we?" he asked. "Are we dating? Are we nothing? What's going on?"

"What do you want us to be?"

Dorian had no idea. He didn't know how any of it worked. He just knew he wanted more than they had. He wanted more than intermittent phone calls and Jules going out with random people, whether they meant anything or not. He'd never admitted any of that to anyone else before. He shrugged in response. "I don't know. I don't want to you to date any more girls. I want something more than this. I don't want to show up and wonder if you want me here."

"I can do that," Jules replied.

Dorian glanced up, hopeful. "So you won't?"

Jules shrugged. "Look, Dorian, I think you're a lot stronger than you've been acting lately, and I really like you, and I'm not nearly the slut you think I am. I am capable of sustaining a relationship for more than a week. You gotta give me more credit."

"I do—"

Jules shook his head. "I get it. I was a jerk during the Olympics. I didn't really make it easy for you to trust me, but you've got to make some changes too. I know your life feels like it's terrible right now, and your ankle and everything just seems like things will never get better, but it will. I like you, a lot, but I can't be your buffer. We're moving on from that, right?"

A pang of guilt hit Dorian's stomach as Jules said it. It wasn't as easy as people seemed to think to let go of his injury, but taking it out on his friends wasn't going to make him any new ones. He needed help.

"Yeah, we're moving on from that," he agreed. He did want to. He wanted to be able to trust Jules, to not be suspicious every time a girl smiled at Jules, every time Jules was nice to someone else.

"Good," Jules said with a soft smile.

"Good," Dorian echoed. "But I want you to come visit me. And I want you to tell your teammates we're dating."

"They won't care," Jules said, and Dorian shrugged.

"I care."

Jules grinned. "Okay."

Dorian slid his arms around Jules' neck as their mouths met in a slow, sweet kiss, something far more tangible than any of their promises.

"Shit," Jules cursed a second later, pulling back abruptly. "The chicken."

He hurried around the counter and flipped it over to reveal a blackened side.

"Now look what you made me do," he huffed, and Dorian merely smiled.

Dorian stood just beyond the entryway to the security line, bag in hand and his cane in the other. People milled past him, hurrying into the line as though they just couldn't wait to sit in a hard plastic chair and wait for their flight. Dorian looked over as Jules returned, a magazine in hand.

"Here," he said, handing it over.

Dorian glanced at the cover, a skeptical eyebrow arching. "Homemaking?"

"Practice for later in life," Jules replied, and he didn't hesitate to lean in and press a kiss to Dorian's cheek.

Dorian didn't bother glaring; his stomach was doing ridiculously stupid flips, and he couldn't bring himself to be annoyed with Jules. It was strange, he thought, considering how much he'd disliked Jules four months ago, and now he didn't want to go home. Looking over unwillingly at the line to security, he sighed. It had gotten longer since he'd stood there.

"Don't look so depressed," Jules said, squeezing his shoulder. "You get to leave the snow."

"I guess I should go then," Dorian said slowly. He didn't know what else to say, and Jules wasn't offering any pearls of wisdom.

"Wait a minute," Jules said, tugging him back and fixing the collar on his jacket. "Better." He shrugged, smiling at Dorian, then he leaned in for a kiss. For a second, Dorian froze, utterly aware how out in the open they were, but most people were too busy heading for security to notice them. It was strange but also nice that Jules didn't care who saw. Dorian didn't really either.

He really didn't want to go now, but he had no choice, he knew. Jules pulled back, grabbing him into a warm hug. "I'll miss you."

Dorian hid his smile in Jules' shoulder. "Me too," he admitted quietly, moving back reluctantly. Hooking his bag over his shoulder, he caught sight of a boy staring at him as he walked past into the security line.

"Mom," the kid hissed, pulling on his mother's arm. "Mom, it's that guy from the Olympics!"

Dorian turned back to Jules' shit-eating grin. "Shut up," he said, and Jules shook his head.

"I didn't say anything, peaches."

For once, Dorian didn't reprimand him. Instead, he sighed. "I guess I'll talk to you later."

Jules nodded. "Text me when you get home. And, Dor, stop taking life so seriously."

"I'll try," Dorian replied, and he meant it this time.

As Dorian stepped into the line, he kept his eyes on Jules until the line grew and Jules was lost. He tried to stretch up, but too many people filled the line behind him, and he was forced to go through the scanner.

Walking to his gate, he passed the same kid with his mother, and he smiled at the kid as he went by. The kid's eyes widened and he waited until Dorian had gone on to babble excitedly to his mother. Dorian merely grinned to himself and headed on towards the gate.

Maybe Jules was right about that too. Dorian would probably have to thank Jason for suggesting this trip, but it was a small price to pay considering all he'd been through lately. Sure, he still had no idea what he was going to do with his life, but at least he had Jules to help him figure it out.

As he waited in the hard, plastic chair, rotating his ankle slowly in preparation for the plane ride ahead, he glanced out the window where a flurry of snow had begun to fall and smiled to himself as the boarding call sounded above him.

Chapter 17

European Rendezvous

"So when will you be back?"

Dorian glanced up at Jason leaning in the doorway then resumed folding the shirts on his bed. After nearly two weeks, he'd finally gotten around to doing laundry which meant clothes piled everywhere. On the floor, his suitcase laid sprawled open, half-packed with jeans and shoes. Dorian wasn't sure he had enough warm clothes to last the week given that the Netherlands were bound to be a lot colder than New Orleans this time of year.

"The World Championships last about a week," he replied, though he had told Jason this ten times already at least. "I'm going early so I can see Jules."

Jason nodded, stepping into the room and settling on Dorian's desk chair. On the desk, homework waited for Dorian — essays to write and textbooks to read. Dorian wouldn't say he was avoiding it, except that he was completely avoiding it. He had an appointment with his advisor later where she would tell him once again that he was on track to graduate in December, a mere two months away.

The idea of graduating only tied his stomach in knots. He had thought that losing his career dreams of being a competitive gymnast was hard, but the thought of graduation made him both happy and terrified at the same time. At least this week, he wouldn't have to think about it. He could just enjoy being with Jules.

The last World Championship Dorian had gone to had been the one before the Olympics. He had won World Champion gold on vault and that had started the predictions about the Olympics to come. This time, he'd be a spectator only, but after three years, he'd come to accept it.

Jason didn't reply to Dorian, and Dorian shoved the folded stack of shirts in the suitcase.

"You'll have the apartment all to yourself so Liz can basically live here."

Jason scoffed. "That's not why I asked."

Dorian raised an amused eyebrow. Liz practically lived there already, but he had no doubt that she would be there the whole time he was gone.

"Are you sure you want to go?" Jason asked, leaning forward on the chair. Dorian paused.

"Yes. Why?" It wasn't like Jason to play the caring friend — he was more likely to be the one pressuring Dorian into going out on the weekends and having a drink to cheer him up.

Jason shrugged. "I don't know. It might be hard for you."

Dorian shook his head and rose from the bed, going to his closet instead. "It's been three years, Jason," he said, opening the doors and searching for the elusive coat his mother had bought him years ago. He wasn't even sure it was still in there. "I can walk mostly normally now without the cane or my brace. I've come to terms with my inability to compete. It's okay. In a few months, I'll have graduated and I'll be working full time at the gym."

"Coaching five year olds to do somersaults," Jason pointed out. "What a dream."

Frowning, Dorian turned back. It wasn't exactly his dream, but as everyone told him, he had to put in his time first before he could get the job he actually wanted. Being a gymnastics coach wasn't as simple as walking into a training center and asking for a job. "Well, what do you want me to do? A job is a job."

Jason didn't seem to have an answer, and Dorian finally spotted the coat in the back of the closet. Pulling it out, he shook out the dust and the creases. It would have to do.

Dorian didn't expect to get a great job right out of school. He was lucky to have one now. Even if his dream job was still far away, at least he was on the right path to get there. A few years in the gym and maybe a spot would open up in a Center. Until then, he would stick it out with the five year olds. At least they didn't sidestep the subject of his injury or give him sympathetic looks when he told them why he had a slight limp at the end of the day.

He shoved the coat into the suitcase and zipped it shut. This week wasn't about him; it was about Jules, and he was sure Jules was going to do well. After all, he'd been training non-stop for weeks. Coach Harper had him in the gym almost every day, so much so that Dorian had barely talked to Jules except to confirm what time his flight arrived.

Coach Harper had his team's noses to the grindstones, which Dorian understood, but he couldn't shake the feeling that it was too much. "No such thing as too much preparation!" he had heard Harper say one time to Jules. Dorian wasn't so sure.

He turned to Jason, who was still in the desk chair, tapping a pencil against the tabletop. "You still gonna take me to the airport?"

Jason smiled. "If you ever finish packing." He rose from the chair. "Hurry up. Liz is coming over and we're gonna order pizza. If you're nice, we'll let you pick the movie, but it better not be 'Stick It.'"

Dorian tossed a sock at Jason as he left and it bounced off the doorframe. Turning away from the stack of homework on his desk, he grabbed a pile of shirts off the bed and went to put them away.

The flight to the Netherlands seemed to take forever, and Dorian found himself squished between a German man and a woman with a Scottish accent so thick that he could barely understand her when she spoke to him. It was raining when the plane landed and outside the airport windows, everything seemed covered in a grey mist as Dorian walked towards the exit. A mixture of languages surrounded him and he passed numerous duty-free shops. He'd never been to Rotterdam before, or the Netherlands for that matter, but it seemed similar to many other European cities. At least the airport did. The town was filled with circular roads and white brick buildings lining the roads. Flower pots lined all the windows, but the flowers inside drooped in preparation for the oncoming winter. Dorian was glad he'd brought the coat.

His hotel wasn't far from the arena, and he lugged his suitcase up several flights of stairs, his ankle protesting by the time he reached the last step. He should have booked a hotel with an elevator. As he slid the key into the slot, his only thought was of taking a nap and maybe finding some food.

The lock clicked, the light turning green, and he pushed the door open to a small room, just big enough for a bed, a miniature dresser... and Jules.

Dorian dropped his suitcase as he stared. It had been months since he'd seen Jules, and he certainly hadn't expected him to show up in his hotel room, not when there was training to be done. There he was, though, grinning at Dorian's surprise. He looked the same; his head shaved again, skin tan despite the lack of sun up in Connecticut.

"What are you doing here?" he asked finally, unable to come up with anything else as his heart swelled and a smile tugged his lips.

Jules pushed off the little dresser and shrugged. "I heard the Netherlands was a great place to get weed and there's a little competition I'm involved in."

Dorian tried not to laugh, shutting the door behind him finally and moving into the small space. Really, it was just a room big enough for sleeping. "I meant here, in my hotel room."

"Oh, did you want me to go?" Jules asked, taking a step towards Dorian and making to go around him. "I think I saw a café around the corner. I wonder if they serve absinthe."

"No." Dorian laughed, catching Jules' arm and pulling him back. "No absinthe for you."

Jules tried to pout, ruffling Dorian's hair. "You're no fun. I don't know why I missed you."

Warmth filled Dorian, the same way it always did these days when he saw Jules. His hand slid down to Jules', entwining their fingers together. "I'm just really miss-able, that's all."

"I guess so," Jules agreed, leaning down finally to kiss him. Dorian smiled into it, rising up on his toes to meet him.

Months, he thought. Months had gone by since he'd seen Jules. They just couldn't afford to, and they were both so busy that it was unfeasible to travel so much. Every time they got together, though, it was as if nothing had changed, but really, everything had changed. It was hard to believe that a few years ago they'd been at each other's throats.

Dorian liked to think he'd matured since then, but when Jules' hand slid down his back and grabbed his ass, he wasn't sure Jules had. He jumped, laughing and pushing Jules back. "Shouldn't you be training right now?"

Jules shrugged, mouthing along Dorian's neck, and Dorian didn't have it in him to make him stop. "Told Coach I had to do a little research."

"On what?" Dorian wasn't really paying attention, not when Jules pulled him in closer and kissed him deeply. He wouldn't deny that he'd been looking forward to this, but he could feel jetlag pulling him down at the same time. He'd been awake for almost twenty-four hours already.

"Some gymnast. Something Rutherford," Jules muttered, sliding his hand to Dorian's neck. "Supposed to be the next big thing."

"Mmm," Dorian hummed. He'd heard of Rutherford but hadn't paid much attention. He was just another gymnast and since Dorian wasn't competing anymore, he didn't need to worry about it. At the moment, he was more concerned with Jules' hands pressing into him, smoothing away any thoughts of napping.

He'd be content to stay like that all day, but Jules pulled away first, brushing his hair back and sighing as he rested their foreheads together. His hand moved up to Dorian's lower back and settled there, a warm weight against his skin.

"You hungry?"

Dorian blinked slowly, the jetlag coming back to him. Suddenly the bed looked very inviting. "Shouldn't you be getting back before Harper notices you're missing?"

"Research could take hours," Jules pointed out, turning Dorian around and leading him towards the door, hand still on his back. "Let's check out that café. No absinthe, I promise."

"I don't think they serve it in cafés," Dorian replied, but he let Jules lead him out to the narrow hallway. Food or sleep, he really didn't care as long as Jules was here.

"Maybe afterwards," Jules said. "We'll get some to celebrate my win."

Dorian didn't argue, though he doubted either of them would ever try absinthe. Harper would go crazy if he found out Jules had, and Dorian never planned on trying any green alcohol. That was the kind of thing that would get you in big trouble, whether on purpose or not.

"Yeah, maybe," he said finally, and Jules grinned back at him.

The café was as adorable as any postcard Dorian had ever seen with flower boxes outside and warm lighting inside. The rain persisted throughout the whole time they were there, drizzling off the overhang and dripping onto the concrete. His mother would have enjoyed it, he found himself thinking as he drank a tiny cup of coffee and ate some kind of pastry that he couldn't pronounce the name of.

"Here," Jules said as they walked back to Dorian's hotel, pulling a piece of paper out of his pocket. "It's your pass to get into trainings."

"I don't want to distract you." Dorian hesitated to take it, but Jules pushed it into his hand.

"You won't. I'm the distraction, remember?"

"I remember," Dorian muttered, and Jules laughed. The hotel came into sight and Dorian turned to Jules. "You going back to your hotel?"

"Still researching," Jules assured him, sliding an arm around his waist, and Dorian hid his smile as they entered the hotel and took the stairs up to his room.

"I'm so tired," Dorian said, flopping down on the bed without bothering to get undressed. He opened his eyes as he heard Jules taking off his shoes.

"You'll be fine tomorrow." Jules crawled onto the bed, lying down beside him. "Then you'll get to watch me win yet another World Championship."

"I'm glad you've learned modesty these past couple of years."

Jules laughed and slid his hand over Dorian's stomach, thumb grazing under the waistline and rubbing circles into his skin. Dorian closed his eyes at the touch, feeling sleep tugging at the edges of his brain.

"Don't worry," Jules murmured. "I am nothing if not a gracious winner."

Dorian snorted at that. "Oh yeah, and what are you going to say to that Rutherford kid if you win?"

"You mean when. When I win, I will congratulate him on a job well done, then I will announce to the press that he was a great competitor but he just couldn't compete with my experience. Coach says I'm great at getting under people's skin."

Dorian was too tired to roll his eyes and he turned towards Jules, gazing at him through the darkened room, the curtains pulled shut to block out the grayness. Jules had a few more lines than he remembered, around his mouth and at the corners of his eyes.

"Is that what you did with me?"

Jules leaned in and kissed him slowly, a hand on his neck. "Yeah, but you got me right back."

Dorian hummed in agreement. He was tired, but Jules was warm, a steady slide of lips moving down his throat. "Jules," he murmured, sighing and sinking into the feeling of Jules' hands smoothing over his chest, reaching for his jeans and tugging them open.

"I missed you," Jules muttered and pushed Dorian's jeans off. He pulled down his boxers as well, and Dorian merely smiled, eyes closed as sleep tugged at him, but a crackle of heat rose under his skin as Jules reached for his prick. It had been so long.

He still remembered the first time, all those years ago, although he'd had a completely different mindset at the time. Now, he welcomed Jules' touch, craved it after months without. The heat crawled over his body as Jules stroked him off, mouth continuing to work at the patch of skin on his neck.

Dorian's hand slid around Jules' neck as he squirmed in his grip. Pulling Jules' mouth to his, he kissed him long and slow, only breaking it to gasp as Jules tightened his grip. He gritted his teeth through a groan. Far too long to be going this slowly, but after an eight hour flight, he only felt like collapsing in the bed and sleeping forever.

Jules brushed a kiss against his cheek as Dorian shut his eyes tightly against the pressure building in his cock. He hadn't come with someone else's hand on his prick in months, and he couldn't hold back as he did. His grip tightened on Jules' neck and he arched his back as Jules' hand slid over him, strong, firm, and warm.

"Fuck," he muttered as his body wound down, tingly and warm all over. He heard Jules get up for a moment, but he came back and curled into bed next to him.

Dorian rolled into him. "Tomorrow," he promised, kissing Jules again. "When I'm not jet lagged, I'll repay the favor."

"Counting on it," Jules murmured.

Sliding down, Dorian closed his eyes again. He could feel Jules' body against his, warm and solid and comforting. If he listened closely, he could almost hear his heartbeat, and he smiled as Jules' arms pulled him in closer. Listening to the rain, it soon lulled him into a slow sleep, and he didn't wake until Jules pulled away to go to practice many hours later.

Chapter 18
Old Strategies

"Tighten up on your tucks!" Harper shouted as Jules' feet hit the mat and he stumbled. He managed to catch himself, pulling back tightly. He wasn't sure what it was, but his vaults seemed to be getting sloppier, and now was exactly the wrong time for that to happen. Where was Dorian when he needed him to tell him exactly what he was doing wrong? He'd left him earlier, slipped out of bed at the ungodly hour of five o'clock. If Harper knew he hadn't stayed in his own room, he would have his head. He'd managed to make it to training without anyone any the wiser.

Jogging off the mat, he grabbed his water bottle from the bench and took a few gulps, wiping sweat off his forehead. Around him, other gymnasts and their coaches were in the middle of warm-ups and training as well. Jules smiled at the few he knew as Coach Harper came over, clapping a hand on his shoulder and tightening it.

"What's got you distracted, Jules?"

"Nothing." He shrugged. There was nothing distracting him except the fact that he couldn't seem to stick his landing. If things kept going like this, he wouldn't have a shot at the Olympics next year. That was a year away, though. World's was tomorrow.

Harper shot him a slanted glance as though refraining from saying what was on his mind. Instead, he squeezed Jules' shoulder. "I think it's time we talked about your competition. You look into Rutherford?" He nodded across the gym at the tall, muscular kid that couldn't be older than eighteen. He was busy stretching and didn't notice their gazes.

"Cameron Rutherford, holds the record high score on the rings."

That was about all he'd managed to gather between meeting Dorian last night and this morning. He'd asked Russell about him earlier in the locker room. This happened every year. Harper spent months doing research, keeping track of the up-and-comers, learning their habits.

"He's the favorite to medal in the event," Harper pointed out, taking Jules by the shoulder and steering him away from the floor. "We got lucky at the Olympics with Dorian's injury, but bronze is child's play. If you want to be ready for the next one, for that gold we both know you deserve, you've got to win here. You know that, dontcha?" He led Jules over to the bench and sat down beside him. "I'd say if you get yourself together, you've got a pretty good shot at another title. Rutherford's young, though, impressionable. It's important that you don't let him get ahead, you know?"

Jules nodded. Every year it was the same thing. There was always someone new to look out for.

"You know what to do," Harper said confidently. "Make sure he's distracted. Do whatever you need to and you'll win that gold just like you're supposed to."

Jules didn't reply. He had no doubts that he wouldn't win the gold, this kid or no, but a little friendly competition never hurt anyone. He smiled at Harper instead. "I got it," he assured him. Distraction was one of his specialties. He'd successfully distracted Dorian into a relationship with him. This kid would be no problem.

"Good." Harper slapped his shoulder and rose from the bench. "I expect you to be on your game tomorrow. Whatever happens here can play big into the Olympics next year."

Jules gazed across the gym at Rutherford. He was just like any other gymnast: a little young, a little overconfident. Nothing Jules couldn't handle.

As he watched Rutherford talking to his coach, something else caught his eye. Dorian stood in the doorway to the training gym, glancing around.

"Dorian's here," he said, rising from the bench, and Harper followed his gaze, eyebrows furrowing.

"Jules," he said, stopping him from leaving. "Now's not the time to let your guard down. You know I like Dorian as if he was part of my own team, but it's time to focus on Rutherford and on winning."

"I know," Jules assured him. He didn't plan on getting distracted, but it had been months since he'd seen Dorian. He would worry about Rutherford in a little bit. "I'll be fine. I promise." He grinned at Harper, leaving him and crossing the gym. He passed Rutherford on the way, catching his eye and giving him a nod. The kid merely watched him pass, a flash of confusion on his face.

Dorian stood by the door, arms crossed and watching a guy from Sweden do a flip on the rings. He dropped his arms as Jules approached.

"You've got nothing to worry about," Dorian said. "That guy's difficulty level is only a seven."

"Morning to you too," Jules greeted him, squeezing his arm. It didn't surprise him in the least that Dorian was already judging difficulty levels. "Gonna come watch my practice?"

"Thought I might. Give you some pointers."

Jules laughed. Of all the people who would give him advice in the next couple days, Dorian's would probably be some of the most honest. Turning back, he led the way over to where Harper was now shouting at Russell for his handstands. They passed Rutherford again.

"Hey, rugrat," he said, catching the blond kid's attention. "I like your routine. Next time, think about adding some stability on your holds. Maybe someday you'll be able to run with the big kids."

Dorian gazed back as they passed, but Jules kept walking. He didn't even wait to see Rutherford's expression. He knew what it would be—confusion, annoyance, everything that would distract him from the competition and be better for Jules.

"What was that?" Dorian asked as they reached the other side of the gym.

"What? It was Rutherford. I told you about him."

Dorian frowned, but whatever he was going to say was cut off by Harper. Jules was glad. He didn't need a lecture that would inevitably come about being nice. They weren't on a team together. He had nothing to lose by getting under Rutherford's skin, and after all, it was fun.

"Dorian," Harper said graciously, holding out a hand to Dorian and shaking it tightly. Dorian shot a look at Jules, but Jules chose to ignore him. He knew Dorian wasn't exactly fond of Harper, but Harper had done a lot for Jules in the past and he wouldn't forget it.

"Coach Harper," Dorian greeted him, smile slightly strained. "It's good to see you."

"You too!" Harper said, clapping him on the shoulder so hard that Dorian actually jerked forward. Jules smiled at his expression of discomfort. He could never figure out just what it was that Dorian didn't like about Harper. "Came to see our boy compete, eh? I say he's got a pretty good shot at the gold as long as we keep the competition in check."

Dorian's mouth twitched, but it wasn't a smile. The least he could do was be polite.

"Jules is going to do great," he said, meeting Jules' eyes. Something in his gaze made Jules pause but he didn't mention it as Harper led Dorian over to the bench.

"You sit down here and take a load off. Wouldn't want that injury acting up. How long has it been since you stopped competing?"

Jules watched Dorian grimace at the question, but he really didn't have time to worry about Dorian's sensitivities at the moment. The injury was old news as far as he was concerned. There were much bigger things to worry about.

"How's the rest of the team doing?" Dorian asked instead, unskillfully changing the subject, and Jules shook his head. Dorian wasn't the most tactful person all the time.

"Jules," Russell called, and Jules hesitated before leaving Dorian with Harper and jogging over.

"What's up?"

Russell nodded at Dorian and Harper. "You sure that's wise?"

"What?"

"The boyfriend and the coach? They're probably coming up with strategies to take out the competition for you."

Jules shook his head. That was ridiculous. "If I can't win on my own, then what's the point?"

"Harper told you to look out for Rutherford, right?" Russell asked with a significant look, and Jules shrugged.

"He's worried over nothing. Rutherford will be too easy to mess up."

Russell didn't look impressed, but Jules didn't have anything to say. They both knew how Harper could be. He wanted his guys to win and he gave them all the necessary tools to do so. Jules wasn't worried.

"You're not gonna sleep with him, are you?"

"What? No!" Jules scoffed. "Have you forgotten Dorian? He'd murder me."

Russell shrugged. "Harper usually says to do anything you can to beat the competition."

"That's a little overboard." Jules wouldn't go that far. Harper wouldn't suggest that. It was just a friendly competition as with anything else.

"Yeah, well." Russell didn't finish, turning from Harper.

"How about you just worry about your floor exercise and I'll worry about Rutherford for the both of us?"

Russell merely shrugged and headed to the weights. Jules turned back to where Harper and Dorian were still talking. Dorian hadn't opened up anymore, sitting with his shoulders hunched and avoiding Harper's gaze. Jules sighed. It'd be much easier if Dorian would just be friendly to Harper. After all, Harper was like a father to Jules, and he'd been there much more than his own father had. They could at least get along. That would be nice.

Dorian finally managed to escape Coach Harper and his veiled comments about his injury and how it was such a shame that he couldn't compete anymore. Every time he said it, Dorian thought he heard a bit of joy behind his words. It just made him angry and leaving was the only way he could stop himself from saying something he would regret later.

The gym was filled with gymnasts, some he knew and some he didn't. He was glad when no one else asked about the ankle. You could hardly tell he'd been injured these days anyway, although he had put on the brace that morning just in case. It helped to keep him on his feet for long periods of time.

He rounded the gym, watching a few people practicing their routines and paused as he caught sight of Rutherford. The kid was definitely good. He held his positions just the right amount of time, and he was definitely on par with Olympic gymnasts. He could see why Harper was worried.

Rutherford caught sight of him and dropped off the rings. His coach was working with someone else at the moment and Rutherford came over to Dorian.

"You're Dorian Stuart," he said, a smile lighting up his face. It only made him look younger. "Wow, I didn't think I'd ever meet you, you know, since you don't compete anymore. This is so awesome. What are you doing here? I've watched your Olympics tape, like, a million times. You were so good."

Dorian couldn't help smiling. If he'd been competing, he would have seen the fawning as a ploy, but Rutherford was just an overexcited kid.

"It's nice to meet you," he said, holding out a hand.

"Oh, uh, Cameron, Cameron Rutherford," Rutherford said. "Sometimes my friends call me Cam, but really, it's just Cameron."

He was rambling, and Dorian held back his laughter. It reminded him of the first time he had met Jules, nervous, intimidated, and with a huge crush. He could barely speak then.

"So," Cameron said when he finally dropped Dorian's hand. "What are you doing here?"

"I came to see Jules." He nodded over to where Jules stood with Russell.

"Oh, right, you were on the team together," Cameron said, gazing at Jules with an unreadable expression. "You still keep in touch with your teammates?"

"Some more than others," Dorian replied vaguely. It wasn't as if he and Jules had announced to the whole gymnastics' world about their relationship. It wasn't a secret, but it wasn't public knowledge either.

Cameron looked away from Jules, smiling at Dorian. "What's it like at the Olympics? I'm really hoping to get on the team next year. My coach says I have a good shot if I win here. How hard was it to make the team? I just really want to go. London is going to be amazing."

"I hear you're pretty good," Dorian said simply. "Just keep training and watch out for injuries."

Cameron nodded seriously, and Dorian smiled. He was so young, so eager. Dorian had been like that once.

"Having a little party over here?" Jules appeared at Dorian's shoulder, and Dorian noticed the way Cameron stiffened slightly. "Rutherford, we haven't officially met."

"I know who you are," Cameron muttered, then straightened his back. "I'm Cameron."

"Right," Jules replied. "I've been watching you. You've got a good routine."

Cameron looked surprised at the compliment. "Thanks."

Jules nodded. "When I was your age, my difficulty level was already a ten, so you're almost there. I'm sure your coach is doing the best he can."

Dorian frowned at Jules' words. What was he doing? He couldn't say anything, though, not with Cameron right there. He saw the way Cameron reacted, though, unable to come up with a response.

"Hey, we'll find out in the next couple days, right?" Jules grinned. "Now's the time that separates the strong from the weak, the Olympic contenders from the casual gymnasts."

"Er, right," Cameron replied. "I should get back to work."

Dorian didn't say anything as he left, although he did shoot Jules a look. "What the fuck was that?"

"What?" Jules shook his head as though he had no idea what Dorian was talking about.

Dorian opened his mouth to respond, but someone else interrupted before he could ask about Jules' peculiar behavior.

"Well, if it isn't my two most competitive boys having a reasonable conversation."

Dorian was surprised to find Brian approaching them, although all things considered, it shouldn't have been a surprise that he was there. Most likely he'd be coaching at the Olympics again, and he needed to scope out the potential athletes.

"Brian!" Dorian said, a smile spreading over his face. He hadn't seen Brian in almost three years, although it felt much longer.

The years hadn't changed Brian except to add a little more grey to his hair. He was still athletic and strong, still stood with his hands on his hips as he surveyed them both.

"I take it you haven't ripped each other's throats out since I last saw you?" Brian asked, grabbing Dorian by the shoulder and pulling him into a brief but crushing hug. He grabbed Jules next. "Nice to know you're still alive."

Dorian rubbed the back of his neck and smiled nervously. He hadn't been the best at staying in touch with people since the Olympics. For a while, he'd been too focused on his own problems, then it had just seemed too long to get back in touch. "I was just..."

"Busy," Brian filled in for him, glancing between him and Jules knowingly. "A little bird told me."

Dorian frowned. He hadn't exactly been forthcoming with many people about his and Jules' relationship, especially people in the gymnastics world. It wasn't as if they'd sent out a press release. He looked at Jules, but Jules seemed just as clueless as he was.

"Speaking of, Georgia is around somewhere," Brian went on, and it hit Dorian. He had mentioned it to Georgia, although he couldn't remember when since they hadn't talked in a while either. "You better say hello or she'll hunt you down." He clapped Dorian on the shoulder. "I've got to get going. Stay out of trouble, boys. I'll be watching." He walked away, leaving them alone.

Jules turned back to Dorian. "I'll see you for dinner, right? Coach wants me to work on my bars routine. We all remember how challenging those are." He grinned at Dorian. "I'll see you later."

Dorian let him go. Between Brian showing up and Harper, he wasn't sure what exactly was going to happen at this competition. It was great to see Brian, but Harper's comments stuck in his mind. Something told him that Harper was going to be difficult, but he had nothing but a gut feeling to prove himself right, so he left without talking to anyone else, shutting the door behind him and walking through empty hallways until he reached the crisp, cool air outside.

Chapter 19

Better than Phone Sex

Darkness pressed in against the tiny window in his hotel room, and Dorian watched Jules strip off his shirt and toss it on the dresser. Sitting on the bed, he debated bringing up what had happened in the gym earlier with Cameron. All through dinner, he hadn't said anything, deciding if he should or not.

"What's with the face?" Jules asked, pushing Dorian back and climbing on top of him. Dorian was still fully-clothed, although he doubted he would stay that was for long.

"Nothing. Just tired," he said, deciding not to say anything for the time being. It wasn't going to help anything, not right now with Jules' hips pressed to his.

"Yeah?" Jules dipped down, brushing his lip against Dorian's chin. "I thought you were going to show me how much you missed me?"

"And inflate your ego some more? I don't think so." Dorian moved, pushing Jules onto his back and straddling him instead.

Jules grinned up at him. "I could show you. Phone sex just doesn't cut it anymore, peaches."

"What have I told you about that name?"

"That you hate it, and I love that you hate it."

Dorian tried to frown, but he couldn't when Jules arched an eyebrow and wiggled his hips up.

"Come on," Jules wheedled. "Can't you feel how much I missed you? I know you did too even if you're too stubborn to say it."

"I'm not," Dorian replied. "I just have more restraint than you do."

"Please," Jules scoffed, reaching for Dorian's hips and pulling him in closer. Dorian felt Jules' cock pressing through his jeans and a lick of heat began to spread from his stomach. "You have the libido of a rabbit and you know it."

"Shut up," Dorian muttered, leaning down to kiss Jules finally.

It had been months since they'd done anything other than phone sex, jerking off to the sound of each other's voices, and Dorian wanted so much more than that. He ignored the way Jules laughed against him. Jules' body felt warm under his hands as he slid them down to the hem of his shirt, sliding underneath. His muscles were taut, defined as Dorian ran his palms up his stomach, humming against Jules' mouth as their tongues slid together. Jules' hand pushed under his shirt, pressing against his lower back, urging Dorian's body down as their mouths slid together, slow at first, then harder. It had been five months after all.

"Mmph." Jules made a noise in the back of his throat, biting at Dorian's mouth and sucking until it was red and swollen. His fingers dug into Dorian's back, pulling their hips together and pushing up against him.

Flushed, Dorian pulled away to gaze down at Jules, feeling the rush of heat in his cock as their hips ground together through too many layers of clothing. He swallowed the lump in his throat, breathing out slowly and biting his lip as their hips slid together.

Dorian let out a soft noise, half a moan, a quiet exhale as he felt his cock hardening against Jules' cock. He'd missed this, this feeling of heat that stole over him as he felt Jules' mouth close over his neck, sucking until he'd have a mark. Dorian would curse at him for it later, but right now, he didn't care. He wanted Jules' mouth on him, marking him wherever he could.

"Mmm," Jules hummed against his mouth, pushing their hips together harder than before, rocking up into him.

"Fuck me," Dorian breathed a second later, moving his hand down and squeezing the outline of Jules' cock through his jeans.

Jules smirked, pushing up into Dorian's hand before he reached for Dorian's shirt, tugging it over his head. Dorian didn't waste time getting Jules' jeans off either.

He got Jules' pants down, shoving them over his hips and down his thighs. Jules' hands struggled with his jeans, and Dorian helped, kicking them off and coming back, their naked bodies pressing together. Dorian moaned softly, his eyes fluttering shut as Jules' hands skimmed over his backside.

Jules pushed up against him, rolling them over, hand sliding around the back of his neck, pulling Dorian's mouth to his for a wet, messy kiss that Dorian fell into, digging his hands into the muscles of Jules' back. He loved Jules' back, how smooth and muscled it always was. That was one perk of dating a gymnast.

Jules took control now, pushing Dorian's shoulders back and bearing down on him, mouth working at his throat, leaving a hot trail of kisses down his collarbone and sucking on his nipple as Dorian pushed up against him, desperately needing more.

His face felt hot — his whole body felt hot — and he moaned softly as Jules sucked on a nipple, tongue flicking over it until Dorian couldn't take it anymore. "Jules," he complained breathlessly, pressing on his shoulders to get him to move.

Finally, Jules moved back up, capturing his mouth for a hot, breathless kiss that left Dorian panting against his lips, following his mouth when he pulled back.

Scrambling over, Dorian rummaged in his suitcase over the side of the bed, coming back with a condom and lube. He pushed it into Jules' hands.

He watched with eager eyes, watching the way Jules slid his slick fingers over his cock, stroking himself slowly, then he moved his hand to Dorian's ass, moving in against him, pushing up Dorian's thighs. Dorian didn't say anything as Jules slid in a finger, pushing past the tight muscles, and he could feel it deep in his ass. Five months was too long, and toys didn't make up for the real thing as Jules pushed in a second finger, dragging against the sides of his body.

Dorian let out a soft, almost-choked noise, breath wavering as Jules prepared him. He was almost shaking with anticipation.

His eyes met Jules', and he didn't have to say anything as Jules leaned in, licking his bottom lip as his finger pushed in farther until Dorian gasped in return, his hands digging into Jules' sides, cock aching. "Jules," he breathed finally, the word half-panted into the silent room, pushing his hips up against him, urging his fingers deeper. Wrapping his arms around Jules' neck, he pulled him in close, their noses bumping together, and he could feel Jules' heated breath against his cheek, a soft rush of air as Jules' fingers slid away and his hands pushed his legs up further, sliding in against him.

Jules pushed inside Dorian finally, a slow slide that made Dorian moan shakily, closing his eyes and biting his lip.

Jules moved faster and Dorian tried to catch his breath, grabbing for the back of Jules' thighs as he rocked in, pushing his cock through the tight muscles. He felt light-headed as he moaned softly, a sharp breath with each push of Jules inside him.

"Fuck," he cursed finally, reaching for his own cock, stroking quickly as Jules continued to move, their hips meeting in a slap of skin that mingled with each noise they made, each gasp for breath, each half-finished groan.

Jules pushed in harder but slower, taking his time to slide his hips in, rotating his body, and Dorian grit his teeth against the noises that came from his mouth, panting for breath around each jolt of heat that ran up his body, each tightening curl to his stomach as Jules moved in purposefully, drawing it out until Dorian was whining for release, his cheeks flushed pink and his mouth falling open.

"Jules, Jules," he panted, fingers tightening over the back of Jules' thigh with each thrust as he felt blood throbbing in his own cock, skin hot in his hand as he jerked himself. He squeezed the base to keep himself from coming too soon, biting his lip and moaning softly, letting out a shaky breath against Jules' mouth as he leaned in.

"I missed you, baby," Jules whispered, breathless as he pushed in, mouth pressing to Dorian's cheek for a second before he cursed under his breath.

Dorian could feel it when Jules came, the way his body seemed to tighten under his hands, how his hips stuttered but kept going. He could hear it in his breath, the sharp, choked noise he made, gasping for air as his hips slowed. Dorian let out a breath, closing his eyes as his hand moved faster, jerking his cock, needing release as Jules panted against his cheek, hips finally stilling inside him.

"Come on, peaches," Jules said a second later, sounding tired but satisfied, and he reached for Dorian's prick a minute later, smoothing his hand up the length and pushing Dorian's hand away. "Come for me."

It wasn't a nickname he really wanted to hear during sex, but the way Jules said it was different than his mother, and dear God, he didn't want to think of his mother at a time like this. Instead, he closed his eyes against Jules' warm hand, letting his head fall back on the pillow as Jules squeezed his cock and stroked him quickly, hand still slippery with lube.

"Shit," he cursed a minute later as he came, Jules' hand pulling him through it, massaging his cock as he came, the heat exploding in his stomach, and he could only pant for breath when Jules finally pulled away, drawing his prick out from his body and rolling the condom off.

Dorian was surprised a second later as Jules leaned down and licked the come off his stomach, but he didn't stop him, stretching back instead and closing his eyes.

Jules licked up his chest, pausing on his nipple again even as Dorian smiled and sighed contently.

Reaching for him, Dorian pulled Jules up to eye level, kissing him slowly and humming softly against his mouth.

"That was good," he murmured when they broke apart.

"You've certainly improved," Jules replied with a grin, catching Dorian's hand as it came up to hit him in the chest. He pulled him in for another kiss, and Dorian succumbed to him easily. It was such an easy routine to fall into with Jules.

Lying there, he didn't say anything for a moment, but something deep inside him knew he had to say it. He had to ask about Jules and Cameron.

"Why were so mean to that Rutherford kid?" he asked as Jules' fingers swept over his shoulder.

"What are you talking about?"

"Earlier in the gym." He pushed himself up. "You were talking down to him."

Jules shrugged. "It wasn't a big deal. If he can't handle the pressure, he shouldn't be competing."

"He's barely seventeen."

Jules didn't seem to understand Dorian's annoyance, and he wasn't sure he could explain it. He didn't want to argue with Jules either, not with the competition so close. He hadn't come all this way to argue.

"Come on," Jules said, pulling Dorian back down, mouth brushing against his shoulder. "If it was you, you probably wouldn't even be talking to him. You'd be too focused on winning. Don't you want me to win?"

"Of course," Dorian agreed, "but you should win because you're the best."

Jules grinned, kissing him slowly. "I am and I will."

Dorian wasn't complete appeased, but he didn't argue anymore as Jules closed his eyes. Maybe it had just been a fluke. Maybe he was just making a big deal out of nothing. Shaking himself, he put it out of his mind for the time being. He was here to support Jules, not question his decisions. If only Jules would make the right decisions.

A part of Dorian still wished he was competing out there, spending hour after hour training. He used to sleep really well after a hard day's training, but these days, he often found himself lying awake for hours instead. It gave him time to think although Jules probably would have told him he thought too much.

Thinking was mostly what he had to do, though, as he sat in the gym watching Jules work on his routines, watching the other competitors size each other up. He hadn't forgotten what it was like. There was a lot of pressure riding on the championship. Winners from their respective countries would become frontrunners for the next Olympics. It'd be one more notch in their belts.

Dorian watched Cameron practice — he seemed to keep to himself and spoke primarily to his coach despite other gymnasts coming up to him.

"I should be insulted," someone said as they plunked down next to him on the bench.

Dorian's face split into a grin. "Georgie," he said, accepting her hug. "It's good to see you."

"You too," she said. After three years, she still looked the same: a spitfire ex-gymnast.

"Why should you be insulted?"

She nudged his shoulder with hers. "You didn't even bother to say hello. I had to find you on my own, although I suppose I shouldn't be surprised. You were never very sociable."

Dorian grimaced. "I was just busy, that's all."

"Yes, you seem to be quite busy," she said. "How long has it been? Two years? Have you finished school yet? Taken the coaching world by storm? I hope you've at least learned to appreciate travel by now."

Dorian laughed. "Considering I hardly get to travel anymore, I do appreciate it a lot more. Not done with school yet, although I've only got about a month left. I'm graduating early so I can start working on paying back those student loans."

"And the coaching?"

"It isn't like coaching jobs grow on trees," Dorian said with a shrug. "Gotta pay my dues first."

"I'm sure you'll be a spectacular coach," she assured him, turning to watch the gymnasts practicing. "How's Jules? He doesn't call either, but I'm less surprised about that."

"He's good. I think he's got a pretty good shot at medaling here and for the Olympics next year."

Georgia glanced at him, almost sighing. "And you're good?" she asked sincerely. "I saw some interviews after the Olympics."

Dorian ducked his head. "That was years ago. I've gotten over it. It was just an injury."

Georgia seemed to understand it wasn't, but she didn't say anything. It was something he had always appreciated about her. She knew when to push and when to stop.

"I'm glad you're doing well," she said, watching Jules do a vault.

For a second, Dorian considered telling her about his suspicions of Harper, but what was there to say, really? He only had vague notions that something was going on with him and Jules and Cameron, but he couldn't say what. Bringing it up would just make him look paranoid and jealous. If anyone would listen to him, though, it would be Georgia.

"That kid's pretty good," she commented, nodding at Cameron.

Dorian almost laughed, but he stopped himself. "Yeah."

"Well, I've got to go find Brian," Georgia said, pushing off the bench and turning to Dorian. "Don't be a stranger."

"I won't," he promised, watching her go. When she was gone, he turned back to Cameron. On his phone, Dorian pulled up the internet and looked up Cameron, scrolling through pictures of him as he sat on the bench.

"Should I be jealous?"

Dorian switched off the phone and glanced up at Jules. "Hardly. You don't get jealous."

"Then maybe you're jealous," Jules pointed out, taking the seat next to Dorian and cracking open his water bottle.

Dorian laughed. "Of what?" Reaching out, he snatched the water from Jules and took a drink, ignoring Jules' fond expression.

"I'm having lunch with Rutherford."

For a second, Dorian could only stare at him, and Jules took back his bottle, slipping it out of his loose grip.

"What?" he asked finally, coming to. "Why?"

"Told you," Jules said knowingly, but Dorian shook his head.

"I'm not jealous. I just—*why*?" It didn't make any sense. Jules didn't even seem to like Cameron, and the more Dorian thought of it, the less it seemed right. So far, he'd only seen Jules be kind of an asshole to Cameron, and a lunch wasn't going to make up for it. He was surprised Cameron had even said yes considering the way he kept to himself.

Jules slipped an arm around his shoulder. "It's just a lunch to get to know him. You know, find his weaknesses, his soft spot."

"Jules," Dorian protested, but Jules wasn't listening, rising from the bench as Harper called to him.

"I'll see you later," Jules promised, trotting off.

Dorian stared after him. Something just wasn't adding up here, and Jules didn't seem to see anything wrong. As he watched, Harper muttered something in Jules' ear, and Jules nodded back. Something was very wrong.

The official competition started tomorrow which meant Jules had a very limited amount of time to get to know Rutherford. In reality, he allowed, he didn't need to get to know him beyond understanding his shortcomings and where he could poke and pry enough to get to him. It was all good-natured teasing as far as he was concerned. He could tell Dorian disapproved, but Dorian had never really understood the purpose. It made things more fun, more competitive. He would have thought, given how competitive Dorian was, that he would have liked it. It didn't matter, though. He wasn't competing against Dorian.

Cameron Rutherford was a whole lot more innocent than Jules had guessed, cloistered away with private coaches instead of using a Center. It meant he had no friends inside the gymnastic world, no teammates aside from those he joined for special competitions. He was about as socially graceful as a baby giraffe, even worse than Dorian had been.

The kid fumbled through lunch, more interested in his food than talking to Jules. It would be so incredibly easy to get under his skin. It almost made Jules laugh, but he didn't. Instead, he texted Harper under the table.

Rutherford scared of his own shadow.

His phone pinged a few minutes later.

Meet me in the gym. Half an hour.

Rutherford glanced up at the noise.

"My coach," Jules explained, waving his phone. "Always working." He tossed his napkin on the tray. "I gotta go. But don't worry, I'm sure that despite the fact that you don't know many of the gymnasts here and their strengths, you'll be okay. Everything's a learning curve, especially when you're going up against former Olympians. Don't try to compare yourself. It'll only make it worse, trust me." He winked at Rutherford's worried expression.

Sweeping away, he smiled to himself. Too easy.

Back in the gym, he found it empty except for Harper standing at the edge of the large, blue mat. As he approached, Harper didn't turn around.

"You see that?" he asked as Jules stepped up to him. Jules didn't see anything except the mat. "That right there is your future, Jules. This mat, those bars. That's what is going to make you great, and I'll be here to see it. Your parents couldn't make it this year?"

"They never make it." Jules couldn't remember the last time his mother had been able to afford to come to a meet, and he hadn't heard from his dad in over ten years. His dad had a new, better family somewhere else.

Harper nodded. "You're like a son to me, Jules. I've watched you grow up. I know what you've got in you. You're not going to let me down."

Jules's heart swelled with pride at Harper's words. He'd never let him down.

Harper turned to him finally, his once rock-hard stomach-turned-pudge protruding even in his sweats. "So Rutherford's soft as a pillow?"

"He'll take everything to heart." Jules knew it. Rutherford wouldn't last a day in a real competition, talented or not. Being a true athlete wasn't just about abilities: it was a mental toughness that not everyone had and not everyone was cut-out for it.

"Good," Harper agreed. "Keep at it. You're going to win. I can feel it."

Jules nodded and gazed out at the mat again. Harper was right. This was his future and it was up to him to make it happen.

Chapter 20
All About Winning

"How are the Netherlands?" Jason asked on the other end of the phone. "You buy any special brownies to bring home?"

"Pretty sure that's illegal," Dorian replied. Flopping down on the bed, he peered out the small window at the rain drizzling down the pane. Out the window, it merely looked out onto a small interior courtyard of the hotel, the flowers bent from the water and fading.

"Not in the Netherlands!"

"To bring home." Dorian shook his head. Of course Jason's biggest worry was how much pot he could smuggle back. Dorian had bigger things to worry about besides getting high.

"I was thinking," Jason said instead of answering, and Dorian gratefully let him change the subject. "Remember when you asked what you should do instead of working in the kiddie gym?"

"I didn't ask, but yes."

"You should just move in with Jules!"

He said it as though it was the simplest answer in the whole world, as if it would magically solve all of Dorian's problems. Instead, Dorian rolled his eyes at the window.

"You think I haven't thought of that?" He had been dating Jules for three years. Of course he had thought of moving in with him. It would have been so simple to pack up his measly belongings, fly to Connecticut, and move into Jules' crappy one bedroom apartment.

"Then what's the problem?"

Jason still had a whole year left. Jason didn't have to think about graduating for another seven months. Jason had a girlfriend who lived ten minutes away. It wasn't quite as easy for Dorian. The shelter that school provided was about to be torn away, and he had to find something else to support him.

"I don't have a job up there, for one," Dorian pointed out. "And for another, I don't want to just barge into his life and his apartment and have to be *that* person."

"He's your boyfriend," Jason replied flatly. "You aren't *that* person. Jesus, Dorian."

Annoyed, Dorian didn't reply. He didn't want to be the guy who had to rely on his boyfriend for somewhere to live. If circumstances were different, if he wouldn't feel like a burden, he might consider it. After all, it wasn't as if they had ever talked about it.

On the other end, he heard Jason sigh. "Anyway, tell Jules good luck from me, and seriously, man, get over yourself."

Dorian hung up after Jason. There was nothing to get over. He had a plan for after graduation. Jules was in it; Dorian was just not in his apartment.

Tossing the phone behind him, he lay down on the bed and stared at the off-white ceiling. Tomorrow, the competition started, and for some reason, the thought twisted Dorian's stomach and he rolled over, sighing into the silence.

Even though it had been three years since Dorian had competed, he still remembered what it felt like, the anticipation the night before, the nerves that settled low in his stomach before an event, the apprehension that went along with everything. Jules was different, though. Jules didn't have any of those things, Dorian knew. Jules took everything in stride, rolled with the punches, and his stress level was always three notches below Dorian's when it came to competitions.

Dorian didn't bother asking if Jules was nervous when he saw him that morning. He knew what the answer would be. Instead, he wished him good luck and took his seat in the stands.

It was always different on this side of the competition, being a mere spectator rather than participating. Most of the gymnasts were people Dorian already knew, but more than a few were newcomers to the scene. When he wasn't actively involved in it, he found that he paid less attention to the new names and faces. Jules was the only one that mattered.

Sitting in the stands, Dorian watched Cameron prepare for his bars routine. He looked nervous, slapping his hands together and barely nodding at whatever his coach was saying. Dorian remembered feeling like that, feeling like he was going to be sick moments before his first event. He supposed everyone felt that way at some point or another. Not Jules, though, he reminded himself, watching Jules walk over to Cameron and say something. Whatever it was, it didn't seem to bolster his confidence, and he looked worse for the wear when Jules turned away.

Dorian didn't like the feeling that crawled into his stomach as he watched Cameron step onto the mat. Jules stood off to the side watching, and Coach Harper patted his shoulder, his mouth curled into a cat-like grin.

Cameron's routine started off shaky, worryingly so. His arms shook as he caught himself, and Dorian frowned as he glanced at Jules. Jules appeared to be enjoying the mess of a show, though Dorian couldn't understand why. Of course, it was nice to see an opponent doing poorly, but there was something else going on. As he watched, a word came to mind — manipulation. Hadn't Harper said something along those lines already? Three years ago, the first time they'd met, he'd said that Jules had to give himself a leg up. Was Harper so concerned with winning that he'd do something as bad as sabotage to ensure it happened? Even to Jules, his shining star? Especially to Jules, Dorian thought as he realized. Jules was Harper's biggest success story since he'd made an Olympian of Christopher Norell back in the eighties.

Cameron made it through the routine, though it certainly wasn't the best he could have done. Dorian had seen him in practice and this was half of what he was capable of. As he came off the mat, Jules grinned at him and said something else that only seemed to make Cameron deflate even more.

Dorian didn't like it one bit, and when Coach Harper winked at Jules, something heavy settled in his stomach and there was no avoiding it this time. He'd have to say something. He couldn't let it slide. He wouldn't. Resigned, he leaned back in his seat. So much for a relaxing trip.

"Today went pretty well, huh?" Jules asked, tossing his bag on the hotel bed and grinning at Dorian. He reached out and pulled him down onto the bed, pressing a kiss to his jaw. "A few more days like that and I'll have another World Championship under my belt. Not too shabby."

Dorian didn't reply. He pulled away from Jules' mouth, though. A part of him didn't want to say anything, didn't want to ruin anything, but he had to. "What'd you say to Cameron today?"

"Rutherford?" Jules slid a hand up Dorian's back, pressing under his shirt, but Dorian didn't let himself get sucked into Jules this time. "Nothing, why?"

"You said something and he fucked up his whole routine," he pointed out. He knew he wasn't imagining it when Jules' smile widened slightly.

"He did fuck up pretty bad."

"Why are you smiling?"

"Why aren't you? It's good when other people don't do as well. Gives me a better chance at winning."

As much as Dorian understood the mentality — hell, he'd had the same one for years — something still didn't add up.

"You're targeting him," he said, and Jules sighed, letting his hand drop from Dorian's back as though preparing himself for a resigned conversation. Dorian didn't think Jules had the right to be annoyed here. He was the one picking on some poor kid who had done nothing to deserve it. "You're trying to make him mess up."

"If he can't run with the big dogs, he'll never make it," Jules pointed out. "It's just friendly competition."

"It's bullying," Dorian said flatly, crossing his arms and not budging an inch when Jules shot him a look. Jules couldn't talk his way out of this one. Dorian had seen it with his own eyes. He knew the sting of it deep down in his heart.

Jules shook his head, pushing himself up and rubbing a hand

over his head. "You're being a little overdramatic here."

"I don't think I am." Dorian stared at Jules, at Jules' nonplussed expression. How did he not see it? "You're running him down so he'll do worse, so you'll win easier. You've done it before."

"When?" Jules scoffed, and Dorian shot him a look.

"You did it to me three years ago."

"That was completely different," Jules argued. "Plus we were fucking."

"And I hated you," Dorian added, anger building in him as Jules brushed him off. "I hated what you were doing, and now you're doing it again to someone else, someone young and inexperienced, someone who could be a threat to you."

"It's not that big of a deal." He sounded annoyed now, as though what Dorian was accusing him of was preposterous.

"It is. It could get you in big trouble." Dorian shifted on his knees, pausing a second. "I know Harper's got something to do with it."

Jules' eyebrows came together at the mention of Harper. "Why do you think that?"

"Because he's always talking about your competition, and he's extremely competitive, and just, things he's said in the past make me think that he'd do anything to win, even if it meant turning you into something terrible."

"That's ridiculous," Jules said bluntly, pushing Dorian off him and standing. "He's always looked out for me. He's the only one who ever has."

"Excuse me?" Dorian asked incredulously. "Where have I been the last three years?"

"I just meant—"

"You just meant that if someone's not giving you continuous praise, it means they don't support you. Well, I have been there. And maybe Harper's not," Dorian replied, watching Jules cross the room. He didn't know how to get to Jules, to make him see what he was doing. "Maybe he's only looking out for himself. You're being a dick to Cameron because he wants you to. I know you're not that stupid. I know you wouldn't do it on your own."

Jules turned towards him, eyes narrowed. "You're just saying that because you think Harper doesn't like you, so you don't like him."

"He *doesn't* like me," Dorian snapped, anger getting the better of him. "Every time I talk to him, he makes some comment about how terrible it is that I got injured, like he's happy about it or something. Like he's glad I did so I couldn't be your competition anymore."

Jules rolled his eyes. "You're so fucking sensitive, Dorian. Not everything is about you and your injury. Coach doesn't care about it. Not everyone cares about it. It's time you finally got over yourself about it. You can't compete anymore, okay?"

Dorian couldn't believe Jules. He couldn't believe what was coming out of his mouth.

"What is wrong with you?" he demanded. "You're so blind to what Harper's doing to you that you can't even be rational. He's poisoning you. Did he tell you to be a dick during the Olympics too? Is that why you were such a monumental jerk? And when you win over Rutherford because you've gotten inside his head and torn down his confidence, will that make you feel better?"

"I don't have to listen to your crazy theories," Jules said instead of answering Dorian. He grabbed his bag off the floor and tossed it over his shoulder where it bounced off, the force giving away the annoyance that didn't show on his face. "I don't have time to fight with you right now. If you're upset because you can't compete anymore, then you shouldn't have come if you couldn't be supportive. What I do to win is my business. Rutherford or not, I'll win, and Harper will be there to support me because he always has."

"I'm trying to support you," Dorian replied, glaring at Jules, "but it's impossible when you're being so stupid. You're being a jackass to Cameron, and to me, and you refuse to listen to reason!"

Jules' eyes narrowed and he reached for the doorknob. "When you're done being selfish, why don't you call me? Until then, I'd rather be around people who are on my side."

He left before Dorian could say anything else. The door shut behind him, and Dorian stared. That hadn't gone as planned, but he couldn't say he'd expected it to go any better. Harper would always be a sore spot if Dorian pushed, but he couldn't let Jules go on being a jerk to Cameron, not when he'd done the exact same thing to him. It wasn't all Jules' fault, but Jules would be the one taking the blame if it went on much longer. If anyone caught on, if Cameron reported it, Jules could be kicked out of the competition. He could be banned from gymnastics entirely if the Board felt it necessary.

Annoyed, Dorian huffed and sunk onto the bed. Clearly Jules didn't want to listen to him, and there wasn't much he could do now that Jules was pissed at him. He'd just have to hope that Jules came to his senses before something terrible happened. As he sat back, he scoffed into the silence. He certainly wasn't holding his breath.

Jules had stopped fuming about ten minutes after leaving Dorian's hotel room, but that didn't mean he found Dorian's accusations any less wrong. How could he think that Harper was manipulating him? It was the most ridiculous thing he'd ever heard. Coach Harper was the one person in his life he could completely rely on, and it didn't make things better when Dorian accused him of sabotaging another competitor. Harper was just looking out for him like he'd always done.

Pacing around the locker room, Jules had to get out of his head. He shouldn't have been thinking about Dorian and his stupid theories. He had more important things to focus on. Still, he couldn't get Dorian's words out of his mind. What he was doing with Rutherford — the teasing — it was just for show, good old-fashioned hazing. It happened to everyone. There was nothing malicious in it, and if it affected Rutherford that much, he wasn't cut out for this kind of competition in the first place.

It had happened to Jules when he first started. It had happened to everyone. He'd never let it affect him, and people who did were just being sensitive. Dorian was overreacting.

The noise of a slamming locker brought Jules back to reality. He had to focus. He couldn't let himself be distracted by Dorian's petty thoughts. Dorian had never like Harper in the first place. He was just letting his prejudices get to him.

Across the room, Rutherford stood staring into his locker, shoulders hunched slightly.

Jules rose to his feet and crossed to him. Rutherford shot him a careful glance as he approached, and Jules smiled reassuringly. He could be nice.

"You've been doing pretty well," he said. Rutherford looked up carefully, almost confused. "Aside from that bars routine yesterday, you haven't fallen."

Rutherford jerked slightly and turned away from Jules. "Thanks," he deadpanned into his locker.

"You'll get by. Rings are today; that's your best event, right? Make sure you don't fall on that one." He winked at Rutherford, but Rutherford didn't reply.

See, totally nice. Turning away, he grabbed his towel and headed for the gym. Dorian was completely wrong about him, and he would regret ever saying anything once Jules won the championship.

"Jules." Coach Harper caught up with him outside the locker room, clamping a hand on his shoulder. "You ready?"

"Of course."

"Good." He shook him, then paused. "What's wrong?"

"Nothing." Jules flashed him a smile, but Harper could always see through him.

"What happened? Who got in your head?"

"It's nothing," Jules assured him. It really wasn't. He could handle Dorian and his delusions. He had for three years already. "Just Dorian being Dorian."

Harper's lips pressed together, hesitating as though debating whether or not to say what he was thinking. Jules knew that he would. He always did.

"I know how much you care for him," Harper said with a slight grimace, "but sometimes I wonder if he has your best interests at heart. We both know he can be a little self-centered."

Jules huffed out a laugh. 'A little' was an understatement for sure. Sure, Dorian had improved over the years, but all roads always seemed to lead back to him.

"I'm not sure he wants you to win all the time. I think he might be a little jealous that you get to compete and he doesn't. You're a great athlete and you deserve everything you get. Don't let him bring you down. You know what's best for you. Only you can choose that."

Jules nodded. It was exactly what he needed to hear. Dorian was making a mountain out of a molehill and putting Jules on top of it. It was exactly where Jules didn't need to be, not right now when there was a medal to win. Dorian knew that, so why was he making such a big deal out of nothing? Jealousy was the only answer that came to Jules' mind. Most of the time, Dorian pretended he was okay with not being able to compete, but Jules knew that deep down he hated having to watch and not participate. That was just the way Dorian was. It was how he would always be. Just the fact that he couldn't muster up enough support for Jules was insulting.

"You'll be fine," Harper assured him, leading him to the bench and sitting him down. "How's Rutherford?"

"Dorian thinks I'm being too hard on him." Jules rolled his eyes. "I'm completely nice. You know me."

Harper paused. "Don't be *too* nice. After all, you know what happened last time you were nice."

"What?"

"You ended up with Dorian." Harper guffawed, though Jules didn't. Even if Dorian was sometimes extremely annoying, he did love him. He forced a smile, though, when Harper looked at him.

"Yeah," he agreed simply, raising his gaze to the stands and scanning the seats for Dorian. He didn't see him immediately and looked away. Of course Dorian wouldn't come after their fight. He was just that stubborn. Oh well. He had other things to think about, like winning. It was important, after all. If he didn't win, his chances at competing in another Olympics could slip significantly. Dorian or not, he needed this.

Chapter 21

Growing Suspicions

Standing in the hall to the gym, Dorian hesitated. A part of him wondered if he should go in. Jules was probably still mad, probably didn't want to talk to him. Then again, Dorian hadn't come all this way to sit and pout in a hotel room.

He had come to watch Jules compete, to support him no matter how blind he was to the manipulation going into his career. He wished he could just hit Coach Harper and force him to admit his real goal. Dorian wasn't naturally violent, though, and the few times he'd been driven to violence, the consequences hadn't been good. His mind flitted briefly to that moment three years ago at the Olympics when he'd slammed Jules up against the locker. It had only served to make his teammates think he was losing it and to make himself feel stupider than normal for letting his emotions get the best of him.

Taking his seat, he searched for Jules on the mat—he always stood out with his shaved head and his red uniform. From far away, Jules didn't look worried. Maybe he'd already forgotten the fight. Maybe Dorian's words had had absolutely no affect on him. It wouldn't have surprised Dorian, after all; Jules wasn't one to hold grudges or take anything to heart. It almost annoyed Dorian, that Jules could let go of something so easily, that he didn't even care enough to really think about what Dorian said.

"Move over," Georgia said as she came down the row and took the seat next to Dorian. She took a moment to survey him and paused. "What's wrong?"

Hiding his emotions had never been Dorian's strong suit, and he sighed. "Nothing. Jules and I just had a fight."

"Uh oh," she said, patting his arm. "How bad was it?"

"Pretty sure we're not talking," Dorian muttered, but he paused. He could tell Georgia his thoughts on Harper. Maybe she would have some insight. After all, she'd been around the gymnastics world for a lot longer than he had. Turning away from the floor where Jules was getting ready to do his routine, he faced Georgia. "If I tell you something, do you promise not to tell anyone else?"

"Not even Brian?"

Dorian hesitated. "Maybe. Let me tell you first."

Georgia turned her full attention to him, and Dorian took a breath. He hoped this wouldn't sound completely paranoid.

"I think Coach Harper is using Jules to manipulate and possibly sabotage Rutherford."

For a moment, Georgia said nothing, gazing at Dorian, then glancing down at Jules in the pit. Her mouth pressed together and she tapped a finger against the armrest. "What makes you think so?"

"Just, the things Harper says to me, to Jules, the things Jules says to Rutherford. It's not something he would usually do. You know Jules. He's a nice guy usually."

Georgia raised an eyebrow. "He wasn't always nice to you."

"I know," Dorian admitted. It hurt to remember even though they'd long moved past it. "I think part of that might have been Harper too, but Jules doesn't see it. He looks up to Harper. He won't listen to me."

For a moment, he was afraid Georgia was going to brush this off as paranoia when she paused for a long minute.

"Do you have any proof?" she asked finally.

Dorian shook his head. Harper had never outright said anything about manipulating other competitors, not to Dorian anyway. Even if he had to Jules, there was no way Jules would admit it. Jules might not have even noticed it. Harper had such a slick tongue.

Georgia shook her head as well. "You could take it to the Board, but without real, hard evidence, there's not much anyone can do."

Dorian's heart fell, although he hadn't expected much better. She was right, of course. At this point, it was just suspicions. He couldn't prove anything, and even if he could, if he turned Harper in, Jules would probably never speak to him again. All he had was a feeling and the rumors that floated around. Georgia wouldn't be one to listen to gossip, but he wondered what she had heard. After all, coaching circles were different than gymnast circles.

"I'll talk to Brian," Georgia promised, "but without any proof, we just have to hope that Jules stays out of trouble and no one reports his behavior."

"You've never heard anything?"

Georgia paused. "Just murmurings. You know how people love to talk, but it's just talk."

It wasn't the answer Dorian wanted to hear. If only they could find someone to back him up. Jules wouldn't do it, but maybe there was someone else.

Crossing his arms, he sat back in his seat to watch Jules' floor routine. He'd seen it enough times before that he knew every step, every element, every pause. Jules did it flawlessly, as good as he'd ever done it, and if Dorian had been a judge, he would have given him a near perfect score.

Other gymnasts congratulated Jules as he jogged off the mat, and even Dorian could see his grin from this far away. As much as Dorian was glad he hadn't fucked anything up on his routine, he couldn't bring himself to feel completely happy. Jules had just ignored him, written off his concerns as petty jealousy. He'd thought they'd moved past that but apparently not.

His eyes drifted to Rutherford across the gym. The kid looked nervous, and it didn't seem to help when Jules went over and said something to him. If anything, he looked worse. Shaking his head, Dorian didn't know what to do. Jules wouldn't listen to him when it came to Coach Harper. Harper was like a father to him — he could do no wrong in Jules' eyes, and an attack on Harper was an attack on Jules.

He jumped at Georgia's hand on his.

"You'll get through it," she assured him.

Dorian wasn't going to give up. Even if Jules pissed him off, he'd find a way to help Rutherford and show Jules the truth.

"Hey, Rutherford," Jules said as he passed Rutherford along the benches. "Maybe someday you'll be as good as me. After your routine, how about you and I get a drink? I could show you a few tricks."

"I, I don't," Rutherford started to stutter.

Jules grinned, reaching out and grabbing his arm. "Relax, kid. I'm not as scary as you think. We'll have a good time, I promise."

Rutherford's eyes seemed to widen, and Jules released his arm. He could be nice. He'd show Dorian. He wasn't being a monumental jerk. He was just being a good competitor.

Leaving Rutherford, he headed to change and meet Harper for dinner. There were only a few days left in the competition and he needed all the strength he could get. He'd considered going to find Dorian and give him a hard time for not showing up today, but he didn't really want to get into another argument over something stupid.

"Good job today," Russell said, catching up to him outside the gym. "I hear you're the favorite now that Rutherford's been stumbling."

Jules smiled. "That's always nice to hear."

Russell cast him a sidelong glance but didn't comment. "How's Harper feeling about your chances?"

He said it the same way everyone always did — as though Harper wasn't their coach too. For some reason, it had always been different with Jules. They were closer than any of the other guys. They were more like father and son than coach and athlete.

"He seems happy."

Russell nodded, more to himself than to Jules. "I bet. Rutherford's been messing up a lot."

Jules smiled. "He's not the most confident kid. When I was his age, I was the cockiest thing ever."

"Still are."

Laughing, Jules elbowed Russell in the side. "Fuck off. At least I win so I can back it up."

"You'll do anything, won't you?" Russell asked offhandedly.

"Sometimes I think you're as focused as Dorian."

"Difference is I can take a joke," Jules replied. "Dorian takes everything seriously. Gotta walk on eggshells all the time."

"Then why do you bother?"

Jules glanced at Russell. He didn't talk much about his relationship with other people. Frankly, it wasn't any of their business.

He shrugged instead. "Despite his moments, I love him. He just makes me want to tear out my hair sometimes."

"You don't have any hair."

Jules grinned and threw an arm around Russell's shoulder as they walked toward the cafeteria. "Precisely."

He could handle Dorian. He could handle anything that came his way.

When the hotel room phone rang at four in the morning, Russell groaned and tossed a pillow at Jules, forcing him to roll over and answer.

"'Lo?" he asked, rubbing his eyes. It wasn't even remotely light outside yet, and they didn't have to be awake for another hour at least. Whoever it was had better have a great reason for waking him up so early.

"Jules." Coach Harper's voice came through the receiver, sounding much more awake than Jules felt. "Get up right now."

"What? Why?" Struggling to keep his eyes open, Jules felt himself sinking back into the warm, comfortable bed.

"We've got a problem."

That made Jules sit up, suddenly alert at the tone of Harper's voice. "What problem?" In the next bed, Russell stuffed the pillow over his head and rolled over.

"It's Rutherford."

As he said it, Jules' stomach sunk with apprehension. He didn't even have to ask as Harper went on.

"He's filed a sexual harassment suit against you."

"What?" Jules barked, and Russell groaned loudly. "That's impossible!"

"He did it last night, and he'll take it to the Board of the championship if we're not careful about how we handle this."

Jules wasn't listening, too wrapped up in the idea of a sexual harassment suit. He'd never come on to Rutherford. He'd never even suggested he was interested. He wasn't interested! *Fuck, fuck, fuck!* This could ruin everything. This could ruin his whole career.

Harper was still talking, but Jules didn't process a word. He was completely fucked.

"...Have a chat with Rutherford," Harper was saying. "We'll get it worked out. He's just taking it too personally. We'll get it all worked out. Don't worry."

Jules was worried, though. A suit like this would follow him around for life. He would lose everything. They had to work it out. He had to. His heart felt as though it had climbed into his throat, thudding tightly against his Adam's apple. For the first time in years, he felt shaky with nerves, unable to put together a comprehensive sentence. He needed to talk to Dorian.

"Hey," Harper said when Jules said nothing, too shaken to reply. "You're not losing because of some naïve kid. We'll work it out."

Jules nodded, then forced himself to speak. "Yeah, okay."

Harper said something else, but Jules didn't hear him and hung up a moment later. Russell had already fallen back asleep. Jules couldn't even think about sleep, though. There were only a few days left in the competition, and if this went too far, he could get kicked out. He could be banned from gymnastics for life if they didn't resolve this.

Kicking off the bed sheets, he rose and rummaged around for a sweatshirt and a pair of pants. They were too short, probably Russell's, but he didn't care. He didn't have time to waste. Instead, he grabbed his room key and left the snoring Russell behind.

He was lucky Dorian's hotel was close by and he didn't have to walk too far in the chilly early morning. He took the narrow stairway up to Dorian's floor and pounded on the door. It took far too long for Dorian to answer, and when he did, he looked entirely disgruntled at being woken up at fuck-all hours of the morning.

"Jules?" he asked, squinting in the darkness. His hair stuck up at odd angles and there were pillow lines on his face. "What are you doing?"

"He filed a fucking sexual harassment suit," Jules said, striding into the room without Dorian's invitation.

"Who?"

"Who?" Jules repeated, turning to Dorian and scoffing. Could he be so stupid? "Rutherford, that's who."

He expected Dorian to do something, to proclaim the injustice of the accusation. He didn't expect Dorian to pause and grimace.

"What?" Jules demanded, a ripple of annoyance piercing the queasy feeling he'd had in his stomach for the past fifteen minutes since the phone had first rung.

"Well," Dorian said slowly. "I mean, are you really surprised?"

"I didn't hit on him." Jules stared at Dorian. How could he be so calm about this? Dorian was the one to overreact and get upset over nothing, and now that there was a real problem, he didn't care? "I never did anything."

"You did harass him."

"I can't believe you're taking his side." This was incredible. Absolutely incredible. He couldn't even count on Dorian to be on his side.

Dorian had the good grace to look insulted at that. "I'm not taking his side. I'm saying he has somewhat of a legitimate claim here. You haven't been the nicest person. Every time you walk past him, he flinches."

"He does not," Jules sneered. That was a little overboard. "Why are you arguing with me? You're supposed to be..."

"What?" Dorian asked suddenly. "Consoling you? Telling you it's okay that you were a complete ass to him and now you're paying the consequences?"

"Don't you get it?" Jules snapped. "This could ruin my career. It could ruin my whole life, and you're just sitting here like you don't care at all. You're blaming me for it."

"I do care," Dorian insisted. "But you're not getting it, Jules. I could have done the exact same thing if I'd thought about it during the Olympics. The teasing and the joking and the nicknames and all that shit. It's not fun for the other person. It hurts a lot. Rutherford doesn't know you. He doesn't know that this isn't you. It's all

Harper."

"Just leave him out of this!" Jules had had enough of blaming Harper. "I don't know why you hate him so much. He's looking out for me, unlike you apparently. After everything we've been through, I thought you'd be a little more interested in helping than blaming everyone."

"You just can't see it!" Dorian snapped, hands balled into fists, and Jules didn't care if he was mad. He didn't care if Dorian wanted to put his fist through a wall or into his face. He didn't need any of this shit. "All you see is Harper being your best friend, your replacement dad, when all he cares about is winning. He'll do whatever it takes. You think every time you win, he has nothing to do with how other people do?"

"So now I can't win on my own?"

"That's not what I meant."

"But it is what you just said," Jules pointed out. The fear of the lawsuit was gone, replaced with anger at Dorian. "I guess I wasn't worthy enough to get to the Olympics on my own. I guess that even if you hadn't injured your ankle, I wouldn't have won?"

Dorian pressed his hands against his face as though Jules was frustrating him, and Jules felt much the same. This wasn't a conversation he'd ever expected to have with Dorian, or anyone for that matter. He was a good gymnast. He'd been training for most of his life, and Dorian couldn't just write off his wins as meddling by his coach.

"Jules, Cameron just filed a sexual harassment suit against you," Dorian said finally. "He's going for the throat. If you don't stop doing what you're doing, if you don't stand up to Harper, you're going to ruin your life. If you don't tell someone about Harper, you'll be kicked out for sure. No more competitions, no more gymnastics. They probably won't even let you within a hundred feet of a gym. Do you want to take the fall for someone who doesn't even care? Harper won't help you. He only cares about winning."

Jules shook his head. Harper wasn't the problem. Dorian was the problem. Why had he thought coming here was a good idea? Why had he thought that maybe Dorian could help? Be a shoulder to lean on? He didn't know where he'd gotten such a ridiculous idea.

"Thanks for your help, Dorian," he said instead, heading for the door. "I guess there's only one person I can really rely on, and it turns out it's not you."

He left Dorian behind, shutting the door too hard behind him. The slam didn't make him feel any better, though, and he sighed in the empty hallway. He had better figure this out and figure it out fast.

Chapter 22
Eye for an Eye

The words "I told you so" had surfaced in Dorian's mouth a few times during his conversation with Jules that morning, but every time, he had bit them down. Why? He wasn't really sure. After all, Jules was being a complete idiot about this whole thing. He refused to see Harper for who he really was, and as a result, he'd been slammed with a harassment suit. Jules was right: this could ruin him. But if he didn't get himself together, he wouldn't be able to stop it.

The championship would soon be coming to an end, and if the officials got wind of this, that could be the end. As angry as Dorian was, he wasn't going to let someone like Harper ruin Jules' career simply because he wanted to win. Even if Jules thought he didn't care, he did. He did care about Jules' career and personal reputation.

He had stewed for a while in his room that morning, debating if he should even bother. Jules had made it perfectly clear that Dorian wasn't someone he thought he could rely on. Why should he bother helping Jules when he was so blinded by his love of Harper? He couldn't see what Harper was doing to him, how far he'd go to win. He'd called Dorian's injury a 'leg up,' as if breaking his ankle had propelled Jules to a medal, as if it had been good luck.

If Dorian had his way, he wouldn't help Harper if his life depended on it. Jules' career did, though. Jules had to get out of this somehow, and if Harper couldn't sweet talk their way out of it, there was a good chance he was screwed. It was that thought, over all the annoyance at Jules, that made Dorian leave his room. He had to do something.

He didn't go to find Jules. They'd said everything they needed to as far as he was concerned. There was nothing more he could say to change his mind. Instead, he went to find Cameron. Maybe he could reason with him.

He found him at the arena, stretching and preparing for the day. Cameron's eyes lit up as Dorian approached, and he set down the weight. "Dorian, hey."

"Hi," Dorian replied, coming over and weighing his words carefully. "I heard about the lawsuit."

Cameron's expression fell slightly and he jerked a shoulder in response. "I didn't want to, but Jules has just been saying so many things, and the other day he invited me out for a drink. I just... my coach thinks it's for the best. I can't let myself get bullied, you know?"

Dorian nodded slowly. "Yeah, it's just, don't you think a lawsuit is a little harsh?"

Cameron shook his head, turning away from Dorian. "I know he's your friend, but he chose to say those things. He chose to harass me. My career is important to me and I have to protect it. They'll be taking the suit to the officials this afternoon. It's out of my hands after that."

"Don't you care about his career? This will ruin it."

Dorian was surprised when Cameron only shrugged, mouth set in a firm line.

"Why should I? He tried his best to ruin mine. If I lost here, I'd have no shot at the Olympics next year. Everybody knows that. He took it to another level and now I have, too. Once the press gets a hold of it, he'll never be allowed in another competition. He'll be banned from gymnastics and I won't have to worry anymore."

It hadn't been what Dorian had expected. He'd expected Cameron to be a pushover, to somehow just agree to drop the suit, but instead he was met with a stubborn response.

"Jules isn't a bad guy," Dorian said instead. "He's actually one of the nicest guys I know. He doesn't always come off that way at first, but he really is. Sometimes he just gets competitive and says things he doesn't mean."

Cameron glanced up. "So he was nice when you met him?"

Dorian hesitated. "Well, like I said, sometimes it takes a while." For the most part, he ignored how he and Jules had been at first. A part of him blamed Harper, though, suspected he'd had a hand in it.

"How can you defend him?" Cameron asked, abandoning the pretense of stretching. "You've heard what he said. You've experienced it firsthand, yet you're standing here telling me I should give him the benefit of the doubt."

"It's complicated." It really wasn't, but Dorian didn't feel like explaining his relationship with Jules to Cameron. He looked away at Cameron's inquiring gaze.

"Oh," Cameron said instead. "I'd heard a rumor…"

"What rumor?"

Cameron shrugged vaguely. "I heard you were gay, but I didn't think you'd be stupid enough to fall for Jules."

Dorian stared, taken aback at the words coming out of his mouth. "Excuse me?"

"You were one of the best gymnasts in the world, but then you injured yourself because of him. I don't know how you can care about him when he doesn't care about you. He only cares about winning."

"Jules didn't make me injure myself." It was just an unlucky coincidence.

"But you did injure yourself with him around. He's bad news. So I'm sorry you're mad about the lawsuit, but I'm not taking it back. He ruined his own career."

Dorian couldn't find anything to say to that, and Cameron appeared to have finished talking as he returned to his warm-up. He couldn't believe this was happening. This week was supposed to have been fun and relaxing. He wasn't supposed to be worrying about sexual harassment suits.

Pinching the bridge of his nose, Dorian left Cameron to his warm-up and stepped out of the gym to the crisp cool air of Rotterdam. There were only a few hours to fix this before it went public, before everything blew up and Jules took the fall. What could he possibly do? Jules didn't even want his help at this point, and sometimes he couldn't see why he was even bothering. He was bothering because he loved Jules and he didn't want to see his career go up in flames. That was why.

He needed to find proof. Good, hard solid proof that Harper was behind all this, but where to start? Maybe a long walk would help clear things up. At least it might give everyone some time to cool down.

"We can fix this," Harper said confidently, dropping a croissant onto Jules' plate. Jules could barely think of eating. The fight with Dorian was still fresh in his mind, and the thought of the lawsuit made him feel queasy. "It's just a matter of perspective."

"What does that mean?"

Harper leaned over across the table and lowered his voice. Jules leaned in as well. He really didn't want everyone in the cafeteria to know what was going on, although they probably would soon.

"Rutherford wants to slap you with a harassment suit? You turn around and put one on him. He's young. He's voracious. He'll do anything to win. If it means making up a lawsuit, he would do it."

For a second, Jules frowned. He didn't like the sound of that. "Isn't that what we'd be doing?"

Harper shrugged and reached for his orange juice. "An eye for an eye. We do whatever it takes to fight this thing. You're the much more respected figure in this sport, Jules. If you say he's made it up, people will believe you. If you countersue, it'll be his career that's ruined."

"I don't want to ruin anyone's career," Jules argued. He reached for the croissant, but the nausea resurfaced and he set it back down. Ruining someone's career wasn't his goal. He was just here to do gymnastics.

Harper only laughed, as though this wasn't a big deal. "You did it to Dorian three years ago. And look how that turned out. You won the bronze and you're on the way to another Olympics next year."

"I didn't ruin Dorian's career," Jules said, frowning.

"Don't be hard on yourself," Harper reassured him. "You did

what you had to do, what we had to do to win."

"So it's all about winning?"

"Now you're getting it." Harper grinned, but something rock hard dropped into Jules' stomach at the sight. He didn't want to believe it. Dorian couldn't be right about this. Harper was looking out for him. He always had. "Don't worry about this suit. I'll take care of it."

Something in the way he said it made Jules nervous, though. He didn't want another lawsuit. He didn't want this to become a huge mess. He just wanted it resolved so he could compete and win and go on with his life. Any more and things would get too complicated and it would become something that would follow him around for life. Just like Dorian's injury.

"Just don't make it worse," he told Harper, and Harper scoffed.

"Hey, I'm here for you, Jules. You can count on me." It went unspoken, but in his head, Jules heard, 'Unlike Dorian.'

Was that his voice or was it Harper's? He couldn't tell anymore and he didn't like it.

Sitting in his hotel room, Dorian scrolled through lists of video interviews on his phone from the past twenty years. There were too many to watch them all, but somewhere in all those competitors, there had to be his answer about Harper.

His first thought was Christopher Norell, the silver medalist Harper had coached back in the eighties. He had abruptly left gymnastics after his second Olympics and was hardly ever seen at events anymore. It was like he'd dropped off the face of gymnastics. Bringing up an interview, he set it to play on his phone.

A handsome man in his late twenties sat with a red backdrop, answering run-of-the-mill questions from reporters. Typical Olympic interviews, Dorian thought vaguely. He'd done enough of them himself to know. He was just beginning to think there wasn't anything there when the reporter asked about Norell's coach.

"Coach Harper is one of the premiere coaches in the world," the reporter said, and Norell nodded along, looking mostly bored with the questions. "Can you tell us some of his tips and tricks for winning?"

There it was. The hesitation. Dorian caught it, just for a second as Norell opened his mouth to respond. "Harper is a, uh, tough coach," he said, not looking at the camera. "He gets what he wants and no one gets in his way." He tried to play it off with a smile, but he couldn't fool Dorian.

If Norell knew it, then all of Harper's gymnasts knew it. None of Jules' teammates had ever mentioned it, but neither had Jules. If he could get them to talk about it, there might be a chance they could save Jules from his fate.

He clicked on another video, an interview done after Norell had retired. Norell looked a little older, a little more tired as he answered the questions.

"Why did you retire?" the reporter pressed. "You were at the top of your game."

Norell huffed and leaned back in his chair. "It just wasn't worth it anymore. There are people, some people in the sport, who will do anything to win. It's not particularly pretty. It's not particularly nice, but it happens. I was tired of being a pawn in someone else's scheme, so I left gymnastics."

"What people?"

Norell paused. "The people you think you can trust the most have their own motives that don't always align with yours. Coaches, friends. At some point, someone has to say stop."

He hadn't said Harper, but he'd implied it. Would that be enough?

Dorian's phone rang as he sat there, contemplating a way to bring this to the Board.

"Hello?"

"Dorian, it's Brian." He sounded serious which only made Dorian's heart beat a little faster in dread.

"Oh, hey," he said, trying not to sound nervous about Brian calling him out of the blue, but he couldn't help the way his voice wavered and the knot in his stomach tightened.

"I don't know if you've heard about Jules…"

"Yeah," Dorian muttered quickly.

"Well, it's gone to the press," Brian said. "Georgia told me about your suspicions. There won't be much time to do anything, not without hard evidence. You know as well as anyone that once the press gets a hold of the story, they never let go. It could take this one instance from a simple reprimand to a full-out ban from gymnastics."

Dorian's heart sunk into the hollow pit in his stomach. That was exactly what he'd feared.

"What can we do?" There had to be some way.

Brian huffed on the other end of the phone. Even though he wasn't Dorian's coach anymore, he still felt that Brian had to have some magical solution, some answer to this problem. "Not much," Brian replied. "It'd be your word against Harper's, and he's got a lot more sway with the Board."

"What if there was someone else, someone else who had experienced Harper's coaching firsthand?" It was desperate, but it was all Dorian had at the moment. Even if he could find Norell, would he talk about it? Would he be willing to sell out his former coach?

"Who?"

Dorian hesitated. "Christopher Norell?"

There was a pause while Dorian waited impatiently, glad he was sitting down because he wasn't sure he'd do too well standing right now. The anticipation, the worry caused him to feel shaky. He hadn't felt like this since his first day at the Olympics, so scared and determined at the same time.

"Norell, huh?" Brian said slowly.

"Yeah, you know him?"

"Actually, I do," Brian said after a moment. "We were on the Olympic team together one year. Good guy, Norell. Hasn't been around much since he retired."

It was Dorian's only hope. There was always Russell, but Russell wasn't Harper's favorite. He wasn't like Jules. Still, he may have experienced some of Harper's "encouragements."

"If he could testify," Dorian said, a little desperately. "Maybe it'd be enough. Him and Russell maybe. Harper is Russell's coach too. He has to have seen it."

"But would he?"

Dorian hesitated. He had no idea how loyal Russell was to

Harper. "It's our only shot."

"Hmm," Brian murmured. Dorian hoped he would help. Brian was the only one with enough of a standing to even think of leveling these charges against Harper, and he wouldn't do it unless he was absolutely sure it was true. "I'll call around, see what I can find out. In the meantime, keep an eye on Jules and Harper, if you can manage."

Dorian nodded. "Okay," he said. He didn't allow himself much hope as Brian hung up. If they couldn't get Norell, if they couldn't get Russell, Jules would be screwed.

Setting down the phone, Dorian rubbed his temples and sighed. He tried to tell himself it could be worse, but he didn't see how.

Jules could hear the whispers following him as he crossed the arena floor. It was like being back in the training center when he'd made out with the assistant coach in the locker room. Except this time they weren't whispering about his accomplishment but rather his failure. The lawsuit had gone to the officials. He knew because he'd received a call an hour ago asking him to come to the offices. It had been half an hour of grilling and questioning about Rutherford. He'd answered them as honestly as he could, but no decision had been made. He'd just been left to dangle.

He passed Russell on his way into the arena, and Russell only shook his head at him, as though he'd known something like this would happen. Even Russell wasn't with him. A pit started to form in Jules' stomach as he looked around. Everyone avoided his gaze as he passed. He was truly alone.

He jumped when a hand came down on his shoulder, but it was only Coach Harper falling into step with him. Harper easily ignored the furtive looks as they passed.

"It's good to get the people talking," he said, and Jules wondered for the tenth time that day why he wasn't worried, how he could be so confident that it would all blow over. "Keeps you fresh in their minds."

Jules didn't want to be in their minds for this reason. He'd rather be there for winning. That didn't seem to be the case at the moment, though.

"You talked to Dorian?" Harper asked as they passed the benches.

"Not since this morning."

"Best to keep him out of this," Harper went on. "He might be blinded by all the attention you're getting."

"I don't think he cares about the attention." Jules was more worried about the fact that he didn't even have Dorian in his corner anymore. He'd ruined that.

"Of course he does! He's an Olympian. They all want attention and now you've got it. Don't let his jealousy get in your way."

Jules wouldn't call it jealousy, not from the way Dorian had looked insulted when he'd brought it up. A few years ago, maybe, but now Dorian had matured. He remembered what Dorian had said before, about Harper not liking him. Before, Jules had always written it off as something stupid, but now he wondered if it wasn't true. Harper had never been completely supportive of their relationship. He'd never said as much, but Jules could tell.

"You think Dorian would have beaten me if he hadn't injured himself?" he asked finally.

Harper shook his head. "I won't say yes, but I will say we got damn lucky with that. You did a good job."

Jules' eyebrows furrowed at Harper's words. A good job? Lucky? How could Harper say something like that? Didn't he have any faith in his talent? He hadn't had anything to do with the injury. As he thought about it, more details came back. He remembered Harper's encouragements before he had left, his warnings about Dorian and Dorian's talent.

Maybe Dorian was right after all. What kind of a coach warned him to take down his opponents? Didn't he believe he could do it on his own? The horror of realization washed over him, and he felt sick to his stomach. Suddenly, he couldn't stand the weight of Harper's hand on his shoulder. It felt repulsive, like ten pounds of expectations, all the trust he'd put into Harper only to be thrown back in his face. Harper had used him, manipulated him into hurting other competitors just so he could win, so Harper could look better. It couldn't be true, though. Harper would never do that, not to him.

"We'll get Rutherford for this," he assured Jules. "This isn't the end."

Jules couldn't even formulate a response, too conflicted between horror and disbelief. His whole world was falling apart right in front of him and Harper acted like it wasn't a big deal, like it could be easily fixed.

It seemed like it was the end, and when they reached the bench, an official was waiting for them.

"Mr. Gardener, I'm afraid you've been pulled from the event."

"What?" Jules snapped, eyes widening, and the pit in his stomach grew. This couldn't be happening. He couldn't be pulled from an event. Harper laid a hand on his arm. He shook it off, though, his skin crawling where Harper had touched him. Luckily, Harper didn't notice.

"It's temporary until the charges against you have been investigated, but I'm going to have to ask you to leave the premises."

Jules couldn't believe this. It was impossible. He shook his head at the man. "No, that's wrong," he said. "I can't be pulled. I have to compete."

"I'm sorry," the man just said, his face stone cold. "I must ask you to leave. Make this easier on everyone, Mr. Gardener. You don't want security called, do you?"

"Come on, Jules," Harper said quietly, pulling him away despite the fact that Jules didn't want to go anywhere. When they were out of earshot of the official, Harper lowered his voice. "You're not out yet. I'm calling my lawyers and filing a suit against Rutherford. We do whatever it takes to win, okay?"

Jules didn't nod, letting himself be pulled past the other gymnasts. He felt all of their eyes on him as they went, the whispers that grew into barely concealed mutters as he passed. He was completely fucked.

Dorian pushed his way through the mob of reporters gathered around the front doors of the arena. He hated reporters, and when all they wanted to talk about was the rumors of a sexual harassment suit, he didn't want any part of it.

"We've been hearing reports that a sexual harassment suit has been filed against Jules Gardener, the former US Olympian," a reporter nearby said into a camera as Dorian passed. "This has yet to be confirmed by the Board of the championship, but Gardener was pulled from an event earlier today. Reports speculate that he will be banned from gymnastics if the rumors are true of sexual harassment."

Dorian pressed on. He didn't want to hear anymore.

"Has Jules ever made inappropriate advances?" another reporter asked, and Dorian turned to see Cameron standing in front of the camera. Cameron nodded gravely.

"I hate to say it, but it's true. I felt my safety was in question."

Dorian's blood boiled at that and he bristled, turning to face Cameron from behind the camera. Cameron caught sight of him, and for a second he looked uneasy, but then the reporter asked him another question and he was wrapped up in the attention again.

Dorian couldn't stand it. He strode away quickly, pushing out of the mob and into the street. This was getting completely out of hand.

"We're just getting reports that James Harper, Jules Gardener's coach, has countersued Rutherford!"

Dorian turned sharply, but he couldn't hear anymore over the clambering of the other reporters to get the new story. A huge mess, that's what it was. How could anyone hope to fix this? The only way was to go to the Board, to unveil the truth about Harper, but even then it wasn't as though he could just walk into the offices and demand to see the president of the USA Gymnastics group. Even Jules couldn't.

He needed Brian. Reaching into his pocket, he pulled out his phone and scrolled down, stopping on Brian's name. He hadn't heard back yet, but they were running out of time. Dorian had called Russell, left a message, but he had no idea if Russell would even help. His thumb hovered over Brian's name but Dorian's phone beeped with a new text message.

Ten o'clock—come to the conference room at the arena. The message was short and to the point, but it made Dorian's heart jump with hope. Maybe all wasn't lost quite yet.

Chapter 23

Standing Trial

The day had gone on forever, quite possibly the longest day of his life, and Jules had shut himself up in his room. He had tried watching TV, but all it was was news about the competition. He hated seeing his face like this, plastered over the sport's channels with that sniveling Rutherford playing the victim. Now he knew how Dorian had felt when he'd injured himself. So he hadn't been the nicest person ever. He had never threatened to do anything sexual to him. It was a complete lie.

Harper's news of the countersuit hadn't made him feel any better either. Countersuing for libel and defamation of character. It was all getting out of control. Jules didn't like it. He didn't like not knowing what was going to happen to him, if he was going to be banned from gymnastics for life. Would he be like Lance Armstrong, a blight on the sport?

Groaning, he sunk down on the bed. He'd been pacing for hours, long enough that his muscles were beginning to cramp. He should stop before he ruined anything more in his life. Reaching down, he massaged his calf and tried to focus on something positive. There wasn't much that he could see at the moment. Either way, he was screwed. Even if the Board didn't expel him, he'd still be forever branded as a sexual harasser. That would be great for sponsors. No one would touch him. He hadn't found it in him to call Dorian or go see him. Dorian would probably just tell him he'd known it all along and that he deserved what he got for trusting Harper so blindly. Admitting it made him feel even worse, and he rolled over onto his side. He still felt queasy. He truly was stupid and Dorian had known it all along. Besides, Dorian was probably enjoying his fall from grace. He did deserve that, at least.

Jules grabbed a pillow and stuffed it over his head, trying to block out his thoughts, the worries that ate at the edge of his conscience. There was no escaping them and after a while, he merely lay on the bed, gazing blearily at the ceiling and praying that the decision would come quickly and put him out of his misery.

Dorian wasn't sure he'd ever been this nervous in his life, waiting before the Board of the championship. He felt like a child at a recital, sure he was going to forget whatever he was supposed to say, afraid his knees were going to buckle.

They sat there, a group of twenty or so men and women in suits and looking particularly grave as Brian rose from his chair to speak. Dorian recognized Christopher Norell in the chair next to him, along with Russell, who shifted in his chair and met Dorian's eyes briefly. Georgia shot him a small, encouraging smile from her seat.

Brian stood before the Board, looking completely calm — exactly the opposite of how Dorian felt at the moment. "I'd like to bring forward evidence against James Harper in the manipulation of Jules Gardener and the Rutherford harassment suit."

The Board muttered amongst themselves until a tall man in a sleek suit spoke up. "What evidence do you have to support this claim?"

Brian nodded at Dorian. This was it. Dorian felt his knees shaking as he rose from his chair and stepped into the middle of the room. This was his only shot.

"I've known Jules for over three years now. He's one of the best people I know, and I know that he wouldn't purposefully be mean to someone without help." He hesitated. He wasn't good at talking. He never had been. "Coach Harper has encouraged disparaging actions towards Jules' opponents in the past and in the present."

"What do you mean in the past?" the man asked.

"When I first met Jules, he was, well, he wasn't very nice," he said lamely. "He said things and did things that could have been considered harassment."

"Such as?"

Dorian frowned. He really wasn't helping Jules' case. "Name-calling, mental games, some physical discomfort... but he's not like that. It was just because of Harper."

"Coach Harper told him to do this?" the man asked, sounding skeptical. "He has told you this?"

"Well, no, but—"

"You're saying that Mr. Gardener's actions resulted in the injury of your ankle and further forced retirement from gymnastics?"

"What? No!" Dorian said, shaking his head sharply. "My injury was purely my fault. Injuries happen all the time. Jules had nothing to do with that."

The man still looked skeptical, raising an eyebrow at his neighbor. Dorian felt something well up inside him, a fierce desire to prove that Harper had done this. Harper had to be held accountable for his actions.

"I've talked to Harper plenty of times, and every time, he seems happy I was injured, as though it was part of his plan all along to get Jules a medal at the Olympics. He called it a 'leg up' like it was good luck, as though he couldn't have done it better himself."

"Despite that," the man said, "it doesn't prove anything."

Dorian felt his stomach drop, a hollow pit taking its place. There was nothing left. There wasn't much more he could say to prove his point. "Look, Jules is one of the most loving, caring people I've ever met. If it wasn't for Harper, he would never sabotage anyone for his own personal gain. Harper is like a father to him, he looks up to him, and that's why he went along with it."

His heart fluttered in his throat as the Board muttered to each other. Glancing over, he sought out Georgia. She nodded at him.

Brian stood again, interrupting the chatter. "We have other testimonies to support Dorian's."

The man in the suit nodded gravely, clasping his hands on the table. Dorian was glad to leave the middle of the room and collapse into his chair, legs feeling like jelly. Georgia took his hand and gave it a light squeeze of reassurance.

Norell stepped up, looking much more impressive than Dorian

probably had. His face was older than the videos, more lined, but he still had a gymnasts' body under his clothes.

"I trained under Coach Harper for many years," he said, voice serious. "I can't count the number of times he encouraged me to look down on another competitor, to find their weak spot and exploit it. It wasn't for my benefit but for his. If I did well, he did better. My second year at the Olympics, Harper pointed out a gymnast on the Russian team, the favorite to win, and he told me to do whatever it took to bring him down: emotional blackmail, even physical harm." Norell sighed deeply. "I refused to follow his advice. That was when Harper threatened to tell the Board that I was unfit to compete. As most of you know, I'd been injured a few months before the trials. I'd been working hard to get back into competitive shape and I'd lied about the amount of damage. Harper had helped pay off the medics to allow me to compete. If I didn't go through with his plan, he would have told the Board about the pay-offs and blamed them solely on me when he helped do it."

For a moment, there was absolute silence in the conference room. Dorian had never imagined that Harper would go that far, especially with someone like Norell, someone who had been his pride and joy. It seemed to come as a shock to the Board as well, and Dorian allowed himself to hope for just a second.

Norell shrugged after a minute. "I decided then and there that I didn't want to continue competing, not if this was what I had to do. It wasn't worth the potential injuries, the damage to others I could have done, and had done in the past. I retired and Harper told everyone that he'd made a champion and I just couldn't take the pressure. It saddens me that he's still at it twenty years later. I have no doubt that he has encouraged this Mr. Gardener to do the same."

Without waiting to be dismissed, Norell returned to his seat. Dorian met his eyes, and Norell nodded briefly at him. A wave of something like relief washed over him, but it wasn't over yet.

"Russell?" Brian prompted.

Russell moved to the center of the room. Dorian's heart climbed back in his throat. What would Russell do?

Russell glanced at him for just a second, but then he turned to the Board. "Harper is my coach and has been for several years now.

Same with Jules. He's been training with me for a while now. Harper doesn't like me the same way he does Jules. I guess he doesn't see the same potential." He huffed, almost a laugh. "It's no secret that Harper is a hard coach to please. He wants all his gymnasts to be champions, and if he thinks they can't be or that there's something in his way, he finds a way to make it happen. I know before the last Olympics, he brought up Dorian to Jules. He talked about this up-and-coming gymnast that Jules had to beat, that he had to do anything to unseat him. I guess that one sort of blew up in his face." He smiled at Dorian.

"So Coach Harper has directly told you to exploit other gymnasts in an effort to win?"

Russell nodded. "He says it's a strategy, but..." He trailed away with a shrug.

"Why haven't you come forward before?" the man asked, and Dorian felt his hope drain out of him. Why hadn't they? Why hadn't anyone?

"Would you accuse your coach, a man who's coached more Olympians than anyone else, of sabotaging other competitors? No one would believe you."

"And why have you come forward now?"

Russell looked the man straight in the eye. "Jules may not be perfect, but he's my teammate and he doesn't deserve to take the blame for Harper in any situation."

Dorian stood abruptly, propelled from his chair by a desire to support Russell, to prove that this wasn't just a waste of the Board's time.

"Please," he said as he joined Russell. "You've heard testimonies. You've heard what Harper does to his gymnasts. It's not fair to expel Jules and not look into Harper. You have to consider it."

The man held Dorian's gaze for a long moment, then arched an eyebrow. "The Board will discuss what we've heard before making a decision. Please take your seat, all of you."

Dorian and Russell returned to their chairs as the Board drew together. Georgia smiled at Dorian as he sat.

"What?" he asked at her misty eyes.

"I'm just so proud of how much you've grown," she said. "Who would have thought that you, the boy who couldn't brush off a single comment three years ago, would stand up for someone else, someone you care about."

"Why wouldn't I?" Dorian asked. "I love Jules, even when he's insufferable."

Georgia laughed and pulled Dorian into a hug. Dorian returned it, smiling into her shoulder. No matter what happened, at least he'd tried. That was as much as he could hope for anymore. At least he'd tried.

Jules didn't know how many hours had passed, but it was enough that his joints were getting stiff. His back cracked as he pushed himself up from the bed. It was agony waiting, the torture of knowing that his fate was being decided as he sat there, unable to do anything about it. He should have said something about Harper. He should have told the Board about him, about his "tips" for dealing with Rutherford.

Too late now, though. He'd missed his chance, and now he might be banned from gymnastics forever because of it.

Sitting there, he contemplated getting something to eat, but he wasn't hungry. He just felt empty. He couldn't sleep either. Darkness was already falling outside, but he didn't feel tired. The door opened a moment later and Russell entered, casting a quick glance at Jules and continuing onto his bed.

"Alright, say it," Jules said when Russell said nothing.

"I've got nothing to say."

"Sure you do." Jules pushed himself up from the bed and arched an eyebrow at Russell. Russell wasn't known for keeping his mouth shut. "Harper's a bastard who only cares about himself and now I've got myself in deep shit for ever listening to him. Isn't that right?"

Russell arched an eyebrow at his words, so unexpected. "He did it because he thought you had the most potential. You're his prize. He's obsessed with winning."

Jules groaned, flopping back down on the bed. He felt terrible. His stomach was tied up in knots. It made him sick to think about all the time he had spent looking up to Harper. How could he have been so stupid? Harper didn't care about him. He only cared about winning and doing whatever it took, even if it meant running others down and making up lawsuits. "Fuck me," Jules muttered.

Russell was silent for a moment, then, "He's been expelled."

"Who?"

"Harper."

Jules sat up abruptly. "What do you mean, expelled?"

"The Board expelled him from the competition. They had a meeting earlier. They pulled in other gymnasts to give testimony on him, me and Christopher Norell. He's expelled pending an investigation by the Board."

"How is that possible?" No one else knew about Harper, about what he'd done.

Russell shrugged. "Brian Dunaway called it in."

"Brian?" How would Brian have known—he stopped himself. There was only one answer to that question. Dorian. After everything he'd said to Dorian, everything he'd accused him of, Dorian had been the one to come to his rescue this time. He only felt worse now, and when his phone rang, he nearly jumped out of his skin. "Hello?"

"Mr. Gardener, the Board would like to speak with you," came a woman's voice through the receiver. "Please be at the conference room in half an hour."

"Uh, yeah, okay," he said before she hung up with a crisp, "See you soon." He set down the phone slowly.

"What was that?" Russell asked as Jules rose from the bed.

"The Board wants to see me." It couldn't be good, whatever it was, but he had to go. His last march. The thought didn't make him feel better.

"Good luck," Russell said, and for once, Jules knew he meant it.

Chapter 24

Going for Gold

Dorian couldn't believe he'd done it. He couldn't believe it had actually worked. It had taken hours for the Board to make up their minds, but they finally had. It felt almost as if he was living in a dream. Harper would be investigated. Jules would be safe.

Jules was probably still pissed off at him, but Dorian didn't care. He wouldn't let him ruin his career for someone who didn't care about him. Harper would get what was coming to him.

Outside the conference room doors, press clamored, waiting and hoping to get a glimpse of Jules when he came out. Dorian hadn't seen him go in, but he knew he was in there from the way the reporters kept talking. It made him sick to listen to them speculate about Jules' career, the fate of gymnastics.

Rutherford was busy enjoying the attention, answering any and all questions put his way. As much as he had seemed like a nice, naïve kid, Dorian wasn't sure anymore. He couldn't tell who was genuine and who wasn't.

"Do you think Jules will be banned from gymnastics?" yet another reporter asked, and Dorian turned away. He didn't want to hear any more speculations. He felt a hand on his shoulder and turned to find Georgia there.

"Should be over soon," she assured him. Dorian wasn't sure he could take the wait much longer. He just wanted to make sure Jules was okay. Even if Jules didn't forgive him, at least he'd done all he could. Georgia patted his arm and moved away. "I have to find Brian. It'll be fine." She disappeared into the crowd and Dorian stood back against the wall to wait.

"Aren't you Dorian Stuart?" one of the reporters asked abruptly, turning to him, and Dorian frowned. They were the last people he wanted to talk to at the moment. As a camera swiveled into his face, his stomach swooped as he was reminded sharply of all the interviews he'd been forced to do after the Olympics. The woman pressed forward with her microphone. "Do you have a comment on Jules Gardener's situation? How do you think it will affect the reputation of gymnastics?"

Dorian hesitated. "I've known Jules for the past three years, and he may be many things—cocky, a smartass, a great gymnast—but he's not a predator. He cares about his competitors and he wants them to do well. I'm sure everything will turn out fine. Gymnastics has weathered scandals before. It always seems to come out alright." He didn't have the charm Jules had with the press, but at least he could form words with a camera shoved too close to his face. He managed to flash the reporter a smile. She opened her mouth, no doubt to ask any number of inane follow-up questions, but behind her, the door to the conference room opened and Board members spilled out.

"Thanks!" she said flippantly, waving at her cameraman to push through the crowd to where the men and women in suits were attempting to leave.

Straining on his toes, Dorian searched for Jules. He couldn't have slipped out.

"Jules!" a reporter shouted, practically barreling Rutherford over in their haste to converge around Jules as he stepped out. "Jules Gardener! What do you have to say to the accusations of sexual harassment?"

Dorian grimaced at the question, and he couldn't understand how Jules merely brushed off the question with half a smile.

"Haven't you heard that gossip is bad for your health?" he replied simply, pushing through the reporters instead of answering their shouted questions. Cameras flashed and Dorian couldn't hear himself think over the garbled questions that Jules clearly had no intention of answering.

By the time he reached Dorian, even he looked frustrated by the sheer amount of questions being thrown at him.

Dorian opened his mouth as Jules reached him, but no words came. Jules glanced around briefly.

"Come with me," he said, jerking his head down the hall. Dorian didn't even question it as he followed Jules, ducking out of the crowd and dodging cameras and microphones. From behind him, he heard someone spot Brian.

"Mr. Dunaway! How will Mr. Gardener's actions reflect on the Olympics? Will it hurt his chances at another bid in London in 2012?"

Dorian rolled his eyes, but Brian at least provided a distraction from the reporters still trying to get Jules to comment.

"In here," Jules said, opening a door and nodding Dorian inside. It was just a long, empty meeting room, the windows overlooking a canal. Dorian shut the door tightly behind them as Jules turned to face him.

"You were right about Harper and me," he said without hesitation. "You were right about everything and I owe you a huge apology." He sighed, and Dorian felt his heart swelling with relief. "I'm sorry, Dor, for being such a jerk and not trusting you."

"I forgive you," Dorian said simply. "I'm just glad they didn't kick you out."

Jules smiled, rubbing his head. "Thanks for that. I hear it was your turn to be the knight in shining armor."

"Well, you needed it."

Jules nodded, wrapping his arms around Dorian's waist. "I did." He leaned in and kissed him.

Dorian sighed into it, the tension draining out of his body as he pulled Jules in tighter. The past few days had been some of the worst, not being able to talk to Jules. At least it was over now.

"You're an idiot," he murmured against Jules' mouth.

Jules just grinned. "Yeah," he agreed. "And I really am sorry. You were totally right about Harper. You know he said we got lucky you were injured."

Dorian didn't have much to say to that. "What about the competition?"

"I'm not banned," Jules replied. "The Board agreed that Harper was the main problem, although I was given a very strong reprimand and warned that if anything like this ever happened again, they wouldn't think twice about banning me from the sport."

"Good to know."

"Don't worry," he assured Dorian. "I don't plan on ever reliving this experience."

It was certainly a relief, Dorian had to say. He hoped he would never have to go through this again. Dorian jumped at a knock on the door a second later and pulled away from Jules. "If that's a reporter, tell them to fuck off."

Jules laughed but moved to the door anyway. He opened it to reveal Cameron standing there, looking more nervous than he had so far the entire week.

"Rutherford!" Jules exclaimed, looking glad to see him. "I just want to say that I am so deeply sorry for what I said to you this week. You had every right to file that suit."

Cameron scuffed his shoes against the floor, looking young once more. "I'll drop the suit," he said finally. "I don't want to ruin your career. I-I guess I was kind of jealous." He looked at Dorian, and Dorian frowned.

"Of what?"

"Of you, peaches," Jules supplied when Dorian didn't get it. His eyes widened as he understood. He certainly hadn't seen that coming, but then again, Jules would have said he had the observation skills of a dead turtle.

Cameron cleared his throat, looking awkward, as well he should. What kind of person did such a thing out of jealousy? Then again, he'd been overdramatic more than a few times when it had come to Jules in the past. "I thought maybe if you and Jules broke up... if you thought he'd done something..." He shook his head. "I'm sorry."

"I know Jules better than that," Dorian pointed out.

Cameron nodded, staring at the ground now. "I am sorry to both of you."

"Hey, who's getting all mushy?" Jules interrupted, slinging an arm over Dorian's shoulder. Dorian wouldn't so easily forgive, but it had never been a problem for Jules. "How about we all get a drink and forget this ever happened."

"No drinking. You're still competing," Dorian said, and Jules pressed a kiss to his cheek.

"Yes, dear."

Dorian stirred his small cup of coffee, less interested in drinking it. Across the table, Georgia enjoyed a pastry while Brian sipped his coffee.

"I just can't thank you guys enough," Dorian said after a moment. "For helping me and Jules. I know you didn't have to."

Brian stopped Dorian with a raised eyebrow. "We're all part of a team," he said simply. "That means helping each other out."

Dorian nodded. He wished there was more to say, a way to truly thank them. Buying a cup of coffee just didn't seem like enough.

"What'll happen to Harper?" he asked instead.

"There'll be an investigation," Brian said, shrugging. "Most likely he'll be banned from coaching."

"So Jules won't have a coach." He supposed he should feel guilty, but considering the harm Harper had done, he didn't feel bad at all.

"Jules can always shop around," Georgia put in. "There are plenty of great coaches out there. Speaking of, what are your plans after graduation?"

"I have a job coaching kids for now, at least until I have enough experience to become an assistant coach somewhere."

"You know," Georgia said, her eyes lighting up. "If they promote Jules' assistant coach to head coach, there'll be a spot open." She looked at Brian expectantly.

Dorian wouldn't allow himself to hope, but he couldn't help the spark of excitement that burst within him. It would be perfect, too perfect.

Brian nodded as he contemplated the idea. "I'm pretty well-acquainted with the hiring board at the Center. I could see what I can do."

"No, Brian, you can't," Dorian said despite himself. "I don't want any favors."

"It's not a favor." Brian waved him away. "You're a talented kid,

Dorian, and you have a great eye. You'd be doing them a favor."

Dorian opened his mouth to argue some more, but Brian shot him a look and he stopped himself. Instead, he sighed. "I'm glad you guys were here this week."

"Oh, you barely need us anymore," Georgia said with a pat on his arm. "Just try not to make us too irrelevant in our own sport?" She grinned.

Dorian laughed. "I'll try not to." Sitting back in his chair, he reached for his cup and smiled. This week hadn't turned out so bad after all.

"Maybe we shouldn't leave," Jules said, lying across Dorian's bed as Dorian packed the last of his clothes in his suitcase.

"And what exactly would we do here?" Dorian asked, reaching for his jeans. He was never sure how things could get so scattered after only a few days in a hotel room, but things always managed to get away from him.

"Buy a little house by the canal." Jules shrugged. "Plant sun-flowers and watch them grow."

"And be bored out of our minds," Dorian pointed out. It was a nice idea, but there were too many responsibilities to take care of back home. "Plus I have school. Finals start in a few weeks and you have to start preparing for the Olympics."

"It's months away," Jules dismissed him. "What am I supposed to do about my lack of a coach anyway? Harper's most likely going to be fired by the Board."

"You'll find another coach." Like Georgia had said, there were plenty of great coaches in the country and any of them would be glad to have Jules as their athlete.

"Fuck," Jules groaned, rolling over and sighing at Dorian. "It would be so much easier if you were my coach."

"I don't have enough experience," Dorian pointed out.

"You have more experience in competing and training than half the coaches out there."

"Yeah," he agreed with a smile. He hadn't told Jules about Brian's offer yet. After all, nothing was set in stone. He didn't even know where he'd be in the next few months.

Jules shifted up, wrapping his arms around Dorian's stomach. "Have I told you lately how grateful I am for your little speech?"

"Yes."

"Well, I am. I know you hate the press."

"All they want is a story and they don't care who they hurt in the process." Dorian leaned into Jules' grip. He didn't want to go back to school where only tests and papers waited for him. He'd rather stay in that tiny hotel room with Jules. Unfortunately, reality had to set in sometime, and if he didn't leave soon, he'd miss his flight.

"What are you doing after graduation?" Jules asked abruptly.

"I applied for a few jobs in New Orleans, at real gyms, not kid gyms, but we'll see," Dorian replied. "Maybe I'll just become a male stripper."

Jules huffed a laugh into his shoulder. "I'd like to see that."

"Maybe I'll get a real coaching job," he said. "You never know. I do know a lot of people in the gymnastics world, if anyone misses me." The thought of going back to the gym, back to normal life after this week seemed surreal. He missed this part of his life — the competitions, seeing Jules on a regular basis. When would he ever have that again? Could he even get it back?

"You know who misses you?"

"Who?"

"Me," Jules replied. "And I was thinking that after graduation, you should move in with me."

Although Dorian had considered it before, it still came as a surprise when Jules suggested it. They'd never discussed it before, and a few days ago, it had seemed like such a huge step.

"Move in with you?" he repeated instead of answering, his mind whirring with the possibilities, what it would really mean to move in with Jules. Hadn't he just said a few days ago that he didn't want to be that person? Living with his boyfriend with no job? Then again, he thought as Jules watched him through big, brown eyes, what did he really have to gain by not moving in with Jules? He'd spend the next few years working at the gym, coaching little kids, and he'd never see Jules except a few times a year. Who was he really punishing here?

Dorian didn't have a good answer for his question. There was absolutely no valid reason why he shouldn't move in with Jules.

"What about this week?" he asked, though. "You really think we could make it work?"

"I trust you," Jules assured him. "I was a jerk and you were right. Everything worked out okay, so now you just gotta trust me that this is a good idea. You can move in with me and you'll find an awesome coaching job, not something a high schooler could do."

Dorian smiled slightly. "You think so?"

"I know so." Jules paused. "Is that a yes?"

There was really nothing for it, and Dorian couldn't help smiling as he nodded. "Yeah, it's a yes."

Jules laughed and hugged Dorian around the middle, pressing a kiss to his cheek. "Alright. I'll expect you on the first flight out after finals."

Dorian grinned at his enthusiasm, but it had already spread to him. Despite their differences and all the obstacles they'd had to overcome, Dorian knew it would work out. They'd come too far to go back now, and he looked forward to what the future would bring.

Epilogue

Three years later

"Have you always had this much shit?" Jules asked as he lugged in the last of the boxes.

Glancing around the apartment, Dorian took a deep breath. At the moment, it was filled with cardboard boxes, ready to be unpacked and settled into their new place.

"I still don't understand why we couldn't have stayed in my apartment."

"Because it's an hour from the Academy. Since they closed the center, there's no reason to stay there anyway."

"Yeah, yeah," Jules agreed reluctantly. "Harper really screwed everyone over. I can't believe they shut down."

"Gave them an opportunity to open up the Olympic Academy," Dorian pointed out, pushing a box off the couch and sinking down. It had already been a long day of moving, but it had at least distracted from the nerves he felt about Monday— when he'd take his new position as Head Coach at the Academy. After three years of working his way up the coaching chain, he'd landed a great position. In fact, the Academy had contacted him about the job.

Jules hummed and took the seat next to Dorian. "You get to mold young minds, terrorize them with visions of injuries."

"I'll just show them my Olympics tape."

Jules laughed. "That'd scare 'em straight." He slid an arm over Dorian's shoulders. "You'll be fine. You'll scare them even without a tape."

Dorian smiled. "Thanks."

It was nice, being in a new apartment in a new city. Even if Dorian was nervous about starting, he knew he'd do fine. After all, he almost always succeeded at the things he tried.

Dorian paused, glancing at Jules next to him. The years hadn't changed him much. Dorian elbowed him gently in the side.

"You're okay with moving, right?"

"I would go anywhere you would, peaches, even to New Jersey." He said it in all seriousness and Dorian shook his head.

"I would never force you to go there."

"And that is why I love you."

Dorian smiled. "I thought it was because of my ass."

"That too," Jules agreed, pressing a kiss to his cheek. "We're moving for your career. It's not like mine requires I live anywhere specific. I don't have to start training again for another year."

"You should stay on top of it," Dorian reminded him, but Jules ignored him.

"You worked hard to get here, and soon, you'll be training your own Olympians. I can handle a new apartment. Besides, it's bigger. Got a nice view of a... parking lot. When it snows, you won't even be able to tell."

"That's the spirit." Dorian grinned.

"Now, let's get unpacked," Jules said, staring around at the boxes.

Dorian paused for a moment. Unpacking wasn't exactly what he had in mind. Leaning over, he pulled Jules into a slow kiss. "Or we could break in the new apartment."

Jules made a curious noise, grinning against his mouth. "I like the way you think, peaches."

"Don't call me that," Dorian said, and Jules laughed.

Author's Notes

It's been a long journey on this novel, starting way back in 2012 when the first draft was written. Although it was (unsurprisingly) inspired by the Olympics airing at the time, I remember watching the 2008 Olympics four years before, staying up until 2AM just to watch the gymnastics events. I even visited the Bird's Nest and Olympic Village in Beijing a few years later which certainly helped writing this. I've always been a fan of gymnastics, women's mostly, thanks to my cousin who coached for many years. Writing *Vaulted* was a great insight into the sport. *Vaulted* has been through many versions in the past two years, and the character of Dorian took quite some time to evolve. Some may see him as an unlikeable protagonist, but he holds a special place in my heart. At times, it felt like this novel would never come to fruition, but I'm glad it finally has. Thanks to everyone who worked on it and made it better, and to those who had to listen to me talk about it for two years straight: you are what keeps me going.

About the Author

E.E. Grey started to write fresh out of high school, but the hobby grew over time. Now Grey has completed six novel-length works and over three hundred short stories. When not writing, Grey likes to travel, having visited twenty countries already with several still on the list for the future. Baking sugar-filled desserts for friends is Grey's other favorite pastime.

Works by E.E. Grey:

Cigarette Burns
Brush with Death
By the Hour
Checking Out
Vaulted

About the Publisher

www.ingramcontent.com/pod-product-compliance
Lightning Source LLC
Chambersburg PA
CBHW060735180626
46819CB00001B/41